Prai̇̃

Washington Whodunit Series

GORE IN THE GARDEN

"Engaging characters, a captivating story, set in an awesome place, will have readers rapidly flipping the pages. The twists are exquisite and our protag has guts, knows how to think on her feet and doesn't back down."
—*Escape With Dollycas Into A Good Book*

"With plenty of suspects and a few red herrings, Kit had her work cut out for her. The story was very well-written with all the sub-plots coming together nicely at the end."
—*Carla Loves To Read*

"Another edge of your seat Cozy. Colleen Shogan continues in book 5 of the series to give the reader a page-turning Cozy Murder Mystery."
—*My Reading Journeys*

"Altogether this is an enjoyable read with an authentic touch that comes from the author's experience on Capitol Hill . . . It definitely is not your normal cozy mystery . . . more like a cozy thriller. And the final scene at a little known place in DC is creepy-suspenseful."
—*Here's How It Happened*

"The mystery, the writing and story development is simply superb. I really enjoyed reading *Gore in the Garden* and I hope you will, too."
—*The Book Decoder*

Other Books in the Washington Whodunit Series

Stabbing in the Senate

Homicide in the House

Calamity at the Continental Club

K Street Killing

Gore in the Garden

Larceny at the Library

Larceny at the Library

A Washington Whodunit

COLLEEN J. SHOGAN

CAMEL
PRESS
Seattle, WA

CAMEL
PRESS

Epicenter Press
6524 NE 181st St., Suite 2
Kenmore, WA 98028

A Camel Press book published by Epicenter Press

For more information go to: www.epicenterpress.com
www.colleenshogan.com

Cover and interior production by Scott Book and Melissa Coffman

Larceny at the Library
Copyright © 2020 by Colleen J. Shogan

ISBN: 978-1-60381-835-3 (Trade Paper)
ISBN: 978-1-60381-305-1 (eBook)

Library of Congress Control Number: 2019945304

Printed in the United States of America

This book, a fictitious, light-hearted attempt to draw attention to the institution and its valuable work, is dedicated to the staff of the Library of Congress.

Acknowledgments

———

WRITING A BOOK is a team effort. I would like to thank my family and friends, who are unwavering in their support of Kit Marshall and her continued adventures. My agent Dawn Dowdle and fellow authors at the Blue Ridge Literary Agency provide sound, helpful advice at every turn of the publishing process. Editor Jennifer McCord has worked on the series since the very beginning and I am grateful to her patient guidance. Thank you to my husband Rob and my entire family for continued support of my inspired pursuits.

I always wanted to write a murder mystery with the Library of Congress as the setting. The Library is known for its beautiful architecture and unparalleled collections. Indeed, there is no other place like it in the world. My favorite part of the Library of Congress, however, is not the awe-inspiring Main Reading Room or Great Hall. As much as I enjoyed the occasional opportunity to view the draft of the Declaration of Independence or Lincoln's Second Inaugural, such treasures are not my favorite component of the Library, either.

Rather, the best part of the Library of Congress is its people. Over the past decade, I had the privilege of working with many different programs and divisions of the Library. It was an honor to serve alongside such a talented and dedicated team of librarians, analysts, managers, senior leaders, development officers, event coordinators, curators, congressional specialists, and book lovers.

Special thanks to Librarian of Congress Dr. Carla Hayden, a supporter of creative endeavors of all Library staff, including these books. Before I started writing *Larceny at the Library*, I mentioned to Dr. Hayden I was having difficulty coming up with yet another clever plot twist involving Clarence, the beagle mutt who appears in the series. Without missing a beat, she encouraged me to give Clarence a Capitol police dog friend. The idea for Murphy was born, and he makes his first appearance in *Larceny*. Also, kudos to Roswell Encina, who read an early version of the manuscript and provided valuable feedback.

A character in this book, Joe Malden, is dedicated to the memory of Joseph M. Alden, a classmate of mine at Boston College who passed away in 2010 at an early age from cancer. His parents are supportive fans of my books and asked if I would construct a character in Joe's memory. I think I did a pretty good job with Joe Malden: a smart, Red Sox-loving lawyer and dedicated public servant. I hope Joe is enjoying the book and laughing at its best moments.

Chapter One

———

"**K**IT, PLEASE BE careful. You almost knocked the Lincoln Bible off the table."

Those weren't words you heard every day from your husband. Reflexively, I backed away from the ornate wooden table inside the Librarian of Congress's ceremonial office.

"Sorry," I murmured. "I'll try to be more careful."

Doug was referring to the actual Bible owned by the sixteenth President of the United States, Abraham Lincoln. With a dark red velvet cover, the small book itself wasn't particularly valuable. Nonetheless, its provenance made it a national treasure. Lincoln was sworn into office in 1861 with it, as was Barack Obama and Donald Trump.

I knew this historical fun fact and dozens more because I was married to the head of the scholarly center at the Library of Congress, who was also a Georgetown American history professor. Right now, he was bustling around the Librarian's ornate office, preparing for a VIP pre-show displaying several of the Library's top treasures.

He stopped and walked over next to me, giving my hand an affectionate squeeze. "The food and drink should be set up right outside the office," said Doug. "Why don't you wait there for our guests?"

As a chief of staff for a member of Congress, I knew how to take a subtle hint. Before I instigated the destruction of a cherished item with national significance, perhaps a walk outside was in order. Besides, I was thirsty and hungry. Doug had promised a high-end bar and tasty treats. History could wait until I'd had a glass of wine and three or four fancy canapés.

Before I could grab a Chardonnay from the waiter, my phone buzzed.

My best friend and congressional staff colleague Meg had texted me.

Trevor and I are headed over now.

I typed back a response.

It's Trevor's date night?

Three dots appeared, indicating Meg was writing a response.

He wouldn't miss this.

I chuckled. Meg had started dating our former Senate colleague Trevor just over six months ago. Their relationship could be described as classic love/hate. For years, they bickered, each claiming he or she detested the other. Then, Trevor professed his romantic infatuation with Meg last summer, and she agreed to go out with him. Much to Trevor's chagrin, it wasn't an exclusive relationship on Meg's part. She was dating one other guy, a current House chief of staff. Such insular amorous intrigue could get exhausting, but long ago I'd learned not to tell Meg what to do in the dating department.

"Hey, big sister."

I looked up from my phone when I heard my brother's voice. Sebastian had recently moved to the Washington, D.C. area and now worked as a tech guru at a local non-profit. Tall and trim, Sebastian had arrived in his hipster millennial work attire, consisting of tartan plaid pants, a grey cardigan, deep red tie, and white button-down shirt. At least he'd listened to my advice that an invitation to a swanky, intimate reception at the Library of Congress meant he couldn't wear a stylish sweater, skinny jeans, and slip-on loafers.

"Looking sharp, little brother." I reached up and gave him a hug. After years of living apart, we'd recently become reacquainted with each other. We had more in common than we initially thought, although our physical appearances didn't peg us for siblings. Sebastian had a lean build with sandy locks that made him seem as though he belonged on a surfing beach in California. With long, brown straight hair, I was average height and build, although I routinely thought my obituary might one day read: "Kit Marshall, congressional staffer and amateur sleuth extraordinaire, who courageously tried to lose ten pounds."

We walked over to the bar and each ordered a glass of wine. After taking a sip, we placed our glasses on a high top table covered with a fancy white cloth. Sebastian's eyes wandered. "Fancy digs here. I've never been inside the Library of Congress."

As if on command, a middle-aged man dressed in a traditional dark suit appeared next to us. "Sorry to interrupt, but I overheard this was your first time visiting us."

Sebastian nodded. "My brother-in-law is helping with the reception tonight. My name is Sebastian and this is my sister, Kit Marshall."

Our eager guest smiled widely. "You must be married to Doug Hollingsworth. I'm Joe Malden, the general counsel for this great institution." He tipped his tumbler of amber liquid in our direction.

"Doug has mentioned you," I said. "The Red Sox fan, right?"

Joe Malden's smile grew. "Absolutely. And I'm stuck here in Washington, the land of the Nationals. Doesn't stop me from cheering for my Sox."

"What's the deal for tonight?" asked Sebastian. "Doug and Kit invited me, but I'm not sure what I've gotten myself into."

Malden leaned forward with a glint in his eyes. "First of all, you're standing inside the Great Hall of the Thomas Jefferson Building. It opened in 1897 and it's arguably the most beautiful room in Washington."

Malden wasn't exaggerating. The surrounding open space was ornately decorated in a style reminiscent of the Italian Renaissance, although uniquely American at the same time. We were standing on the bottom floor of the two-story building, surrounded by colorful murals, statues, mosaics, and a vaulted marble ceiling. If I didn't know where I was, I might have thought I was enjoying a glass of wine in a far-flung European capital art museum.

Sebastian swiveled his neck around. "Can't disagree with you, although I haven't seen as much of the sights as I'd like since moving here."

"This is our country's pantheon of knowledge. Authors, inventors, scientists, and world cultures are represented," said Joe. "Every sculpture, engraving, and entryway has significance. At the turn of the century, it was built to show the United States was equal to Europe in matters of knowledge and culture."

"It must have cost a fortune to build," I muttered. The member of Congress I worked for, Maeve Dixon from North Carolina, had recently been appointed as the chair of the committee which provided oversight to Capitol Hill itself, including the Library of Congress. We were constantly fretting over authorized expenditures, cognizant that the American people didn't want Congress spending lavishly in its own backyard as the federal deficit ballooned.

"Not exactly," said Joe. "Only six point three million dollars. And it was under budget."

Sebastian took a sip of wine. "That's a bargain. You can't even build a reputable data server for that amount these days."

"You'll have to excuse my brother. He's a techie who thinks the world revolves around the internet," I said.

Joe Malden laughed. "We know a thing or two about servers these days. It's not just about collecting old, dusty books anymore. We're putting our digital collections online for everyone to explore."

"Speaking of old stuff, can you tell us more about what we're going to see this evening?" I asked. When Doug had the opportunity to invite guests to this evening's preview, he hadn't given too many specifics, other than it was a rehearsal for tomorrow's big event celebrating Lincoln's birthday.

"I'm not the expert curator, but as I understand it, we will be viewing one of the Library's most treasured collections," said Malden.

He had just taken a breath to continue when a high-pitched feminine voice interrupted. "One of the crown jewels," she said.

A well put-together middle-aged woman with professionally styled, shoulder length blonde hair joined us at our standing table. She wore a long sleeve expensive-looking print dress perfectly fitted to her well-proportioned frame. I guessed Dolce & Gabbana, but I was no fashion blogger. Her makeup was expertly applied, and I noticed she wore diamond earrings with a matching necklace that tripled the carat count. I'd eat my hat if this woman worked at the Library of Congress. If she did, I needed to consider a career change. Pronto.

We scooted over to make room for our new guest. She placed her tumbler aside and offered her hand. "Lea Rutherford."

I accepted it, noticing that diamonds also adorned her slim fingers, along with other brightly colored gems. I introduced myself, and Sebastian followed in turn.

"What is your relationship to the Library of Congress?" asked Sebastian innocently.

Joe answered before Lea could speak. "Ms. Rutherford is one of our most generous donors. A true patron of the humanities in Washington."

Big shocker. "I'm happy to support *worthy* institutions." She glanced sideways at Malden. "You wouldn't think it, but sometimes my assistance isn't welcome."

"Really? Funding is scarce on Capitol Hill these days. I'm surprised they're not beating down the door for help," I said.

Joe raised his eyebrows and wiggled them in my direction. I took it as a clumsy sign to drop the issue, so I quickly changed the topic. "Back to Sebastian's question. What will be on display tonight?"

Joe took advantage of the opportunity to steer the conversation back to safer ground. "The contents of Lincoln's pockets."

Sebastian interrupted. "The Library owns Lincoln's personal possessions?"

Joe smirked. "You didn't let me finish. The contents of Lincoln's pockets the night he was assassinated."

Sebastian and I gasped at the same time. Both Joe and Lea laughed at our reaction.

"I don't mean to be a bore, but I'm going to repeat my brother's question. Why does the Library of Congress have these items in its collection?"

Joe motioned toward an older, slightly built gentleman walking inside the ceremonial office. "I'm sure you'll hear the story from him tonight."

"Who's that?" asked Sebastian, draining his drink.

"Gustav Gaffney," said Lea. "He's the Assistant Librarian of Congress. The number two around here."

"And our host for this evening," said Joe. "He's been a librarian for decades and makes it his business to know our collections inside out."

"You can say that again," muttered Lea.

Joe patted Lea's hand. "You have to forgive Ms. Rutherford. She and the Assistant Librarian occasionally disagree concerning where to focus resources at the Library of Congress."

Lea smiled tightly. "No need to apologize, Joe. You know I've made alternate plans for my dollars. As Kit mentioned, there's plenty of places who welcome my financial support these days."

I hadn't met Gustav Gaffney before, but his name was familiar. As I recall, he hadn't enthusiastically supported Doug's selection as head of the scholarly center, believing that Doug would only serve in the position for a short period of time before returning to his tenured professorship at Georgetown. However, Gaffney's boss, the Librarian of Congress, had overruled him and made the appointment. As the chief of staff for an important member of Congress, I'd steered clear of the matter entirely. I knew a conflict of interest when I saw one.

Doug emerged from the ceremonial office and approached our gathering. "We'll begin our short program in about ten minutes. We're waiting for a member of Congress to arrive. Once he shows up, we can start."

I turned to Joe. "I thought the congressional event was tomorrow. That's when my boss plans to attend. You know, Maeve Dixon."

Joe's eyebrows furrowed. "Of course, we know Chairwoman Dixon." He glanced around nervously, and then spotted a tall woman in her early fifties with short, light brown hair and a substantial build. Waving at her, he said, "Janice, can you come over here for a moment?"

She hustled over and, ignoring everyone else, spoke directly to Joe. "I'm looking out for our congressional guest. What's wrong?"

Joe motioned in my direction. "Janice, you must know Kit Marshall."

I stuck out my hand, and she politely accepted it. "I've heard the name."

Joe cleared his throat. "She's a chief of staff in the House." He paused for a beat. "Maeve Dixon's chief."

Janice's entire visage changed in an instant. Her face lit up, a wide smile spreading across her face. "Certainly. We work with Chairwoman Dixon's committee staff and Meg Peters from your office. I'm Janice Jackson, the head of congressional relations for the Library."

"Meg is our legislative director, and she's assigned to liaise with the committee from our personal office," I explained. "But I have another connection to the Library of Congress. My husband is Doug Hollingsworth, the newly appointed director of the scholarly center."

Janice hit her forehead. "Yes, of course. Doug told me about you when we chatted after his appointment. So glad to welcome you to the Library of Congress this evening. You certainly do have a lot of connections here." While her voice and expression seemed genuine on the surface, I felt like the warmth was forced.

I introduced Sebastian and explained that Meg and her guest would be arriving soon. "I heard that we're waiting for a member of Congress to arrive. I didn't think members were invited tonight." I didn't want to appear difficult, but if my boss found out she missed an exclusive viewing, she'd be annoyed. After all, she was the chair of the oversight committee with Library of Congress jurisdiction. It might seem petty, but Maeve Dixon suffered from extreme FOMO, otherwise known as "fear of missing out."

"Members of Congress weren't invited tonight. Tomorrow is the big day, and Maeve Dixon is going to kick it off for us by introducing the Librarian of Congress." She placed her hand gently on my shoulder. "Don't worry, Kit. We'd never shortchange Chairwoman Dixon. We have one member of Congress who can't make it tomorrow morning and he was quite eager to view the special display we have on tap. As a courtesy, we allowed him to attend the rehearsal this evening."

I pursed my lips. "Representative Henry Chang?"

Janice laughed. "How did you know? Yes, Congressman Chang is quite the aficionado of history. I believe he has his own modest collection of historical items. He's over here at the Library of Congress on a regular basis. Given his intense interest in our collections, particularly related to Lincoln and other presidents, we decided to offer him the opportunity to attend the preview."

My face relaxed. "No problem," I said. "Thank you for explaining that to me."

I heard a female voice over my right shoulder. "Explain what?"

It was Meg, who had arrived with Trevor in tow. The fashion mogul of Capitol Hill, Meg was decked out in a pretty black long-sleeved shirt dress, accented with a multi-colored scarf around her trim waist. Her sleek blonde bob shone underneath the soft lighting of the Jefferson Building.

Janice reached over and gave Meg a half hug. "Thank you for attending, Meg. Who is your guest this evening?"

Meg stepped aside to allow Trevor to join our growing circle. He was dressed in his typical attire: a dark blue suit, neutral red tie, a crisp white collared shirt, and horn-rimmed glasses. Trevor wasn't going to win hunk of the year. Nonetheless, he had a certain smart D.C. smart guy sex appeal that made him reasonably attractive, particularly to a Capitol Hill audience. Before this past year, I would have never thought Meg would have given someone like Trevor the time of day. She usually went for the guy who could have become a Chippendale dancer if he'd chosen a divergent career path. But Trevor's obvious devotion and maturity had resonated with Meg at the right time. Timing was everything in life.

Meg linked her arm underneath Trevor's. After he introduced himself, Meg added, "Trevor is a senior advisor to the C-A-O in the House."

That was Washington, D.C. lingo for the Chief Administrative Officer, who managed all the operations, technology, and facilities within the House of Representatives. Trevor had enjoyed a storied career in Washington, which began in the Senate as our co-worker. Then he'd become a defense lobbyist and a tell-all bestselling author. He'd finally settled into the relatively tame position with the Chief Administrative Officer, where he appeared to excel. Trevor was the master of details, and the CAO relied upon him to keep everything straight.

Trevor patted Meg's arm with his other hand. "Nothing quite as impressive as the work that's done here," he said, his eyes drifting to the ceiling of the Great Hall. "This structure is simply awe inspiring."

As if on cue, Joe Malden piped up. "When the ceiling was restored a few decades ago, they discovered it was inlaid with aluminum plating, not silver. During the period of construction in the 1890s, aluminum was much more valuable than silver. The six skylights were designed to match the patterns on the floor below." He took a breath. "No expense or detail was spared. When the doors to the Thomas Jefferson Building opened, it signaled our nation's arrival on the global stage of knowledge. The United States would no longer be dwarfed by the likes of London, Paris, or Rome."

Janice Jackson chuckled. "Joe, if you ever get bored with legal matters, I could hire you as a tour guide for our congressional V-I-Ps."

Lea Rutherford smiled slyly. "He's certainly a man of many talents."

Joe promptly turned a shade of dark red. "I'd better check to see if Gustav needs help with setting up for tonight's viewing."

"And I think I just saw Representative Chang arrive," said Janice. "Please excuse me." She scurried across the Great Hall to intercept the congressman.

Meg whispered, "Does she mean Henry Chang?"

"The Library gave him special permission to attend tonight because he can't go tomorrow," I murmured.

Meg wrinkled her nose. "He's a pest on the committee. Maeve finds him annoying. He's only a freshman, yet he's always clamoring for tickets to events at glamorous places."

"It's Chang's first term in Congress, so he's eager," I said. "And according to the congressional relations person, he likes American history."

"Janice Jackson," said Meg. "She bends over backwards for Chang because she thinks he'll help the Library of Congress on the committee."

"Isn't that the name of the game, Meg? You understand how it works," I said. "No surprise that she'd want to make him happy. Isn't that the job of congressional relations in a federal agency?"

Meg fiddled with her silver hoop earring. "I'm giving you the background so you understand what's going on, Kit."

I smiled. "Doug gives me an earful about Library politics. But it's helpful to hear it from a veteran like you."

Meg beamed. We'd been best friends for a while, but I was also technically Meg's boss. It didn't hurt to provide well deserved praise every once in a while.

A trim, muscular African American man in his early forties emerged from the ceremonial office. In a demonstrative voice, he announced, "Please join us inside for a preview of our program. Unfortunately, you will need to leave your refreshments outside."

We dutifully left our drinks on the table and made our way toward the entrance to the office. Lea Rutherford appeared next to me. "Lea, who is the gentleman who just spoke?"

"Gordon Endicott," she said. "The head of the rare books and special collections division."

"It seems like he's in charge of the situation," I said.

Lea nodded. "You've got that right. He'll be a force to be reckoned with in the future. I have a feeling he doesn't take no for an answer," she said. "Gustav might have his hands full with him."

I leaned closer to Lea so I could lower my voice. "I get the sense that Assistant Librarian Gaffney throws his weight around quite a bit."

"There's no weight to throw around." She chuckled at her reference to Gaffney's slight build. "But yes, you're right. He has a lot of opinions about everything and he's not afraid to make them known."

"I suppose his job is a tough one," I said.

"No doubt," said Lea. "In my experience, most people think they can catch more flies with honey. That lesson is lost on Gustav Gaffney."

We'd reached the entrance to the ceremonial office, situated adjacent to the Great Hall. Library of Congress staff members, including Doug, Gaffney, and Endicott, were standing behind the Librarian's ornate wooden desk.

Gordon Endicott spoke. "Please, gather around so we can begin." The crowd was small enough that everyone had a front row spot.

Gustav cleared his throat. "Thank you for joining us today. Most of you already know who I am." He peered around the room, reminding me of my middle school English teacher who tried to stare down students who didn't complete the homework assignment. "However, I do not recognize all the faces before me, so I shall introduce myself formally. My name is Gustav Gaffney, and I am the Assistant Librarian of Congress."

My phone vibrated. Thank goodness I'd kept it on silent. If I'd interrupted Gustav, I might not live to tell about it. I pulled it out of my suit jacket pocket and glanced at the text message. Of course, it was from Meg.

Is this guy for reals?

I couldn't risk typing back a long reply, but I did manage to send Meg the emoticon equivalent of a wink.

;)

Afraid Gaffney might rap my wrists with a ruler for misbehavior,

I returned my attention to behind the desk and studied the Assistant Librarian. Slender with a long, dour face, the remaining wisps of gray hair on his head indicated he'd never see sixty-five again. Dressed impeccably in a three-piece vested charcoal suit, I got the impression Gustav Gaffney was a serious man who got the job done, but probably wasn't collecting too many happy hour invitations. This wasn't a man who cared about winning popularity contests.

Gaffney kept talking. "This evening, we will preview the display we will provide tomorrow to members of Congress and select guests of the scholarly and library community. Of course, we do have one member of Congress with us this evening." He paused and motioned with his hand to an Asian man standing next to Janice Jackson. "As I understand it, Representative Chang is a collector of American history artifacts and an Abraham Lincoln aficionado."

Chang nodded, but didn't say anything. That was uncharacteristic of a politician. Usually, they took any opportunity to offer remarks. Maybe Chang hadn't gotten used to his job as a congressman yet. On the surface, he seemed like a fish out of water. From what I could recall, he hadn't been a politician before coming to Congress and seemed way more interested in what happened a century ago than what was going on inside the Capitol today. Other history buffs had occupied key positions in Congress, such as former Speaker of the House Newt Gingrich. Love him or hate him, Newt's head was focused on present day politics, not the past.

"Now, we will turn to the newly appointed director of our scholarly center, historian Douglas Hollingsworth." Gaffney motioned for Doug to assume the floor.

"Thank you, Gustav. First, I'd like to tell you a little about this room, which served as the official office of the Librarian until 1980. There have been many kings, queens, presidents, prime ministers, and heads of state who have visited earlier Librarians inside this room."

Doug took a breath before continuing.

"As you may know, Abraham Lincoln was born on February 12, 1809. Tomorrow, we will celebrate the anniversary of Lincoln's birth by reenacting one of the greatest discoveries ever made within the walls of the Library of Congress."

Doug paused and looked around the room. He had everyone's attention. "On February 12, 1976 inside this office, the Librarian of Congress at the time, Daniel Boorstin, opened a box during a well-attended press conference containing a very important set of Abraham Lincoln artifacts, namely the contents of his pockets the night he died.

"The most interesting fact about these set of items is that they were lost for nearly four decades here at the Library of Congress," said Doug. "Boorstin became the Librarian of Congress in 1975. One day, he walked into the closet inside this office." Doug paused and pointed to a door only steps away from the desk. "Inside, he found a package marked for the Librarian of Congress. Boorstin pulled off a layer of wrapping and discovered the box was marked as the contents of Lincoln's pockets the night he was assassinated.

"Librarian Boorstin was initially skeptical, but it was verified that the items inside the package were indeed authentic. A few months later, the public reveal was held on Lincoln's birthday to share the items with the public. Soon thereafter, they went on display at the Library of Congress so that visitors could experience the discovery." Doug smiled as he concluded his short speech.

"How did the items end up at the Library of Congress in the first place?" asked Lea Rutherford. "Why not a museum?"

Doug adjusted his glasses. "We can only speculate, but we know that the items belonged to Lincoln's son, Robert Todd Lincoln, for many years. His daughter, Mary Lincoln Ishum, donated the items, along with the Lincoln papers, to the Library of Congress in 1937."

"Why was the package misplaced for so long?" asked Representative Chang.

"That's a mystery," said Doug.

Gustav Gaffney interjected. "But the good news is that it's no longer lost, and we have come together to recreate Librarian Boorstin's finest moment as he shared the collection with journalists and scholars."

Gordon Endicott spoke. "Nonetheless, we don't quite trust the collection to reside inside the closet in an unprotected package to recreate the Boorstin unveiling." He walked over to the closet and opened the door. "We have invested in a state of the art biometric safe for this occasion."

We turned our gaze to the inside of the small room. Inside was a grey steel box the size of a mini-fridge.

Gaffney joined Endicott. "This safe can only be opened using fingerprints. It ensures the contents cannot be stolen due to a safecracker. It has been fastened to the floor using our strongest enforcements." He attempted to move the safe, which didn't budge an inch. Given Gaffney's slight build, was he really the best person to demonstrate the safe's security?

Doug must have read my mind. "The safe isn't going anywhere. I watched the Architect of the Capitol install multiple bolts earlier today," he said. "Apparently, when thefts occur, safes are typically not opened on site. Instead, they are removed from the premises and then cracked after hours of work."

Well, if the Library of Congress gig didn't work out over the long term, maybe Doug had a future as a cat burglar. I suppressed a smile as the theme from the Pink Panther ran through my head.

Gaffney bent down and placed his finger on the keypad of the safe. Moments later, the door opened.

"For security purposes, the fingerprints of only two people will operate the safe," said Janice Jackson.

Gaffney cleared his throat. "Myself, as you've just seen. Of course, the other person is the Librarian of Congress. She will open the safe tomorrow during our official reenactment."

Gaffney stepped aside as Endicott reached into the safe, wearing white gloves. He pulled out a red velvet tray with a number of items on it. Everyone craned their necks for a closer look.

Gaffney clapped his hands. "Please, no need to crowd around. We're a small group this evening. Gordon will place the contents on Librarian's desk and explain each item."

Lea Rutherford's description of the Assistant Librarian seemed dead on. In the absence of his boss, he'd certainly assumed the role of the alpha male in the room. He called the shots and the rest of the world knew it.

Endicott was now positioned directly behind the desk. "First, we have a handkerchief." Pointing to it, he explained. "His name is embroidered in red, as you can see." I craned my neck. Sure enough, in tiny scarlet stitch, the words "A. Lincoln" adorned the handkerchief.

Beside me, Sebastian muttered, "That's too cool."

"Notice Lincoln carried two pairs of glasses with him and a pocket-knife, as well," said Endicott. He signaled to the next objects on the tray.

"But perhaps the most curious item in the collection is this," said Endicott, pointing to a rectangular piece of paper. "This is a Confederate five-dollar bill. Lincoln had it inside his wallet the night he died."

Trevor couldn't contain his curiosity. "Why would the President of the United States, the commander in chief of the Union Army, carry a Confederate note?"

Endicott motioned for Doug to take the question. "We don't know for sure, but the capital of the Confederacy, Richmond, had just fallen into Union control. Lincoln had recently traveled there, and it might have been passed along to him during that trip."

"As a souvenir?" asked Representative Chang. He was leaning on the desk, his body moving dangerously close to the treasures. Gordon Endicott winced. If it had been anyone but a member of Congress, I'm sure he would have received a sharp rebuke.

"Perhaps," said Doug. "We can't know for sure. It's certainly the most infamous item in this collection."

"Finally, even Abraham Lincoln was concerned about what the press said about him," said Endicott. "He also carried several newspaper clippings with him about the Union cause during the last days of the Civil War."

Doug added, "I might add that the articles were favorable commentaries on the President."

"I guess even Abraham Lincoln was human," said Meg, almost to herself.

She must have spoken loud enough for Gustav Gaffney to hear. "Exactly right, young lady. At the Library of Congress, we feel this collection greatly humanizes our sixteenth president. He carried everyday items with him, which demonstrates he was much more than a myth. He was a living, breathing person. That helps Americans relate to Lincoln, even today."

Meg beamed. She might have liked that the Assistant Librarian signaled out her comment as insightful. It was even more probable she appreciated the "young lady" comment. In her late thirties, Meg was starting to become age sensitive, particularly amongst the youthful culture of Capitol Hill, where the median age of a congressional staffer gravitated around the mid-twenties mark.

"There's also a watch fob, a wallet, a button with the letter 'L' on it, a glass lens cleaner, and a case for his glasses. Please, feel free to take turns walking around the desk so you can inspect the items," said Endicott. He motioned for Doug and Gaffney to move over so that the rest of us could get a better look. Doug obliged and positioned himself on the periphery. Gustav Gaffney didn't budge.

I bent down to examine the contents of the tray. The stitching on the handkerchief was extraordinary. Despite sitting in an unattended box for decades, it had been preserved perfectly. The two pairs of spectacles were equally curious. The gold-rimmed spectacles had a bit of string holding them together.

"Did Lincoln repair his glasses with this string?" I asked. "You would think the President of the United States could have had a better fix."

Endicott motioned for Doug to answer. "We don't know precisely, but yes, the string was an attempt to fix the left hinge. Those were his reading glasses," said my husband. "Perhaps he was too busy saving the Union to have his spectacles properly repaired."

After taking another look, I stepped out of the way and whispered to Doug. "How long do you have to stay here tonight?"

"Unfortunately, I was busy this afternoon making sure everything is settled for tomorrow's congressional event. I need to return to my office to catch up on some paperwork after this is over," he said.

After examining the artifacts, Meg and Trevor joined us. "Dinner plans?" asked Meg. She had a one-track mind, and most of the time, it was focused on happy hour or eating out.

Trevor steered her outside the ceremonial office. "Let's have a drink first. It's bad form to rush off after viewing priceless treasures, darling."

A few years ago, Trevor's sarcastic comment would have sent Meg reeling. Now, she simply giggled and followed Trevor's lead.

"They seem happy," said Doug. "I guess things are working out."

"It's not an exclusive relationship, though. She's still seeing Clay Donovan, too. Tonight is Trevor's night." I shook my head.

"Is Donovan the Republican chief of staff?" asked Doug.

I nodded. "About ten years older than her. Nice guy. Honestly, I don't know how much longer Trevor is going to stick around. Three's a crowd."

Gustav Gaffney's clipped voice interrupted our conversation. "Dr. Hollingsworth, will you please join us to answer additional questions about the Lincoln assassination?"

Doug muttered under his breath. "Gotta go. Gaffney will cry bloody murder if I don't follow his order. Be sure to say goodbye before you leave for dinner."

Neither of us realized how foreboding Doug's words would turn out be.

Chapter Two

RETURNED TO THE reception area outside the Librarian's ceremonial office. My stomach grumbled. As Trevor noted, rushing off to dinner would be viewed as rude. Small talk was part of the Washington, D.C. game, although my patience for it had grown thinner over time. It seemed like there were a hundred things to accomplish, and never enough time to get it all done. Schmoozing as a sleuth was valuable, less so when I wasn't trying to solve a case. On the other hand, my brother Sebastian had adapted well to Beltway life. He was standing alongside Trevor, Meg, Joe Malden, and Janice Jackson, chatting away at the speed of a POTUS tweetstorm.

"Thank you for including me this evening," Sebastian said. "Six months ago, I was just a tech guy making his way in Silicon Valley. And now I've seen the contents of Lincoln's pockets the night he died." He shook his head and took a sip of his drink.

Trevor piped up. "I'm normally as blasé as it comes, but that was definitely a pinch-me moment."

"Tomorrow's event will go over really well with members of Congress," said Meg.

Janice beamed. "We certainly hope so. The Librarian wants to make a splash." She emphasized the last word by flashing her hands in front of us. Someone had drunk too much coffee this morning.

"I haven't met Gustav Gaffney before," I said. "Is he always so. . ."

I paused to search for the right word.

Joe Malden finished my sentence for me. "Stuffy?"

"Yes," I said, smiling. "But I wasn't sure if I should say it."

Malden blushed. "I certainly shouldn't be saying it. After all, he's our boss." He motioned to include himself and Janice. "But to answer your question, he's pretty much always that way."

"Gustav is an acquired taste," said Janice. "He's worked in the librarian profession for a considerable time and has a lot of opinions about how we should accomplish our work."

"He certainly seems to take a lot of pride in his position," I said, choosing my words carefully.

"He was named the Assistant Librarian about six months ago," said Janice. "Let's just say it didn't take him very long to settle into the role."

"Was he the only person suitable for the job?" asked Sebastian.

Janice shrugged in the direction of Joe Malden. "Except for one other qualified candidate."

I raised my eyebrows. "You were considered for the position?" I directed my question at Joe.

"I've worked at the Library of Congress for three decades," he said. "Some people thought I had the experience and background for the job."

Lea Rutherford approached our group from the side. "Let's not mince words. *Many* people thought Joe was the *best* candidate for the position."

Joe's face turned pink. "That's all water under the bridge. Gustav got the job, and he obviously has the right demeanor for it."

That was debatable, but given Joe's obvious embarrassment, I decided to change the topic of conversation. "What about Gordon Endicott?"

"As you know, he's the head of our noteworthy rare books and collections division," said Joe Malden. "He arrived about the same time as Gustav. Very well connected in the world of antiquities. We think he will help us make strategic connections to acquire impressive items for the growing collection. He has a keen eye for the changing demands in the rare book market, and we hope he can keep the Library of Congress ahead of the curve." Joe added, "As part of my job, I often work on these acquisition agreements. They're often legally complex."

"Certainly very impressive jobs," I said. "We spend so much time with politicians, sometimes we forget there's all types of people working on Capitol Hill."

"Well said, Kit." Trevor extended his hand to Joe, and then Janice. "Thank you for hosting us this evening. You must have a lot of details to attend to before tomorrow morning's event."

"I wish I could go home, but I'm afraid you're right," said Joe. "I'm going to head back to my office in the Madison Building to finish some work."

Lea Rutherford made a face. "All work and no play, Mr. Malden. It's not good for the soul."

Malden laughed. "That may be the case, but it's good for my bank ac-count. I want to make sure I keep my job here."

"I need to make sure Representative Chang has successfully retrieved his coat," said Janice. "I'm glad you enjoyed this evening. Please excuse me."

I whispered to Meg. "I'm going to say goodbye to Doug. Then we can head to dinner. Why don't you speak with Sebastian and Trevor and find out where you want to go?"

I poked my head inside the Librarian's ceremonial office. "We're head-ed to grab a bite nearby. Are you sure you can't join us?"

Doug glanced uneasily in the direction of Gustav Gaffney. "Afraid not. I need to finish up here and then go back to my office to finish up some work."

Endicott was moving the contents of the red velvet tray from the desk back toward the closet. "Dr. Hollingsworth, please come over here so you can be a witness to the return of the items to the safe," said Gaffney.

"Text me and maybe we can share a ride back home?" asked Doug.

"Of course." I resisted the urge to give him an affectionate peck on the lips. Somehow, Gustav Gaffney didn't seem like the romantic type, partic-ularly if it caused him to wait a few precious seconds.

I exited the office and returned to my brother and friends. "Doug has his hands full in there, both literally and figuratively. He can't join us for dinner."

Trevor sighed. "Alas, same for me. I'm afraid I must return to the Capitol to finish a memo for my boss." He gave Meg a kiss on the cheek and took off in a flash.

"And then there were three," I said, an obvious reference to Agatha Christie's novel *Ten Little Indians*.

Meg waved her hand. "Never mind them. I'm famished."

"Let's not go too far," I said. "Doug and I will drive home together, so I will need to swing back to the Library to pick him up."

Meg pressed a manicured red nail to her chin as she pondered the op-tions. "What about Bullfeathers?"

"Let's do it," I said, linking my arm underneath my brother's. "We can introduce Sebastian to it."

"I'm not sure I can take all this excitement today," said Sebastian.

Meg hit Sebastian playfully on the shoulder. "Bullfeathers won't be as exciting as viewing the contents of President Lincoln's pockets."

Ten minutes later, we walked into the classic restaurant and bar on

First Street, two blocks south of the Library of Congress. The restaurant owners renovated several years ago, and the establishment benefited from a rebuilt bar, new tables, and an overhaul of the kitchen.

The waiter gave us our menus, and Meg leaned in. "I read online that Bullfeathers received more campaign fundraising visits than any other restaurant on Capitol Hill."

"How would anyone know that?" asked Sebastian.

"Filings with the Federal Election Commission," I said. "All campaign or political action committees have to file reports to explain their expenditures."

"That's right," said Meg. "Bullfeathers had the highest number of entries. It was particularly popular amongst Republicans."

Sebastian crinkled his forehead. "Why would that be?"

"Tradition mostly," I said. "The name of this place is tied to Teddy Roosevelt, and Republicans are big Teddy fans."

After the waiter took our drink and food orders, Sebastian ran his fingers through his dishwater blond locks, now trimmed neatly. A political activist at heart, my brother used to have a shaggy look about him, but since relocating to the Washington area and accepting a full-time, permanent job as an IT specialist for a non-profit, he'd adapted to the more conservative D.C. culture. He now confined his protesting activities to nights and weekends, which seemed to provide him with a satisfying balance of stability and anarchy. When he tired of his nine to five existence, there was always another corporation to picket or politician to phone bomb in his free time.

"You got me again," said Sebastian. "How is the name 'Bullfeathers' tied to Teddy Roosevelt?"

"It was his preferred euphemism for bullshit," I said. "Teddy was a classy guy. He didn't want to swear all the time."

Meg laughed. "The better question is how you know all this arcane information, Kit."

I sat up straight. "I am married to a historian. And now Doug works on Capitol Hill. I'm picking up new information all the time."

"How's that job working out for him?" asked Sebastian. "Those people at the Library of Congress are a real cast of characters."

"Pretty well. He was getting bored at Georgetown and wanted to stretch his wings. Managing the scholarly center fits the bill," I said. "It was rocky for a while. Gustav Gaffney didn't want Doug to get the permanent job as director."

"I don't understand it," said Meg. "I mean, Doug is perfect for that position." She ticked off her points with her fingers. "He's boring, likes old stuff, and loves talking about obscure topics with weird people."

Meg liked Doug, but she also enjoyed giving him a dig or two when the opportunity presented itself.

"Perhaps you have a future as a Human Resources professional," I said.

"You know what I mean, Kit," said Meg. "Doug had all the qualifications, no matter how you want to describe them."

Our waiter approached, interrupting our conversation with the arrival of our food. Sebastian's mouth watered as our server plunked down a huge Reuben sandwich with fries in front of him.

"Now I understand why the Republicans are spending so much money here," he said eagerly.

I'd gone for the Teddy Cobb, which made me feel virtuous while still enjoying fried chicken, cheese, and ranch dressing. Meg had ordered only an appetizer portion of mac and cheese. It was uncharacteristic of my best friend to not indulge in a full meal. Svelte as she was, Meg possessed an appetite of epic proportions.

I eyed her suspiciously. Motioning toward her plate, I asked, "Something the matter with you, Meg?"

With a puzzled look on her face, she shrugged. "Me? Nothing."

"Come on," said Sebastian. "I've only known you for a short time, but even I know you never pass up the opportunity for a good meal."

"Boy troubles?" I asked.

She pushed her plate away and sighed. "As you know, I'm dating Trevor and Clay Donovan at the same time." She paused to take a sip of her water. "I just can't decide what to do. They both want me to decide about who to date exclusively. Pronto."

Quite frankly, it didn't seem like an unreasonable request. We were in our late thirties, after all. Maybe a decade ago, Meg would have gotten away with dating several guys casually at the same time. But probably not at this station of life.

Sebastian stuffed a few fries in his mouth, put up his finger while he was chewing, and then swallowed. "Let's approach this analytically. You shouldn't get so emotional about it."

Leave it to a tech professional to remove emotions from love. "Oh, brother," I said. It was one of my favorite expressions to use around Sebastian.

"Kit, just let me handle something for once. You're not the only one who can solve problems," he said.

Ouch. Nice dig, Sebastian. Growing up, I'd always been the "fixer." Gradually, I was trying to teach myself that I didn't always have to solve the world's problems. Sometimes, it was better to let others take a crack at it.

"Let's make a list concerning both Trevor and Clay. What do you like about each of them? That will help you decide who to stick with," he said.

Sebastian made it sound like Meg was selecting a new sofa for her apartment. But I kept my mouth shut.

Meg seemed willing to play along. She ticked off items like a grocery list. "Let's start with Clay. He's handsome, accomplished, understands politics, and loves to plan fun dates."

"Great start," said Sebastian. "What about Trevor?"

"Trevor is intelligent, earnest, hardworking, and quite funny once you get to know him. Plus, he really likes me," she said. "I mean, he *adores* me."

Sebastian raised his eyebrows. "Clay doesn't *adore* you?"

"He does," said Meg quickly. "Just not in the same way."

Sebastian wrinkled his nose. "What do you mean, not in the same way?"

"Clay has a lot of options. Women are dying to go out with him on Capitol Hill," said Meg. "I practically had to wait my turn to get a chance to date him."

"You don't think Trevor has other options, too?" I asked. Trevor might not be as attractive as Clay, but he had a certain *je ne sais quoi* that Washington women might find alluring.

"Sure," said Meg casually. "Just not as many."

Sebastian rapped the table with his hand. "Let's keep on point. What about negatives for both?"

Meg hesitated for a beat. "Clay might not want to commit longer term. He's ten years older than me and has never been married."

Sebastian rubbed his chin, deep in thought. "And Trevor?"

Meg sighed. "Trevor is the opposite end of the spectrum. He's super committed. It's intimidating."

Sebastian finished off his sandwich and pushed his plate away. "Objectively speaking, this is a draw."

Meg threw up her hands. "That's what I've been trying to tell you!"

"But that doesn't mean it's an impossible problem to solve," said Sebastian. "You need to decide what *your* priorities are. Then you can decide who you want to be with longer term."

This was the same conversation I'd had over and over with Meg, although I hadn't applied Sebastian's dispassionate objectiveness to Meg's conundrum.

"I know," said Meg, her gaze downward. "I'll figure it out." I patted Meg's hand.

"Of course, you will. Don't fret too much, Meg. Most women would be lucky to have two worthy suitors lusting after them."

Meg's face brightened immediately. "That's true!" She picked up her fork and finished off her food.

Sebastian cleared his throat. "While we're on the subject of love, I have an announcement."

I stuffed the last piece of Teddy Cobb chicken into my mouth and eyed Sebastian suspiciously. Doug and I had thought something was up with him. He'd been busy the last couple of times we'd invited him to join us for dinner or drinks.

"I'm dating someone," he said, his face flush with excitement.

"And who is this person?" asked Meg in a bossy tone. "Why are we only finding out about it now?" Like our boss Maeve Dixon, Meg was also a FOMO-phobe.

"Her name is Lisa Reddy," said Sebastian. "And for the record, I wasn't holding out. I wanted to make sure she was interested in me as much as I was interested in her."

"Well, she'd be crazy not to be interested," said Meg. When Meg first met Sebastian, she'd had a major crush on him. With his sandy surfer locks and lean build, Sebastian was certainly a looker.

"Does she work in the technology sector?" I asked. Secretly, I hoped the answer was yes. Sebastian's life revolved around his job and his political protests. While the latter was admirable, I wasn't sure he needed a significant other to egg him on. I dreaded the late-night phone call to bail him out of jail because he'd chained himself to a tree in front of the World Bank to protest global economic inequality.

"Nope," said Sebastian.

Drat.

"She's one of your hippie anti-government, anti-corporate friends?" asked Meg.

"Nope," he said.

The check came, and we each threw down a few bills. I handed the stack to the waiter, and Sebastian got up to leave.

I motioned for him to sit back down. "Wait a second. If she's not in tech and you didn't meet her at a protest, then what does she do?"

Sebastian grinned. "She's a police officer. You might have seen her around. Lisa's on the Capitol Hill force."

Meg's mouth hung open. "You're dating a cop?"

"It appears so," he said. "She's in the K-9 unit."

My phone buzzed. A text message from Doug.

Ready to go home?

I typed out a reply.

C U @ Neptune in 10.

An American rendition of the Trevi Fountain in Rome, Neptune was located in front of the Jefferson Building on First Street. The bearded Neptune, king of the sea, was the centerpiece of the bronze fountain. He's flanked by his triton sons, sea nymphs riding horses, frolicking dolphins, and turtles spouting water. It was a convenient meeting spot since no one could miss the grandiose landmark.

"I have to run," I said. "Gotta get the car and pick up Doug. He has a big day tomorrow."

"Tell him good luck," said Sebastian.

"I want to hear more about Lisa," I said. "You're not getting off the hook that easily."

Sebastian's eyes sparkled. "I want you to meet her. And her dog. I know Clarence is going to love Murphy."

"Terrific." I purposefully didn't respond to his comment about Clarence, our beagle mutt who had grown attached to Sebastian since he moved nearby. Clarence was a one-man dog. He didn't particularly like to share, and I wasn't sure how he'd respond to Sebastian fussing over another dog.

After giving Meg a quick hug goodbye, I hustled to the garage, retrieved our Prius, and pulled up nine minutes and thirty seconds later in front of Neptune's Fountain. Doug was bundled up in his dark winter coat, tuffs of his bushy brown hair peeking through the hood he had pulled over his head. Minutes later, we were cruising along interstate 395 South, headed back to the Virginia suburb of Arlington where we lived.

"Did you get all your work done?" I asked.

"I'm caught up," he said. "You have no idea how much time it's taken to prepare for tomorrow's event. Gaffney wanted everything planned to the minute."

"It's understandable. After all, he wants the Librarian to look good. A lot of important members of Congress will be there. Miriam Dunlap hasn't been in the position for that long."

The first woman and African American Librarian of Congress, Miriam Dunlap had brought a breath of fresh air to Capitol Hill. In her early fifties, she had more energy than hours in the day. In a little over a year, she'd taken a time-honored institution and made it relevant to the twenty-first century.

"We'll make sure it goes off without a hitch," said Doug. "In the meantime, did you have a chance to look at the listing Jonathan sent us?"

Jonathan, a former Senate colleague who'd changed careers and become a successful realtor, had recently shown us several houses in Virginia suburbs near Arlington. Doug was eager to move into a bigger space than our two-bedroom condo. But I was hesitant to leave our Arlington oasis. At our current residence, everything we needed was within walking distance and our commute to Capitol Hill remained tolerable. A house meant living somewhere less cosmopolitan than Arlington, and I wasn't ready for that degree of domesticity. At least now. Doug had gotten so excited about the prospect of having an office where he could store all of his books and a yard for Clarence. I'd only hinted at my hesitation.

"Not yet, but I will tomorrow." I turned into the garage underneath our high-rise condo building.

"Don't forget, darling," said Doug. "Jonathan said this house is a real keeper."

Five minutes later, we braced ourselves outside the door. Clarence had a habit of trying to escape when we entered. He liked the thrill of running down the long hallway, often barking with glee. Unfortunately, our elderly neighbor Mrs. Beauregard (a confirmed cat lover) disliked dogs and frequently threatened to report Clarence to the condo board.

"Ready?" asked Doug.

I nodded, putting my key into the lock and slowly opening the door. Sure enough, our chunky beagle mutt tried to wedge himself between the door and the frame. Doug anticipated our puppy's move, placing his foot in Clarence's path.

"Not so fast, buddy," he said.

Clarence knew the jig was up. He retreated into our condo, his tail wagging like a souped-up metronome.

"If we could harness the power of that tail, we might solve the energy crisis," I said.

Doug laughed, and we walked into our condo. "I'm beat," he said. "I'd better hit the sack. I have an early day tomorrow."

"I'll take Clarence for his walk and join you soon," I said.

As I strolled with Clarence outside, I considered the evening's events. Doug certainly worked with a lively and assorted set of colleagues. Despite their eccentricities and foibles, it was refreshing to observe a group of people genuinely unified around a common mission. The most delightful part of it was the lack of politics or bitter partisanship. I'd worked on Capitol Hill as a congressional staffer for so many years, I almost forgot what it was like to work somewhere without persistent conflict. Perhaps that was fodder for careful reflection.

Clarence pulled toward our building. After all, it was mid-February. Even with his fur coat, he'd had enough of the cold. When we arrived at our condo, Doug was already fast asleep. We soon joined him for a long winter's nap, blissfully unaware of what awaited us the next day.

Chapter Three

———~~———

$\mathbf{B}$Y THE TIME I rolled out of bed, Doug had already departed for work. Usually, it was the other way around. Nervous about today's reenactment, this time with the Librarian of Congress playing the main part, he must have gotten an early start to the day. Sure enough, I checked my phone and there was a text message from him.

Had to run. Wish me luck.

I wrote back, reassuring him everything would go smoothly. If not, the Assistant Librarian would certainly let Doug know about it. He obviously wanted to test Doug in his new position. After today's event, maybe Gaffney would back off Doug. I certainly hoped so. While I was used to pushy, demanding bosses, Doug's background as an academic had shielded him from such authoritative supervision. He'd either have to get used to it or figure out a way to sidestep Gaffney's overbearing style.

My boss, Chairwoman Maeve Dixon, was headed directly to the Library of Congress this morning for the event. That meant I didn't need to rush into work. As the chair of the oversight committee, she'd linger at the festivities this morning and would certainly give an interview (or two) to the D.C. newspapers covering it. Due to the media interest, our press secretary planned to attend with her. Since I'd gone to the preview last night, I was more than happy to cede my usual duty of accompanying the boss to another staffer in our office.

Furthermore, Maeve wasn't happy to be in Washington this week, and I was tired of hearing the complaints. Congress was usually in recess during the week of President's Day. During recess, Maeve recharged, spending time in North Carolina with family, friends, and constituents. But the Speaker of the House decided to cancel the recess in an effort to pass critical legislation. No one really believed the extra time would have the desired effect, but optics are everything in D.C. these days. No one liked having a break unexpectedly removed from the calendar, including staff and politicians.

After a light morning jog with Clarence, I made myself a double shot cappuccino from our monster espresso machine, which occupied a good portion of our kitchen countertop. We'd have to keep that in mind if we decided to move. There was no way I was giving up our mammoth coffee contraption. I couldn't get moving most mornings without it.

I was about to dash into the shower when my phone buzzed. Hopefully nothing had gone awry at the office.

Thankfully, it was another message from Doug. That was surprising, since the big event was scheduled to start in less than thirty minutes. I punched the code to access my phone and read the text.

Come to LOC ASAP.

"LOC" was the acronym for the Library of Congress. I typed back a reply.

Haven't left condo yet.

Three dots appeared immediately, indicating Doug was responding.

Hurry, pls.

How strange. Maybe something had gone wrong with the congressional attendance and Doug needed my help. Didn't congressional relations guru Janice Jackson deal with those types of problems?

Before I could ask what was so urgent, my other phone, which I used for only work-related business, buzzed. But this wasn't a text message. It was a phone call from Maeve Dixon.

I swiped the phone to answer the call.

"Good morning, Madame Chair."

A little humor couldn't hurt. Maeve liked being called "Madame Chair," and I already knew she was miffed she had to spend the week in Washington, D.C.

"I'm afraid it's not a good morning. I walked over early to attend the Library of Congress event." She paused for second. "Kit, someone is dead."

In an instant, my heart sank. Doug? Then I remembered he had just texted me. It couldn't be him. I squeaked out a question. "Did you say dead?"

"Yes," said Maeve in a clipped voice. "It's a Library of Congress staffer. Not your husband, of course. He's here with the police. They seem quite interested in what he has to say."

I gulped. "I'll be there as soon as I can." I clicked the phone shut. At least I knew the reason for Doug's cryptic texts.

In five minutes flat, I took a lightning fast shower, threw on a black pantsuit and boots, and ran out the door. Clarence had never seen me move so quickly. He barked goodbye as I tossed him a milk bone.

The traffic gods were with me this morning. Thirty minutes later, I was trotting toward the Thomas Jefferson Building. I approached the entrance from the drive adjacent to the ground floor, called the "carriage entrance," reminiscent of the horse and buggy era when the building was constructed in the late nineteenth century.

A Capitol Hill police office stood squarely in front of the door. "Sorry, ma'am. The Jefferson Building is closed," he said. After taking a look at my attire, which screamed Capitol Hill staffer, he continued. "The congressional event has been postponed."

"Thank you," I said. Politeness was always preferable, but particularly useful when dealing with law enforcement. "But my husband works here at the Library and he contacted me about the. . ." I stammered. "Incident. I think he's somehow. . ." Stammering again. "Involved."

The cop narrowed his eyes. "I don't have authorization to let anyone inside the building." He turned away from me, grabbing his crackling radio from his hip holster.

An attractive female police officer stepped outside, her auburn hair pulled back neatly in a ponytail. She was holding tightly onto a leash attached to a large black dog. Surveying the scene, she fixed her gaze on me. "Are you Kit Marshall?"

"That's me."

It only took three strides of her long legs to reach me. "I'm Lisa Reddy," she said, offering her hand.

"Have we met before?" I racked my brain. "I've met a lot of Capitol Hill police officers since my boss became the chair of the oversight committee."

Lisa laughed, her green eyes sparkling. "We've never met. But I know your brother Sebastian."

Duh. This was Sebastian's new girlfriend.

I accepted her hand and shook it. "Sorry, Lisa. It's sort of been a stressful morning."

"I understand. By the way, this is Murphy. Sebastian tells me you're a dog lover."

I looked down. Murphy stared up at me with big, brown eyes. His Capitol Hill police vest said, "POLICE DOG: DO NOT PET."

"Hello, Murphy," I said, pulling my hand back. "I'm not supposed to pet you, unfortunately."

Lisa chuckled. "That's for the general public. Murphy is pretty cute. If we didn't have that sign on him, every tourist would want to stop and cuddle. But you can pet him, if you like."

I rubbed Murphy's head, and he licked my hand. "Lisa, can you help me get inside? I think your colleagues are speaking to my husband, and my boss Chairwoman Maeve Dixon is also there. Quite frankly, I don't even know what happened, except that a Library of Congress staff member is dead."

She nodded. "Let me go inside and check to make sure it's okay."

"Thank you," I said. Lisa turned around with Murphy to enter the building. Before she did, I called out to her. "Nice to meet you!"

I texted Doug to let him know I was trying to find a way inside. I also sent a message to Meg, asking her to hold down the fort at the office. She wrote back immediately.

Why are you at LOC again?

Meg knew that I wasn't supposed to staff the Congresswoman at this event.

Dead body at the Library.

Meg responded with the "surprise" emoticon.

:-0

After promising to keep her posted, the door opened, and Lisa and Murphy emerged. "Good news," she said. "O'Halloran says you can go inside."

"Thank goodness for Detective O'Halloran." I'd worked with him on other Capitol Hill murder investigations. Unfortunately, if he was on the scene, foul play was likely.

"*Sergeant* O'Halloran," Lisa said. "He was promoted."

"Wow!" I exclaimed. "That's great news. I'll have to congratulate him, although today might not be the best time."

"It might not be," said Lisa gravely. We went through the metal detectors to enter the building and climbed the stairs. I shuddered. Lisa's foreshadowing hadn't escaped me.

Despite the swarm of police officers, the Great Hall shone with ornate regality. I scanned the marble expanse, which was now filled with law enforcement and officials in dark suits. Finally, I spotted Doug, deep in conversation with O'Halloran.

Maeve Dixon was here, too, but my first priority was Doug. From across the way, I could see the worry lines on Doug's forehead. In his case, graceful aging wasn't the culprit. My husband was distressed. Calm and collected, Doug rarely became flustered. His apparent anxiety upped my own blood pressure several points.

I hustled over to the two men. Placing a hand on Doug's shoulder, I leaned in. "Good morning," I said evenly, extending my hand. "I understand it's Sergeant O'Halloran these days."

The edges of the beefy cop's mouth inched upward ever so slightly. "Correct, Ms. Marshall. Unfortunately, we meet under difficult circumstances." He added, "Once again."

This could only mean murder. "Can you tell me what happened?"

O'Halloran tried to speak, but Doug cut him off. "I came into work early today, as you know. After dropping off my coat at my office, I walked over here to the Great Hall to make sure everything was in order." Doug pointed to the Librarian's ceremonial office, the same place we'd been last night. I noticed a piece of yellow police tape cordoned off the entrance.

I nodded my head and massaged Doug's shoulder. "Go on. What happened next?"

Doug's face was now flush. "That's when I discovered him."

"Who, Doug?" I asked. Clearly, the shock had affected his thinking. Maybe he didn't realize I had no idea what happened.

"My boss," said Doug, his fingers pinching the bridge of his nose, no doubt in a futile attempt to forestall an impending headache. "Gustav Gaffney has been murdered, and the killer stole the contents of Lincoln's pockets."

Chapter Four

"THAT'S NOT ENTIRELY true," said O'Halloran. He pulled out a handkerchief and wiped trickles of perspiration from his face. Even though it was February, the robust former detective must have been feeling the heat.

"What's not true?" I asked. "Are you sure the Assistant Librarian was murdered?"

"Oh yeah," said O'Halloran with the nonchalance that comes with having worked homicide investigations previously. "Gaffney was definitely murdered. But not everything was stolen from the safe."

"That's right," said Doug. "I'm too upset to think clearly. The confederate note was stolen and the handkerchief."

"Perhaps the thief had to hurry," I said. "And grabbed what he could."

"We're not sure," said O'Halloran. "But your husband here is front and center of this investigation, as you might imagine, Ms. Marshall."

I swallowed hard. Doug had discovered the body, which almost always cast suspicions. To add insult to injury, his relationship with Gaffney had been strained. It wouldn't take an experienced investigator like O'Halloran too long to figure that out.

"I'm sure Doug called the police immediately after finding Mr. Gaffney." I touched my husband's arm lightly. "Right, Doug?"

"Of course," he said, his voice quavering. "I mean, right after I checked his vitals."

"You touched the body?" I asked. As the spouse of an amateur sleuth, he should have known better, right?

"I guess." He added quickly, "But only to see if he was breathing."

"How was he killed?" I asked. There was no way someone could have snuck a gun or knife inside the Library of Congress. The level of security was comparable to the congressional office buildings since tunnels connected the structures underground.

"I shouldn't be sharing information, but since your husband is involved, I might as well tell you," said the newly minted sergeant. "It appears Gaffney was hit on the head with a bust of Thomas Jefferson."

"The bust was inside the Librarian's office?" I asked.

O'Halloran consulted his notebook. "You got it."

"It was a gift from the Archivist of the United States when Miriam Dunlap was sworn into office," said Doug. "She keeps it on display on the bookshelf inside the ceremonial office."

"If that's the case, then a lot of people would know it could serve as a handy weapon," I said.

"True," said O'Halloran. "It definitely points to an insider. Someone who knew his or her way around the Library of Congress."

I couldn't disagree with the Sergeant's reasoning. The perpetrator had taken advantage of the situation and used the opportunity to steal a national treasure. A light bulb went off in my head. If theft was the motive, then maybe there was a way to clear Doug.

I turned to face O'Halloran. "Have you searched Doug?"

"The officer on the scene sequestered him," said the sergeant. "Once we realized the safe was open and items were missing, we did search Dr. Hollingsworth." He added, "After he consented, of course."

I snapped my fingers. "That puts him in the clear! The murderer clearly has the missing artifacts in his or her possession."

"Wait a second, Ms. Marshall," said O'Halloran slowly. "I know you want to clear your husband, but I'm afraid it won't be that easy. First, we don't know when Gaffney was killed. It might have been last night. Second, even if it was this morning, the culprit might have done the deed, removed the goods from the safe, and then stashed them somewhere for safekeeping." He waved his hand around the Great Hall. "God only knows there are about a million places to hide something in this building. We could search for a year and not find all the nooks and crannies."

O'Halloran was right again. The killer could have hidden the stolen items behind a book in any of the reading rooms. Then, when the coast was clear, the thief could retrieve the objects undetected.

"How did the murderer manage to open the safe?" I asked.

"Remember the details from last night?" Doug said. "Only two sets of fingerprints work on the safe. Gustav Gaffney's and Miriam Dunlap's."

"Everyone at the event last night would have heard that," I said. "Are you saying the perpetrator bashed Gaffney over the head and then used his finger to open the safe?"

"I'm afraid so, Ms. Marshall," said O'Halloran. "We're dealing with a vicious criminal who killed Gaffney and then positioned his body near the safe so he or she could gain access to the treasures."

"Who would have known these critical details?" I asked Doug. "Was it widely known that the contents of Lincoln's pockets would be stored in a safe inside the Librarian's ceremonial office last night?"

Doug shook his head vigorously. "Absolutely not. Many congressional offices knew about this morning's event, but not the details. Certainly rank-and-file Library of Congress staff weren't privy to the insider information."

O'Halloran rubbed his chin. "It does point to someone who attended yesterday evening's preview. The details about the safe were discussed, and the perpetrator would have had the opportunity to strike after the event had ended."

"I can make sure you have a list of everyone who was present last night," said Doug helpfully.

As Doug listed the names of the Library employees and guests, I scanned the room. Across the Great Hall, my boss was deep in conversation with a fifty-something woman wearing a worried expression. I recognized Maeve Dixon's interlocutor as Miriam Dunlap, the Librarian of Congress. Doug was still explaining last night's program to Sergeant O'Halloran. Although the police would definitely consider him a suspect, Doug seemed to have things under control at the moment. I touched him lightly on the arm and let him know I needed to speak with Maeve Dixon.

My boss saw me coming and motioned for me to hurry. "Here's the person I was telling you about, Miriam. This is Kit Marshall, my chief of staff."

I offered my hand to the Librarian of Congress. "I'm sorry to meet formally under these terrible circumstances, Ms. Dunlap. You have my condolences."

Dunlap adjusted her glasses and peered up at me. I was no giant, but she was barely five feet tall. Her worried eyes narrowed. "You're the amateur sleuth of Capitol Hill?"

"Yes, ma'am. I've had some luck solving a few cases." My voice quavered.

"I've never been involved with a real murder, but I've read my share of mysteries," said Dunlap. "I hope you're as good as the literary sleuths I've encountered."

All thoughts of Gustav Gaffney disappeared. I was a big fan of mystery novels and enjoyed talking with a fellow aficionado.

"Who do you like to read?" I asked. "Christie? Sayers?"

Dunlap wrinkled her forehead.

"Or maybe you like more modern authors. Lippman? Grafton? French?" I continued.

Miriam Dunlap took me by the arm and gently guided me toward the ceremonial office. "Ms. Marshall, I would like to speak to you about your favorite mystery authors one day in the near future. However, we have important business at hand. Don't we?" She gestured in the direction of the police tape that now served as a barrier blocking the entrance to the office.

"Oh, yes," I said, blushing. "You're absolutely right."

She smiled. "I understand your husband Doug Hollingsworth, the director of our scholarly center, discovered Gustav's body. Is that correct?"

"Yes, ma'am. I spoke to him briefly. The police officer in charge, Sergeant O'Halloran, is asking Doug some questions now." I gestured in their direction.

Miriam Dunlap nodded. "Good. I'm glad he's cooperating." She paused for a moment before continuing. "Your boss speaks highly of your talents. Not only as a chief of staff, but also as an investigator."

"Thank you," I said. "We've found ourselves in several quagmires in the past and I've been able to help the police." I stared at the Librarian of Congress directly in the eye. "I've managed to find the guilty party every time." I conveniently neglected to mention the unorthodox routes to justice involved in these escapades. She could read the newspaper accounts if she wanted all the sordid details.

Dunlap clasped her hands together and then dragged me back toward Maeve Dixon, who was standing several feet away. "Let's talk to the esteemed committee chair."

My boss, whose head was buried in her phone, looked up when we approached. Dunlap spoke first. "Chairwoman Dixon, I've had a brief chat with Kit. I would like to enlist her services."

Maeve was a consummate politician. After experiencing combat in Iraq and Afghanistan, she almost always kept her composure, even in sticky situations. But I could tell that Miriam Dunlap's request caught her off guard. Dixon's head jerked backwards, and she blinked several times. A moment later, she had regained her poker face.

"I assume you're referring to Kit's detective skills?" asked Dixon.

"Of course," said Dunlap. "Given the circumstances, I need all the help I can get." She pulled both of us closer and lowered her voice. "Ladies, this murder must be solved quickly. First, Gustav Gaffney was my colleague and friend." Dunlap's chin trembled as she continued. "I owe it to him to find the person responsible for this heinous crime. Second, I need to recover the stolen items. As you surely know, those artifacts are irreplaceable items of our national heritage. We must apprehend the thief as soon as possible so we can recover everything and make sure nothing has been damaged. Or worse."

"Worse?" I asked. It was hard to imagine how the situation could become more dire.

"If this goes on too long, the thief will find a buyer underground. And who knows what that person will do with our treasures. We may never see them again." Dunlap covered her face with her hands. "I can't believe poor Gustav died because of it."

Maeve took a deep breath. "These are extraordinary circumstances, Miriam." My boss looked at me. "Kit, what do you think?"

I was taken aback by Maeve's question. Her military training usually meant she operated in demonstratives, not questions.

I thought for a few seconds before answering. Doug was nervously standing in the corner of the Great Hall, now chatting with the crusty Library of Congress general counsel Joe Malden. If the culprit wasn't apprehended swiftly, we'd need to find Doug a real lawyer. He'd taken the job at the Library of Congress to give his career a new direction. It would be a very short tenure if a cloud of suspicion hung over his head. There was no doubt about it. I needed to help Doug.

Before answering, I straightened my posture. "I'm sure I can assist. But it will need to be in cooperation with the police."

"Let's not waste any time, then," said the Librarian. "It looks as though the Sergeant has a free moment."

She marched over to O'Halloran, who seemed to be carrying on a conversation with himself as he read through the scrawl in his notebook. As chief of staff for Maeve Dixon, I was used to working for a strong-minded woman. But Miriam Dunlap took the cake. She made General Patton look indecisive. Maeve Dixon and I followed behind her.

Ensconced in his notes, O'Halloran didn't recognize our presence immediately. Dunlap waited patiently for several seconds and then cleared her throat. The sergeant looked up. "Ms. Dunlap," he said. "How can I help you?"

"Sergeant, I don't think introductions are necessary. You know Kit Marshall and Chairwoman Maeve Dixon," said Dunlap.

The Librarian didn't give O'Halloran a chance to disagree.

"The Assistant Librarian, my dear friend Gustav Gaffney, was killed in my office and a great national treasure has been stolen. The criminal behind this outrage must be apprehended as soon as possible," she said.

O'Halloran tried to say something, but Dunlap kept going. "You need all available resources at your disposal. I'm sure there will be numerous federal agencies who will want to make this case their own." She stared at O'Halloran pointedly. "But I'm also certain you have the internal knowledge of Capitol Hill to solve this case."

Miriam Dunlap certainly didn't pull any punches. Nothing like going for the jugular and hitting O'Halloran where it hurt. Overlapping jurisdictions infuriated him and any other self-respecting law enforcement officer. Capitol Hill was his beat. Pretty soon, the FBI would be all over this case, decreasing the chances of the local Capitol cops solving the crime.

"As the head of the Library of Congress, I would like to ask you to collaborate with Ms. Marshall. As I understand it, she's had much success in assisting the police previously with homicide cases."

O'Halloran inhaled and started to speak. Miriam Dunlap didn't give him the opportunity. "This arrangement has the support of *Chairwoman Dixon.*" Dunlap motioned toward my boss as she emphasized her name. "As you know, she leads the committee with congressional oversight authority concerning the Library of Congress." She paused for a beat. "And the Capitol Hill police." Her speech finished, Dunlap crossed her hands in front of her body and took a half step back.

O'Halloran eyed the three of us warily, his hands tightened into fists. He certainly didn't welcome my help. On the other hand, Dunlap had him between a rock and a hard place. After an uncomfortable silence, he finally spoke. "Normally, I wouldn't contradict the wishes of an elected official, particularly a member of Congress. However, in this situation, we have a conflict of interest. Ms. Marshall's husband is a suspect."

Dixon chimed in. "I would never substitute my judgment for a law enforcement officer's expert opinion." She raised a finger. "However, I can vouch for the character of Doug Hollingsworth. Do you have material evidence against him?"

"No, we do not," said O'Halloran, a tone of regret in his voice. He knew where this conversation was headed.

"Sergeant, can I suggest that until you do, Ms. Marshall can work with you on the investigation?" She gestured toward Miriam Dunlap. "After all, the Librarian of Congress is the lead agency official, and she's asking for Kit's help."

O'Halloran sighed. His ploy to oust me from the investigation had failed. These two women were not going to let him prevail. "Very well," he said. "Once again, Ms. Marshall will serve in a liaison capacity." He raised his hand, with his palm facing us as a "stop" sign. "However, she will not interfere with the pursuit of this criminal. We are dealing with a very different scenario than other crimes she's assisted with."

He turned to face me directly. "Homicide is nasty enough business. But this person committed murder to steal artifacts of immeasurable value." He shook his finger. "We don't know what we're dealing with here. A professional killer for hire? An insider working with a crime syndicate?" His voice became higher pitched. "A terrorist plot?"

I couldn't resist. "You really think terrorists want to steal the contents of Lincoln's pockets from the night he was assassinated?"

O'Halloran took his handkerchief from his pocket and wiped his forehead. "Ms. Marshall, for all of your detecting and interactions with killers, you have a sanguine view of the world." He put his hands on his hips, almost indistinguishable from his sizable waist. "I do not have that luxury."

The sergeant's words seemed more adversarial than necessary. Best to diffuse the situation, especially if we were going to work together to find the culprit who committed homicide and larceny at the Library of Congress. "I am an optimistic person, Sergeant. But my positive outlook has never prevented me from delivering justice to those responsible."

Dixon listened to our repartee with a tight smile. I knew my boss. She was amused, but not for long. "It's settled, then." She gestured between me and O'Halloran. "You'll work together to find the party or parties responsible for this travesty. Kit's primary assignment will be providing Miriam with information as the investigation progresses." She grasped the lapels of her suit jacket and gave them a straightening yank. "I will also require regular briefings, since I am the chair of the committee with jurisdiction concerning this matter."

Maeve Dixon spoke with such authority, no one could dispute her pronouncement. Miriam Dunlap seemed satisfied. "Very well," she said. "Ms. Marshall, perhaps we should speak later today, after the dust settles, so to speak."

I nodded. "Detective." I realized my mistake. "I mean, Sergeant."

Dixon and Dunlap walked away, deep in conversation. They couldn't hear O'Halloran's parting commentary. "Doesn't matter if I'm a sergeant or the chief of police. Those two would still be telling me what to do."

We hadn't caught the killer yet, but at least Sergeant O'Halloran had a firm grasp of what it meant to work on Capitol Hill.

Chapter Five

———

I JOINED DOUG AND Joe Malden, still deep in conversation near the marble staircase leading to the second floor. "Well, I have good news and bad news. Which one do you want first?"

Doug wrinkled his forehead. "I could really use some good news."

"Miriam Dunlap asked my boss if I could assist the police in solving the murder," I said. "Dixon agreed and made it clear to O'Halloran I should be kept in the loop."

Doug's face brightened. "That's great news, Kit. With you on the case, this fiasco should get wrapped up in no time."

"I'm not sure about that," I said. "It's a pretty complex situation."

"Wait, what's the bad news?" asked Malden.

"The police apparently consider Doug a suspect." I put my arm around Doug and gave him a tight squeeze. Being considered a murder suspect was stressful. I could practically feel Doug's unease with the situation.

Malden shrugged. "That'll clear up in a flash. Once the authorities realize they're barking up the wrong tree, their attention will be focused elsewhere."

As someone who had been accused of murder a few years ago when my boss was murdered in the United States Senate, I wasn't quite sure it was as simple as Joe suggested. The moniker "suspect" was stickier than flypaper. In my experience, the specter of suspicion didn't lift until the police apprehended the real murderer. I'd been so eager to end the drama, I solved the murder to clear my name.

"Let's hope so," muttered Doug, staring in the direction of the Librarian's ceremonial office, where Sergeant O'Halloran was now chatting with

Gordon Endicott. I followed Doug's gaze, just in time to notice O'Halloran and Endicott glancing in our direction.

"I wonder why they're looking over here," I thought out loud.

"Gordon is probably up to no good," said Doug glumly.

"What makes you think that?" I asked.

Malden answered. "Endicott wanted the job Doug has now as head of the scholarly center. Gustav preferred Endicott. But Miriam Dunlap believed Doug had a higher academic profile and more publications to his name." Malden smiled. "She was right, of course."

"Are you worried that Gordon Endicott might try to frame you for the murder and theft?" I asked.

Doug ran his hands through his dark, bushy hair. "It's possible. He's not a fan of mine."

It was bad enough trying to solve a homicide, but now I had to clear my husband and figure out a way to combat a crafty rare books expert who was hellbent on discrediting Doug. I had my work cut out for me. Reinforcements were in order, particularly since I had missed breakfast this morning. I pulled my iPhone out of my purse and texted Meg.

Can we meet for an early lunch?

Three dots appeared.

Who was murdered at the Library?

Meg's gossip network was impressive. It had only grown stronger now that our boss Maeve was the chair of the House Administration committee. These days, she heard the scuttlebutt from her regular sources *and* the most senior staff in Congress.

We can talk over tacos @ Rosa's.

Ok. Will bring T.

"T" was, of course, shorthand for Trevor. Given current circumstances, I didn't have the time or energy to deal with Meg's love triangle. Nonetheless, Trevor had been at the event last night and was keenly observant. It would be worth the drama to learn if he had any revelatory insights or clues.

"Doug, are you free to leave the Jefferson Building?" I asked. "You might feel better if you had something to eat."

"I'd better check with O'Halloran." Doug scurried over to ask.

Nonchalantly scrolling through his iPhone like he was in line for coffee, Joe Malden looked awfully relaxed for the lead lawyer at an agency where a murder had just occurred. I strained my eyes to spy on what had him so captivated, expecting to find that he was searching Twitter or popular news websites for media reports of the crimes. Instead, I spotted a familiar logo that had nothing to do with the fact that the now former Assistant Librarian was less than fifty feet away, his head bashed in from a fatal blow and a nation's invaluable treasure in the wind.

"Reading about the Red Sox?" I asked, gesturing toward his phone screen.

"Guilty as charged," he said. "Given today's events, perhaps I shouldn't say that phrase too loudly." He chuckled before continuing.

"You must be dedicated if you're following them in February," I said.

"Pitchers and catchers are reporting this week for spring training," he explained. "I'll be headed to Fort Myers next month for games."

"You really are passionate, then. That's refreshing."

Malden smiled. "We do have our share of fair-weather sports fans in Washington. But who can blame them? D.C. residents are used to picking winners and losers. Everyone flocks to the former and no one sticks with the latter, even when it comes to sports."

Harsh words, yet true. Perhaps he could give me some valuable info. "Do you have any idea who might have killed Assistant Librarian Gaffney and stolen the items from the safe?"

His jaw tightened. "No idea." Malden had gone from Mr. Chatty to Mr. Clammy in three seconds flat.

"The killer had to know that only Gaffney's and the Librarian's prints would open the safe," I said. "Doug says that wasn't widely known amongst staff. That might narrow the credible suspect pool to last night's attendees."

"You never know," said Malden. "Any person at the preview might have mentioned the method for opening the safe to a colleague. Or even a person outside the Library of Congress."

Was it just me, or was Joe Malden grasping at straws? Obviously, this crime had been carefully planned. There was no way someone had casually mentioned these facts after the event to someone who impetuously decided to kill Gustav Gaffney and steal the contents of Abraham Lincoln's pockets.

Maybe a more pointed approach would yield better results. "You don't think someone at the event last night had the desire to commit the crime?"

Malden had returned to the baseball scouting report on his phone. He didn't even look up to answer me. In a flat voice, he said, "Nope."

Perhaps I needed to spurn a reaction. "It seemed to me that Lea Rutherford had definite interest in the Library's impressive Lincoln collection."

Malden snorted. "Lea Rutherford could *own* the Library of Congress, if that's what she wanted. She's a very rich woman."

"That might be the case, but no dollar figure could buy the contents of Lincoln's pockets the night he was assassinated. Or other national treasures held within this building." I waved my arm around.

"Of course," said Malden, looking me directly in the eye. "What I'm saying is that Lea can buy any priceless item that's for sale. Why would she bother with something that's not for sale?"

"I don't know. Sometimes we want what we can't have. Right?"

"Perhaps, but you don't know Lea Rutherford. She's not that type of person. She supports *preserving* artifacts, not stealing them."

Before I could respond, Doug showed up at my side. "Sergeant O'Halloran says I can leave." Then he added, "Well, I can't leave the metropolitan area. But I can go to lunch on Capitol Hill."

"That's good enough for now," I said in my most cheerful voice. Doug needed to shed his status as a suspect quickly. O'Halloran had consented to my assistance for the time being. But if Doug's status elevated, he'd make sure my sleuthing days came to an end. Not to mention that Congresswoman Dixon and the Librarian of Congress wanted the killer caught in record time.

"Nice chatting with you," I said to Joe.

"Enjoy your lunch, Doug," he said as he returned to his iPhone. As we walked away, I caught him staring. I had the distinct feeling the baseball-loving general counsel didn't particularly like me. No surprise there. I was asking hard questions, and I wasn't going to take easy answers without pushing back.

Doug and I left the Jefferson Building, turned the corner, and walked east down Pennsylvania toward Santa Rosa's Taqueria. Celebrity chef Spike Mendelsohn, who operated several restaurants in Washington, opened Rosa's a few years ago and before you could say "margarita," it had become a favorite lunch spot on Capitol Hill. We walked through the entrance and found Meg and Trevor already waiting for us.

Trevor started to say something, but Meg cut him off. "Who was *murdered* at the Library of Congress?"

"Please keep your voice down," I said. "They haven't released anything to the press yet."

Meg pursed her lips. "I get it," she said in her version of a hushed voice, which could probably be heard without trouble during a Capitals' playoffs power play.

Trevor caught on. "Let's order our lunch, Meg. Then we can talk." He gently took her arm and guided her to the line.

Doug elbowed me. "We couldn't have enjoyed a private lunch?"

He had a point. Doug had just been accused of murder. Then again, my instinct was to solve the crime so his problem would disappear. "Meg and Trevor have been instrumental in solving previous cases. We need their help." Then I added, "So we can clear your name." I gave Doug's hand a squeeze.

He took a deep breath. "You're right. They will be on our side. And four heads are better than two."

"Most of the time," I said. "What are you going to order?"

"Carne asada street tacos," he said. "With guacamole, of course."

"I'm going for the chicken casa bowl," I said.

"Chips for the table?" asked Doug.

"Of course," I said. "If we're going to ask Meg and Trevor to help us figure out who killed Gustav Gaffney, we'd better make sure they are well fed."

After placing our orders at the counter and picking up our food, we found a spot in the corner of the crowded eatery. Meg had selected the spicy fried shrimp tacos. Trevor, whose fastidious behavior included a healthy diet, had ordered the La Fuerte salad with grilled chicken. Since they started dating six months ago, Meg had loosened Trevor up a bit, but he still had a long way to go.

Meg didn't even wait to take a bite before firing off questions. "Who was murdered? Do the police have any suspects in custody? Are you going to investigate?"

I wiped my mouth before answering. "Settle down. We'll catch you both up."

Doug and I explained this morning's events, including the theft and other relevant details. Meg and Trevor listened intently, not even bothering to eat. Meg's eyes widened as we explained that Doug was likely a suspect.

"But what's the motive?" asked Trevor.

"No matter who the killer is, the motive has to be the theft," I said. "Gaffney was only one of two people whose fingerprints could open the safe. The Librarian of Congress wasn't alone with the safe, either last night or this morning. Therefore, the thief had to kill Gaffney to gain access."

Trevor rubbed his chin, deep in thought. "If the thief was a professional, then he or she could have knocked Gaffney unconscious and then used his fingerprints to open the safe. When Gaffney woke up, he wouldn't be able to identify the person, especially if a mask was worn."

"That's a good point," I said. "It corroborates my original theory that the perpetrator was someone who attended last night's viewing inside the ceremonial office. A mask wouldn't have disguised someone who was already well known to the victim."

"Yes," said Trevor slowly. "The thief had no choice but to murder Gaffney. He or she couldn't risk that he would be able to provide an identification."

Meg took a big bite of a shrimp taco. "Scrumptious," she muttered, her mouth still full. Trevor gave her a sideways glance, but I noticed the twinkle in his eye.

"If that's the case, then who is a likely suspect amongst those whom we met last night at the Library of Congress?" I asked.

"Besides Doug, you mean," said Trevor matter-of-factly.

"Of course, Trevor," I said, no hiding the annoyance in my voice. "We *know* that Doug didn't kill Gustav Gaffney."

Trevor rolled his eyes slightly. He never let friendship or emotional attachment get in the way of rational deduction. Although he'd improved over time, Trevor still scored relatively low on the emotional IQ scale.

Doug ignored Trevor's comment. "My guess is Gordon Endicott," said Doug.

"He did want your job," I said. "But murder and the theft of priceless treasures would be a pretty elaborate plot just to frame you."

"He might have wanted to steal the items," said Meg. "And then figured out a way he could frame Doug in the process."

"Quite ingenious," said Trevor. "He'd accomplish several goals with the crime."

"But Endicott is clearly enamored with the collections at the Library of Congress. Why would he want to steal Lincoln's handkerchief and the Confederate note? It goes against everything in his professional background."

Doug chuckled. "Unfortunately, many antiquities thefts are inside jobs, Kit. It's more common than you'd think."

"Dr. Hollingsworth is correct," said Trevor. "The biggest library theft in recent years occurred at the Carnegie Library in Pittsburgh. The chief archivist of the rare books collection stole over eight million dollars in materials over the course of several years. He worked with a rare books dealer to sell the items."

"That's terrible," said Meg. "Talk about letting the fox inside the henhouse."

"That means Gordon Endicott has to be at the top of our list," I said. "If he did it, he'd have access to the right people when he decided to sell the stolen items."

"He also seemed as though he was in good shape," said Meg. "He's strong enough to kill someone in the way you described."

"Quite frankly, everyone at the party last night would have been able to carry out the homicide," I said. "Remember, Gustav Gaffney was thin and frail. He was at least fifteen years older than everyone else in attendance. I don't think he would have been difficult to overpower."

"Meg, given your work with the oversight committee and the Library of Congress, you knew some of the guests from last night," Trevor said. "What do you think?"

Meg selected a tortilla chip and dipped it in green salsa. She nibbled on it before answering. "Well, Representative Henry Chang should definitely be on the list."

Doug raised his eyebrows. "You think a member of Congress could have done this?"

"Not just any member of Congress," said Meg. "Henry Chang is. . ." She paused while searching for the right word. "Unusual."

"How so?" I asked. Meg had told me last night that our boss didn't care for him. But that was no reason to consider him a murderer.

"He's obsessed with history," said Meg. She looked at Doug. "Not in the dorky, academic way."

"No offense taken," Doug said after swallowing a big bite of his taco.

"Can you be more specific?" I asked. "It's not uncommon for members of Congress to be interested in American history."

Meg shook her manicured red nail at me. "I know that, Kit. Remember, I've been working in Congress even longer than you have. What I mean is that Chang always asks detailed questions about the artifacts or paintings or whatever is on display. He gets really close to them, too."

"You're right about that," I said. "Last night, Gordon Endicott seemed annoyed that Chang invaded his space. From his body language, he seemed worried that Chang might try to touch the items."

Meg snapped her fingers. "Exactly! I've been to several of these soirees with him. As Chairwoman, Maeve gets a lot of invitations to D.C. cultural events and I usually go with her. After all, I do enjoy a good party and it's really the only perk for her as Chair of this committee." Meg repeatedly reminded us she wasn't enthralled about Maeve's assignment at House Administration.

"And he does this each and every time?" asked Trevor.

"Absolutely. He always monopolizes the poor curator or librarian's time, too. It's like he wants to know every last detail," she said, taking a sip of her iced tea. "Even before today, I always thought it was strange behavior."

I trusted Meg's opinion here. She'd been around a fair number of members of Congress and senators over the years. If Henry Chang's demeanor was atypical, she'd know it.

"I'll put him on the suspect list," I said. "We'll need to find out if he has an alibi."

"As soon as we find out when Gustav died," said Doug.

"That's right. We don't know when it happened." I turned to my husband. "Didn't you check Gaffney's pulse when you discovered his body this morning?"

Doug nodded. "Yes, even though I knew he was dead. I wanted to make sure."

"Was the body cold to your touch? Or still warm?" I asked.

"It wasn't warm," said Doug. His face looked a little pale.

"Did he look. . ." I hesitated because I didn't want to upset Doug more. "Stiff?"

Doug considered my question for a couple seconds. "Once I realized he was dead, I didn't look closely at him. It was obvious that someone had bashed him over the head with the Jefferson bust. But if I had to guess, I would say he did look stiff."

"Then perhaps the murder and theft occurred last night rather than this morning," said Trevor.

"Most likely," I said. "But I'll check with the police later today. It shouldn't take too long to establish the time of death."

"If it was last night, then it means that someone hung around the Library of Congress after the event and waited for the opportunity to kill Gaffney," said Meg.

"That's right," said Doug. "You wouldn't have been able to reenter the building if you left."

"Unfortunately, there's a lot of places to hide inside that building," I said. "The corridors are dark, especially without daylight. The perpetrator must needed to wait around until Gaffney was alone."

"But how did our killer know Gaffney would be alone?" asked Trevor. "After all, it's the Librarian's ceremonial office, not his."

Doug chuckled. "Gustav really liked that office. He had a small desk he sometimes used in the anteroom during the evening when he stayed late. I think he was inspired by his surroundings in the Jefferson Building. Miriam Dunlap didn't mind him using it after hours."

"Once again, it points to an insider," I said. "Only someone who was familiar with Gustav's habits would have known he worked inside that office late at night."

We munched on the remnants of chips and guacamole, silent while considering the conclusions we'd just drawn. Meg spoke first. "If we're considering Henry Chang, we should also consider Janice Jackson."

"The head of congressional affairs?" I asked. "I thought you liked her, Meg."

"I do. But one thing I've learned is that doesn't disqualify someone for murder," she said. Meg spoke the truth. Our previous cases had proven that inconvenient fact.

"But why would she want to steal the contents of Lincoln's pockets?" asked Doug. "I don't think she's a collector of rare books or historical items."

"Not that I know of," said Meg. "But she did complain about her boss Gustav Gaffney."

"Off-hand comments?" asked Trevor.

Meg shook her head as she finished off her shrimp tacos. "Nope. She mentioned him a lot."

"Enough to kill him?" I asked.

Meg shrugged. "Who knows? Gaffney wanted stronger congressional support for Library of Congress initiatives. Janice said she was under the gun from Gaffney to make sure it happened. It was one of the reasons I always insisted Maeve Dixon attend these events. I knew Janice needed our support."

"But we're looking for someone who murdered Gustav to steal the contents of Lincoln's pockets," said Doug.

"That's true. It doesn't exactly fit the scenario," I said. "But it's good to know more about everyone who was there last night. Are we missing anyone?"

Trevor cleared his throat. "Lea Rutherford is a person of interest." He stated his opinion the way that most people spoke about facts. An aura of certainty surrounded Trevor, a master of both emotions and information. This had to be what attracted Meg to him.

"Couldn't she *buy* the contents of Lincoln's pockets, if she wanted it?" asked Doug.

"If it was for sale, she could," said Trevor. "But as you know, some things cannot be bought. From what I've read, Lea Rutherford is an aggressive collector. She might want to take her obsession into uncharted waters."

"It's not like she could show anyone what she stole," said Meg. "Everyone would know she was a thief and murderer."

"Remember that Lea Rutherford owns houses in many different countries," said Trevor. "In far flung places, she might be able to enjoy what she'd taken."

"She also didn't like Gustav Gaffney very much," I said. "There was something mentioned last night to that effect."

"She recently decided to give several rare books she bought to Yale instead of the Library of Congress," said Doug. "It enraged Gustav. Ironically, she did it because she couldn't reach an agreement with him about how they would be displayed inside the Jefferson Building."

"It sounds like it wouldn't have bothered her to bop Gaffney on the head," said Meg.

"We'll add her to the list," I said. "Although I don't know how I'm going to investigate a billionaire."

"You always think of something, Kit," said Meg, grinning mischievously.

"I think that's about it for the suspects," said Doug. "I probably need to get back to work. My colleagues will have a lot of questions."

"Wait a second," I said. "We forgot someone."

"Who?" asked Doug.

"Joe Malden," I said. "He was there last night."

Doug waved his hand. "Joe can't be our killer," he said. "He wouldn't hurt a fly."

"Famous last words," muttered Meg.

"I had an awkward conversation with him before we left for lunch," I said. "He swore that Lea Rutherford wasn't involved in the murder and theft. But he couldn't give me any insight about who else might have done it."

"You can't blame him for that, Kit," said Doug, a tinge of annoyance in his voice. "He's the counsel for the Library of Congress. He's not going to sell any of his colleagues down the river."

"That's a good point. But he seemed extraordinarily tight-lipped. Something was off, like he was withholding information. I can't put my finger on it, but that was the feeling I got." Similar to Meg, I'd learned a thing or two after helping to solve several murders. My intuition was rarely wrong. Over time, I'd grown more comfortable in trusting it.

"I wouldn't waste your time on Joe," said Doug.

I reached over and placed my hand over Doug's. "He's your friend," I said gently. "Remember that you're also a suspect. We can't let any stone go unturned until you're cleared."

Doug gulped and said nothing. Not a fan of emotion-laden moments, Trevor stood up. "Speaking of the office, I'd better get back soon. My boss will want an update. He likes to stay informed about what happens on Capitol grounds."

We were clearing our table of trays and garbage when I heard a familiar, whiny male voice behind me. "Kit Marshall, is that you?"

I spun around. I'd recognize that voice anywhere. Sure enough, I was right. I summoned all the good karma left inside my body and plastered a smile on my face. "Dan, it's been so long since I've seen you last. How are you?"

Dan had briefly been my boss in Maeve Dixon's office. After Dixon had been accused of murdering the Speaker's top aide, he jumped ship. When the murder was solved and the guilty party apprehended, Maeve immediately offered me Dan's job as chief of staff. Dan had been such a disaster, we never spoke of him in the office. It was almost like he never existed.

Dan scanned our table nervously. "Team Dixon, I presume?"

"Sort of." I didn't want to give him too many specifics. I turned to everyone else and explained, "Dan was Maeve's first chief of staff."

Doug, Meg, and Trevor knew what a disaster Dan had been. They murmured pleasantries and kept their heads down.

"You're not still working in the House, are you?" I hadn't seen Dan at any chief of staff meetings in a long time. After leaving Dixon, he went to work for a congressman with a reputation for being extraordinarily difficult.

Dan waved his hand. "Nah, my time in Congress is over. I've moved on to the association world."

Washington, D.C. was a city full of associations. Everyone knew the National Rifle Association or Planned Parenthood. But there were literally thousands of organizations in the city, representing the particular interests of businesses, professions, and advocacy groups.

"Really?" I'd always thought Dan would have returned to his native small town in North Carolina. He didn't seem a good fit for permanent residence in our nation's capital.

Dan puffed out his chest. "Absolutely. I'm the executive director."

I raised my eyebrow. "Which association?"

Without missing a beat, he answered, "The National Association of

Pet Sitters."

I blinked. "Pet sitters?" Doug turned his face away, hiding his valiant attempt not to laugh.

"Absolutely, Kit. We have a board of directors and thousands of members. Pet sitting is a growing economic industry in the United States," he said.

I glanced at Meg. For once, we were both speechless. It was a rare occurrence.

I stuck my hand out. "Congratulations, Dan. I'm glad you found your calling."

He accepted my handshake and passed me a business card. "I'd like to visit you and the congresswoman to discuss our organization's most pressing issues."

I took his card and smiled. "Sure thing, Dan."

Trevor stood. "Kit, we should be going." He didn't pull my arm, but by the look he gave me, he was pondering it.

I waved goodbye to my former colleague and followed my friends out of the restaurant. Meg waited exactly five seconds before letting loose. "You're not going to suggest that Maeve Dixon meet with him, are you?"

"We can have someone in the office take the meeting. I'm not going to worry about it now," I said. "Somehow, I'm not surprised that Dan is now the esteemed leader for the pet sitters."

"I can't believe he was your boss," said Doug.

"Neither can I, but it's all water under the bridge now." I grabbed my phone out of my purse and scanned my email. "Looks like Miriam Dunlap would like to speak with me as soon as possible. I'll head to her office now. Let's touch base later to share any information about the murder and theft."

"I'll keep my eyes and ears open," said Trevor. "And I'll let Meg know if anything useful comes my way." Poor Trevor. He'd use any excuse to spend more time with Meg, all in hope she'd decide to make their relationship exclusive.

"Don't say too much," I told Doug. "You don't want to fan the flames of any rumors or gossip."

Doug nodded. "I plan to shut myself in my office until this whole ordeal is over."

I laughed. "That might be a little extreme, but better safe than sorry, I suppose." We split apart in front of the Library of Congress, each of us headed in our separate directions. I entered the Madison Building and got on the elevator for the sixth floor, searching for the Librarian's executive suite. With the modern digital signage added to the Library of Congress recently, it didn't take me more than a few minutes to find the right place. I waited for less than a minute before Miriam Dunlap strode across the waiting area to greet me.

"Welcome again to the Library of Congress, Ms. Marshall. It's the largest library in the world. And now. . ." she said, swallowing hard. In a shaky voice, she finished the sentence. "The scene of a ghastly murder."

Chapter Six

———— ∿ ————

THE DAY'S EVENTS had shaken Miriam Dunlap to the core. "Don't despair too much," I said in a soothing tone. "I've been in this situation before. Every time, it works out."

Dunlap motioned for me to follow inside her private office. With a spectacular view of the historic Jefferson Building and the United States Capitol accompanied by floor to ceiling windows, the Librarian's corner suite constituted prime real estate on Capitol Hill. Her desk was littered with papers and books. I appreciated a disheveled work space and instantly felt at ease with the homey appearance of her personal space.

"Please sit down, Ms. Marshall," she said, pointing to a leather armchair. She took a seat directly opposite me, straining to offer a smile.

"I'll touch base with Sergeant O'Halloran later this afternoon," I said. "I've already done a preliminary survey of the immediate suspects so we can talk freely about where the investigation stands."

"Impressive," said the Librarian, her hands folded neatly on her lap. "How did you come up with such a list?"

I explained that a limited number of people knew that only her fingerprints and Gustav Gaffney's could open the safe. Given Doug's observations, if we assumed that Gaffney was killed last night instead of this morning, then only those already inside the building would have had access to the Librarian's ceremonial office. That narrowed the list of possible suspects considerably.

"Then who are we talking about specifically, Ms. Marshall?" asked Dunlap. "After all, I'm in charge of the Library of Congress, and I need to know who might be responsible for these heinous crimes."

"Of course, ma'am." I ticked off the known suspects with my fingers. "There's Gordon Endicott, Joe Malden, Lea Rutherford, Janice Jackson, and Congressman Henry Chang." After taking a breath, I continued. "The police likely consider my husband Doug Hollingsworth a suspect, too. But I don't." I chuckled. "For obvious reasons."

"Thank you for those names, Ms. Marshall," said the Librarian, now with a pinched expression on her face. "I'm afraid you're going to have to go back to the drawing board."

My head flinched backwards. "Excuse me, ma'am?"

"Many of those individuals are my employees here at the Library of Congress," she said. "None of them could have killed Gustav Gaffney or committed theft."

"It's hard to imagine a colleague you know and trusted could have done this. But I've seen this unfortunate scenario time and time again. You'd be surprised what motivates people to do horrible things."

Dunlap didn't respond immediately. She pressed her lips together and pinched the bridge of her nose. "Gustav was a dear friend. I knew him for many years in our shared professional community of librarianship. We both worked at other institutions but saw each other frequently at conferences. Even before he became the Assistant Librarian, he offered valuable counsel when I first arrived to this position."

I leaned closer to her. "This must be quite difficult for you. I'd be happy to come back another time if you'd rather not talk about it."

"No, no," she said quickly. "I don't want any delay in solving this crime. I owe that to Gustav, after all." She looked directly at me. "What do you need from me?"

"Can you tell me anything about those people I mentioned?" I asked. "Such as details or information that might shed light on who could have done this?"

Dunlap spoke slowly. "I've been here for only a little over a year. I know them professionally, but I don't have too many personal insights to offer, I'm afraid." She shook her head. "I don't understand why anyone would want to do this to poor Gustav."

"Speaking of the victim," I said. Dunlap's face twisted into a somber expression. "I mean, Assistant Librarian Gaffney. What about him? Can you tell me more about what type of person he was?"

Dunlap's expression brightened. "Of course," she said. "What do you want to know?"

"Well, how about his reputation at the Library of Congress?" I asked

"Impeccable," said the Librarian. "Gustav was a respected librarian of the first order."

Okay, this might be a little harder than I thought. I'd have to be more pointed in my questioning.

"Was he well-liked by the staff? Wealthy donors? Any enemies? Of the first order?" I asked.

Miriam Dunlap got my drift. She rubbed her chin thoughtfully. "Now that you mention it, Gustav did not have the *easiest* job at the Library of Congress."

"How so?" Now we were getting somewhere.

"It's never easy being second in command, Ms. Marshall," she said. "Gustav needed to take care of the nitty gritty, so to speak."

"I won't beat around the bush, since I know your time is valuable." After taking a deep breath, I asked, "Was Gustav your hatchet man?"

Dunlap shifted uneasily in her seat. "The term is misleading. Gustav didn't fire people for me."

I chuckled. "This is the federal government. Does anyone get fired?"

The Librarian ignored my snarky remark. "But he did perform certain tasks that some might consider. . ." She paused before finishing the sentence. "Unpleasant."

The adjective "unpleasant" was too vague. It could mean anything from terminating a program to organizing the annual holiday party.

"Such as?"

Dunlap sat back in her high-backed armchair. "Sometimes good people apply for jobs they can't have. There's not enough money to fund all the terrific initiatives staff want to support. Rules and regulations need to be followed, even when they pose inconvenient hardships. Choices must be made between competing priorities." She adjusted her glasses. "In any organization, someone needs to make those operational decisions and communicate them. Gustav performed that function."

"I imagine a high-ranking person put in that position would garner quite a few enemies," I said, more as a comment than a question.

"It's not outside the realm of possibility," said Dunlap. "But Gustav's murder wasn't related to the difficult nature of his work, Ms. Marshall. The motive for this crime is theft. Gustav was caught up in this nasty business because his fingerprints opened the safe. At least that's what the police told me."

"You're right," I said. "It can't hurt to know something about the victim, though. By the way, did anyone else know about the safe and how to open it?"

She shook her head. "For security purposes, we didn't let many staff know about it. The only people who were aware attended the preview party inside the ceremonial office last night." Then she added, "Plus my chief of staff. But he was with me yesterday evening at an event across town. The police have already eliminated his as a suspect."

I perked up. "Who is your chief of staff?"

"His name is Dorian Jones," said the Librarian. "I'm surprised you don't know him."

"My colleague Meg handles the House Administration liaison committee work," I explained. "But perhaps I should speak with Dorian."

Dunlap nodded. "Of course. When we're done here, I will introduce you to him."

"Is there anything else I should know?" I asked. "Obviously, the police will be investigating everyone's background. It's my experience they can miss subtleties that actually matter."

"It's best you speak with Dorian," said the Librarian. "He might be able to help you there."

I rose out of the armchair and extended my hand. "I wish we could have met under better circumstances."

Miriam Dunlap adjusted her glasses and shook my hand lightly. "Ms. Marshall, I'm counting on you to help the Library of Congress at this difficult time. I simply cannot have a serious crime unsolved at this institution." She straightened her posture. "After all, people don't associate libraries with *murder*."

My mind immediately recalled the litany of mystery novels with a library as a setting. Agatha Christie's *A Body in the Library*. Charles Goodrum's *Dewey Decimated*. Margaret Truman's *Murder at the Library of Congress*. Even more recently, Con Lehane's *Murder at the 42nd Street Library* and Jenn McKinlay's *Death in the Stacks*. But one look at Dunlap's forlorn face and I shut my mouth. After all, these stories were fiction and she was struggling with the real deal.

"You're absolutely right," I said. "Libraries are for *learning*. Not murder."

Dunlap's face brightened. "Ms. Marshall, I'm glad we are on the same page." She motioned for me to follow her. "Come this way, and I'll introduce you to Dorian."

I followed Dunlap through the maze of offices inside her suite. We finally arrived at a private office in the rear of the suite. A thirty-something African American man, smartly dressed in a dark grey suit and deep purple tie, was typing at his computer. He completed the look with wire round-framed glasses. Was it me or did everyone at the Library of Congress look like they'd just emerged out of central casting? Obviously, Lasik surgery had not made its way to the hallowed halls of our national library.

"Dorian, please meet Ms. Marshall, who works for Chairwoman Dixon and will be assisting us with Gustav's murder."

He turned to face us. "Pleased to meet you, Ms. Marshall."

"By all means, call me Kit," I replied.

"Ms. Marshall would like to speak with you so she can learn more about the Library and our staff," said Dunlap, ignoring my request.

"Certainly," he said. "Have a seat." He motioned to the empty chair next to his desk.

"I'll leave you to it," said Dunlap. "Please don't forget to keep me updated." She turned to face me. "I will keep my ear to the ground, Ms. Marshall. I've read my share of mystery novels and not much gets past me. If a clue comes across my path, I'll be in touch."

With that, the Librarian exited Dorian's office. "Thank you for speaking with me," I said.

Dorian checked his watch. "I'm afraid I have a scheduled meeting I cannot miss. But I'm happy to chat with you. Are you free at the end of the day? Perhaps we could meet somewhere outside of the Library of Congress." He looked around nervously. "It might enable us to speak more freely."

The offices at the Library of Congress seemed to provide more privacy than the House of Representatives. But Dorian obviously knew best. If he couldn't speak honestly inside his office, it was best to talk to him at another location.

"Do you know my colleague Meg Peters?" I asked.

Dorian's eyes twinkled. Very few men (at least straight men) were unaffected by Meg's beauty and charm.

"Of course," he said. "She's been quite helpful as we work with the oversight committee in the House."

"Would you like to meet us for a drink after work? Since Chairwoman Dixon wants me to prioritize this investigation, we can probably leave work a little early to meet you."

He rubbed his chin. "It's been a difficult day with Gustav's death and the theft. I think a drink would be perfect. How does five o'clock sound?"

"Sure," I said. "Do you have a favorite place? My husband works at the Library of Congress, but I'm not sure he knows the hangouts yet."

Dorian smiled. "I do know the hangouts, and if we want to have a productive conversation, we shouldn't go to any of them." He thought for a moment before continuing. "How about Barrel? It's a few blocks away from here, in the Eastern Market area. I doubt we'll run into too many Library of Congress staff there."

"Perfect. I'll confirm with Meg, but let's plan on meeting there. I appreciate your help."

Dorian showed me the way out and ten minutes later, I opened the door to our congressional office suite inside the Cannon House Office Building. Our staff assistant greeted me. "Good afternoon, Kit. Patsy said you should check in with her."

Patsy was the inviolable keeper of the Congresswoman's schedule. I willingly tussled with a lot of people on Capitol Hill, but not Patsy. She managed to keep a thousand balls in the air and had the complete confidence of our boss.

I breezed through our office suite and dropped my purse on the desk chair inside my tiny office. It was a miracle I had a private office on Capitol Hill; they were rarer than approved legislation in the Senate.

Ten seconds later, I was standing in front of Patsy's desk, which was situated right outside Maeve Dixon's office. "I got the message you wanted to see me," I said.

Patsy scrunched up her round face as she stared at the computer monitor. She was probably trying to figure out how Maeve Dixon could be in two places at once. Such a feat might challenge the laws of physics, but such a trifling complication was no match for Patsy.

She raised her finger in the air. "One moment, Kit." A few seconds later, she smiled. "Mischief managed." She turned to face me and sighed.

"Everything okay, Patsy?" I asked.

"I'm fine, Kit. But I heard you managed to get yourself embroiled in another murder. How is that possible?"

"I suppose it is unusual. I seem to find myself in the right place at the right time, I guess."

Patsy shifted in her chair. "You mean the *wrong* place at the *wrong* time, Kit."

I crossed my arms across my chest. "Depends on your perspective, I suppose."

Patsy ran her fingers through her dyed blonde hair. "I give up. If you like solving murders, then go for it. You certainly work for the right boss." She pointed toward Maeve's office. "She'd like to speak with you about what happened at the Library of Congress this morning."

I gulped. "Is she upset?" Patsy could usually interpret my boss's moods with considerable accuracy.

Patsy shook her head. "Don't think so. You can go on in now. She has a meeting in twenty minutes so keep it brief."

I gave Patsy a two-fingered salute and knocked lightly on the door.

Maeve's voice echoed from the rear of her office. "Come in, Kit." I walked inside and found my boss hunched over her computer.

"Are you working on something?" I usually helped with Maeve's big speeches. I didn't know about anything in the works.

"No," she said, with a pained gaze. "The news has broken about the theft and murder at the Library of Congress."

"Did the media reports say anything about a suspect?" I asked, half-hoping that Sergeant O'Halloran had gotten lucky and found a piece of incriminating physical evidence at the crime scene that enabled him to make a swift arrest. As much as I enjoyed solving murders and bringing guilty parties to justice, Doug would remain under a cloud of suspicion until the real perpetrator was apprehended. I'd gladly trade in my usual sleuthing for a swift resolution of this mystery.

Much to my chagrin, Maeve shook her head slowly. "Afraid not, Kit."

"I met with Miriam Dunlap this afternoon and I'm scheduled to speak with her chief of staff early this evening," I said. "The pool of suspects is limited. Dunlap said only those in attendance at last night's preview event knew whose fingerprints would open the safe."

My boss blinked rapidly. "That's good news, I suppose." With a pained expression on her face, Maeve rubbed the back of her neck.

"Ma'am, is something wrong?" Dixon was usually as cool as a cucumber. Her experience as a combat veteran kept her calm and collected as a politician.

Dixon inhaled deeply. "The stakes have changed, Kit. I'm the chair of the committee responsible for the Library of Congress." Her eyes shifted around the office. "And the Capitol Hill police force."

"Unlike the other crimes that have been committed in the past, this one falls directly under your watch." I'd been around enough members of Congress to understand what they believed was important.

"Precisely. The theft of the contents of Abraham Lincoln's pockets make it a hundred times worse." She drummed her fingers on the desk.

"No one can blame you for that fiasco," I said evenly.

"Not blamed for it," she said. "But they can criticize me if this case lingers or goes unsolved."

I couldn't disagree with Maeve. She'd welcomed the opportunity to become a committee chair. Now she was caught in the crosshairs of one of the most notorious heists in American history.

"I'll start speaking with suspects tomorrow. Hopefully the Librarian's chief will shed light on potential motives."

"Motives?" asked Dixon. "That's one part of this mystery you *don't* have to solve, Kit. The murderer wanted to steal the treasures inside that safe. Gaffney was nothing other than a convenient set of fingerprints for him." Then she added abruptly, "Or her."

"I suppose so," I said slowly. "I still think it's important to understand what makes these suspects tick. Why steal a national treasure now? And why the contents of Lincoln's pockets?"

Maeve waved her right hand absently in the air. "I shouldn't be telling you how to investigate. After all, you're the one with the experience in these situations. But remember that time is of the essence. Every day that goes by that we don't bring those precious items home, I wither on the proverbial political vine."

It was a bit dramatic. To say nothing of the fact that a man was killed and finding his murderer might be the number one reason for cracking the case. For the zillionth time, I wondered if politics was really the right business for me. My boss certainly wanted to serve the United States and help people, but self-preservation was the name of the game.

"I'll check in with Sergeant O'Halloran and see if there are any updates," I said. "And I'll reinforce how important the investigation is to you."

Maeve smiled. It wasn't genuine, but more of a forced grin. She usually made this type of face when she was trying to act politely in front of constituents who she disagreed with.

"Thank you, Kit." She turned back to her computer. I understood Maeve Dixon's body language. I'd been dismissed.

I trotted back to my bijou office. Piles of paperwork had already grown into a chain of mountains on my desk. I stacked everything in a corner and vowed not to worry about it until the larceny at the Library had been solved. Doug's future rested on it, and furthermore, I wasn't about to let Maeve's political future wither on any vine. I'd worked too hard to make sure she had a second act in Congress. Even more importantly, I wasn't going to stand by quietly while a greedy murderer robbed the United States of invaluable historical artifacts.

I grabbed my desk phone and dialed Sergeant O'Halloran's extension, which I'd memorized. It was a long shot he'd be at his desk, and sur enough, he wasn't. Instead of leaving a message, I picked up my iPhone and texted him to call me.

I was about to turn on my computer when Meg popped into my office. "Any luck with the Librarian of Congress?"

I hit my forehead. "Duh, I forgot to text you. Can you join me for drinks with her chief of staff?"

"Dorian Jones?" Her eyes twinkled. "Of course. He's just my type."

"And what type would that be, Meg?" I teased.

"Attractive, successful, and single," she said.

"Spoken just like a woman who has not one, but two suitors."

"There's no harm in making it three." Meg licked her lips.

"Actually, there might be," I said.

Meg wrinkled her forehead. "What do you mean?"

I suppressed a sigh. "Last night, you were lamenting that Trevor and Clay wanted you to decide between the two of them. I don't think they'd appreciate adding a third guy to the mix."

Meg narrowed her eyes. "Because it would reduce their odds?"

"Yes, Meg," I said, not hiding the exasperation in my voice. "And they might also view you as a lost cause if you start dating another guy. It sends the wrong signal."

Meg twirled a lock of her blonde bob. "Doesn't it make me appear more desirable if another guy wants to date me?"

I stood up and placed my hands on Meg's shoulders. "You're missing the point. It will make both Trevor and Clay think you aren't serious about either of them. They might move on…" I paused before finishing the sentence. "To greener pastures."

Before Meg could answer, my cell phone vibrated. Saved by the bell. Or, more accurately, the buzz. It was Sergeant O'Halloran.

"Sorry, I have to take this. I'll swing by your desk in fifteen minutes for happy hour."

Meg nodded and skedaddled out of my office. Not only did Meg help solve murders, she also held down the fort when I got sidetracked on a big mystery. Even though she could be a little dense when it came to men, she was a loyal best friend and a terrific congressional staffer.

"Sergeant O'Halloran," I bellowed into my phone. "Thanks for getting back to me."

"Ms. Marshall, I was at the crime scene this morning and heard what your boss and the Librarian of Congress said. I was instructed to work with you." From the sound of his reply, he was likely saying these words through clenched teeth.

"I'll make sure it's not too much of a burden," I said, somewhat iron-ically. *Without my help, you might still be looking for several killers on Capitol Hill.*

The other end of the line was silent, except for the muted sound of chewing. No doubt it was time for the Sergeant's afternoon snack. He never let a difficult case get in the way of his eating regimen.

I used the pause to ask an important question. "Do you have time of death established for Gustav Gaffney?"

After a gurgle that I assumed was a big swallow, O'Halloran cleared his throat. "Yes, we do."

"What is the approximate time of death, Sergeant?" If the whole in-vestigation progressed as slowly as this conversation, I'd better tell my boss and Miriam Dunlap to settle in for the long haul.

"Gaffney was killed the night before," he said. "Probably not too long after your cozy soirée wrapped up."

That meant Doug wasn't the obvious suspect, given that he'd discov-ered the body the following morning. Unfortunately, it still left him as a potential suspect, since he was working in his office alone when the mur-der likely occurred.

"And the security cameras didn't pick anything up?"

"There's no camera inside the office itself," he said. "The cameras out-side in the Great Hall are focused on the most valuable displayed items, like the Gutenberg Bible and the Buell map. There's no way to monitor every nook and cranny of that building." The fifteenth century Gutenberg was one of only three perfect printed vellum copies known in the world, and the 1784 Buell wall map was the first cartographic representation of the independent United States. It made sense the cameras would be trained on them.

"So, our murderer knew how to elude the cameras?" I asked.

"You could draw that conclusion," said O'Halloran. "Any professional thief would have staked the place out numerous times beforehand. That doesn't mean it was an inside job."

"How would an outsider know that Gaffney would be alone with the contents of Lincoln's pockets, though? Only the people who knew his hab-its were aware that he liked to work late at night inside the Librarian's cere-monial office," I pressed. "Also, why would a thief assume his prints would open the safe? Or even know the safe could be opened through biomet-rics?" My voice went up a few decibels at the end of my speech.

"Ms. Marshall, please refrain from shouting at me. I don't disagree with your analysis. But I need to make sure we're covering all the bases here."

"I understand," I said. "Where do you plan to focus your attention?"

O'Halloran hesitated. "I'll need to look closely at those individuals who attended last night's event who don't have an alibi for the hour or two after it ended."

"That includes Doug," I said softly, almost to myself.

"Yes, it does" said O' Halloran. "I can't get into those details concerning your husband. You've done enough detective work with the police to understand. It's best you let us complete our investigation. If you come across any leads, let us know."

O'Halloran might come off as gruff at times, but he was a good cop. My gut told me he believed Doug was innocent, but he couldn't leave any stone unturned. I needed to keep pressing to find the killer to make sure Doug's reputation didn't suffer irreparable damage.

"What about Henry Chang?" I asked. "Are you going to investigate him?"

"The congressman?" O'Halloran snickered. "That's tricky, Ms. Marshall."

It was politically sensitive, but I had an idea. "I can try that angle."

"Good luck," said O'Halloran. "Don't get fired. In your line of business, accusing a congressman of murder and grand larceny isn't exactly a recipe for career advancement."

"I know what I'm doing," I said. "Or at least I think I know."

"Let's hope it's the former rather than the latter, Ms. Marshall."

Touché.

Chapter Seven

⁓

FIFTEEN MINUTES LATER, Meg and I were walking due east on Pennsylvania Avenue. Given the chill in the air, we weren't exactly taking an early evening stroll. Meg's teeth chattered. "Why do we need to meet Dorian four blocks away? Sonoma is a perfectly good wine bar and it's much closer."

"Since he's our guest, I asked him for a recommendation. He wanted to meet at a place where Library of Congress staff don't hang out." I pulled my wool scarf tighter around my neck.

"I'll need to have a drink just to warm up," said Meg.

"It might help if you dressed more appropriately for the weather." Meg's thin red vinyl jacket was better for a crisp autumn day rather than the February cold.

Meg pouted. "This jacket matched my outfit. How was I supposed to know I'd be battling the Arctic tundra for happy hour?"

"Not to change the subject, but let's make sure we use our time with Dorian wisely. The Librarian felt he might be able to give us more details about the staff who are suspects."

"I agree," she said. "I like working with him on committee business. He seems like a straight shooter."

"He's out of the running as a suspect," I said. "I'm sure he knew which fingerprints opened the safe, but at the time of the murder, he was with the Librarian of Congress at another event across town."

"Thank goodness. I'd hate to have to put a hottie like him in prison. He wouldn't look good in stripes." Meg giggled as she wiped her runny nose with a tissue.

"Let's not use *that* approach tonight," I said. "After all, we do represen the chairwoman who has oversight over the Library of Congress."

Meg pursed her lips. "What do you mean by *that* approach, Kit?"

"You know," I said. "The approach we often use when we interrogate men involved in murder investigations. Where you pretend to be interested in them so they tell us juicy information."

"So that's why you bring me along for these chats?" Meg's steely blue eyes bore into me.

"Meg, don't be ridiculous. You know it's effective and you do it on purpose," I said firmly. "Don't deny it."

We'd reached the entrance to Barrel. Meg reached into her purse to pull out her compact and apply a new coat of lipstick. She stopped before opening the compact. "I'm not going to bother," she said. "After all, we're not using *that* approach, right?"

Meg grabbed the door and walked inside, her blonde bob flouncing in the wind. These minor outbursts no longer bothered me. Meg had literally been a high school drama queen. I'd often thought she'd missed her true calling and instead of working on Capitol Hill, she should have pursued an acting career. She would have been a star on the soap opera circuit, for sure.

My eyes adjusted to the lower lighting level inside Barrel. Exposed brick walls and a wooden bar gave the watering hole a cozy, rustic feel, yet the place was a hipster's paradise. Known for its craft beers, creative cocktails, bourbon, whiskey, and southern food, it was typically packed for happy hour. Luckily, the cold weather and our early arrival meant we almost had the place to ourselves. Dorian was sitting alone at a table in the far corner of the restaurant, and we hustled to join him.

Like any other self-respecting chief of staff, Dorian was buried in his phone and his fingers were flying across the screen faster than members of Congress racing to National Airport after the last vote of the week. After a few moments, he must have realized we'd arrived. His head popped up and a grin spread across his face.

"Evening, ladies. Please have a seat," he said in a warm voice.

We squeezed into the seats opposite him. "Dorian, it's fun to see you outside work," said Meg. As she spoke, she smoothed her hair and returned the smile.

Maybe Meg didn't even realize when she was flirting. It had become so ingrained in her *modus operandi*, flirting was the default rather than the exception.

Surprisingly, Dorian was all business. "Unfortunate circumstances, though," he said as he passed out menus sitting on the table. "Perhaps we should order and then we can have our discussion."

We studied the menu, although I knew what I'd get. Even though this was a bar specializing in spirits, I preferred wine. There was a long list of "brown water" options, namely bourbon, whiskey, and single malt scotch. I couldn't touch the stuff. It made me queasy just thinking about it. Fortunately, happy hour Chardonnay was only five dollars. A match made in heaven.

Our waitress approached. Dorian asked for a Barrel Manhattan, the house specialty. Meg went next. "Make it two," she said, with a wink. "Plus, an order of wings and buttermilk biscuits for everyone."

I squirmed in my seat. So much for keeping it simple. However, the Barrel biscuits were legendary, and it seemed like an awfully long time since lunch.

After I placed my order, I turned my full attention to our guest. "Thank you again for agreeing to meet with us this evening, Dorian."

He folded his hands. "If the Librarian thinks our discussion might be helpful, then it's my job."

Maybe not the friendliest response, but what the heck. At least he *seemed* cooperative. It was an improvement over what I encountered most days in my position as a congressional chief of staff.

"Do you know everyone who was present last night at the preview display?" I asked.

"I think so," said Dorian. "Who are you specifically interested in knowing more about?"

This guy did not beat around the bush. "Let's start with Joe Malden."

"Red Sox fan extraordinaire," said Dorian. "He would have been your guy if it had been something stolen from our baseball collection."

Meg perked up. "Why does the Library of Congress have a baseball collection?"

"You should know this by now, but I'm happy to remind you that we have priceless treasures in many areas," he said. "Including one of the best baseball card collections of the game's early years."

Our waitress arrived with our drinks and food. Meg dove right into the wings and made sure each of us had a plate with a buttermilk biscuit on it. "Don't forget the honey butter," she said in between bites.

"Back to Joe Malden," I said, spreading the butter on my biscuit. "He seemed cagey when I inquired about the murder earlier today."

Dorian raised an eyebrow. "That doesn't sound like Joe. What did you ask him about?"

"He was tight lipped when I asked who could have committed the crime," I said. "Then he became uber defensive when I mentioned Lea Rutherford's name."

Mid-sip, Dorian put his drink down. "That explains it."

Meg had also sampled her libation. She put it down quickly. "Quite strong. Maybe I should have stuck to my usual Prosecco." The Italian bubbly was her favorite, and it was light years away from a stiff Manhattan.

"What explains it?" I asked. The biscuit was a perfect southern concoction, literally melting in my mouth. Thank goodness for Meg's insatiable appetite.

"It's not well known, but Joe Malden and Lea Rutherford are more than Library of Congress acquaintances." Dorian wiggled his eyebrows up and down.

"They're knocking boots?" asked Meg.

I shot my best friend a killer glance. No more liquor for her at happy hour. "What Meg meant to ask," I said, "is whether they are engaged in a romantic relationship."

Dorian laughed. "You don't have to act politically correct around me. And the answer is yes. To both of your questions."

"So that's why Malden clammed up when I started fishing around," I said.

"Because he was trying to protect Lea Rutherford?" asked Meg.

"Could be," said Dorian. "But their relationship isn't exactly well received."

"What do you mean?" I asked.

"She's one of the Library's most affluent patrons. It's not kosher for an employee to be in a relationship with her," said Dorian. "Quite frankly, I don't mind so much and neither does Miriam. You know, live and let live." He paused for a beat before continuing. "But Gustav Gaffney did *not* like it."

I sipped my unoaked Chardonnay as I considered Dorian's comment. "Did Gaffney forbid it?"

Dorian finished a wing and wiped his mouth with a napkin. "That's tricky business. It's hard to forbid a relationship between consenting adults. But Gustav could certainly make sure Joe knew he disapproved."

"How so? By scolding him?" Meg imitated the words by wagging her index finger at Dorian while giggling.

"A little more than that," said Dorian. "He could cut him out of meetings or decisions. You know, make sure he realized what the dalliance was costing him professionally."

"Is that all it is?" I asked. "A fleeting affair?"

Dorian sipped his Manhattan and thought for a moment before responding. "It's a fair question. I'm not sure how to answer it. Like any competent chief of staff, I make sure I know most of the gossip. But I haven't asked Joe directly about his relationship with Lea."

"Even if Joe and Lea are having a serious affair, it doesn't explain the theft," said Meg. "Joe might have had a motive to kill Gaffney, but why would he steal the contents of Lincoln's pockets?"

Dorian nodded. "Meg has a good point. I can't see Joe stealing a Library of Congress treasure. He might hold a grudge against Gaffney but stealing a valuable part of our collection would be really out of character."

"Perhaps he has money troubles," I said. "That's the obvious motive. As a lawyer, he might know how to evade law enforcement when trying to sell the items."

"That would make sense. But if Joe and Lea were hot and heavy, you'd think she'd take care of any financial problems Joe might have," said Meg.

Meg was right. The motive for murder might be there, but why theft? The same reasoning applied to Lea Rutherford. She clearly disliked Gustav Gaffney, who didn't seem to support her philanthropic initiatives and disapproved of her personal relationship with Joe Malden. Given that Lea had gobs of money, would she really need to steal valuable items? She could buy almost anything she wanted that was for sale legally.

"Let's move on," I said. "Gordon Endicott knew about the safe. Do you know anything about him?"

"He's our rare books librarian," said Dorian. "There's not much gossip about him. But given his position, he'd definitely know how to move stolen goods on the black market. He'd have the connections."

"He's one of the only people with the means to profit from the theft," said Meg. "We shouldn't forget that."

"There's another delicate matter concerning Endicott," I said. "Joe Malden told me today that he wanted the job Doug ended up getting."

Dorian took another sip of his drink before answering. "Joe is right. But Miriam thought Gordon's talents were better suited for his current position. She preferred your husband for the job."

"I'm worried Endicott might try to cast suspicion on Doug," I said. "If he's guilty, it would doubly benefit him."

"Even if he's not guilty," said Meg. "It would be a convenient way to discredit Doug and take the job he always wanted."

Dorian shook his head. "That sounds awfully calculating for Gordon Endicott. He's a smart guy, don't get me wrong. But that would be really malicious."

Meg and I exchanged knowing glances. Dorian hadn't been acquainted with as many murderers as we had. Criminals of this caliber were ruthless. A few years ago, we wouldn't have believed seemingly normal people could stoop to such low levels. Now, our eyes were wide open.

"Thanks for your help, Dorian," I said. "The last Library of Congress staff member who attended was Janice Jackson. Given our congressional work with the oversight committee, Meg knows Janice pretty well." I motioned for her to take it over.

"I can't think of a reason why Janice would do this," said Meg. "After all, her job is to promote the Library of Congress with politicians. This debacle will raise a ton of questions about security and other matters. It will prove a real challenge."

Dorian drained his drink. "Don't remind me." Meg's comment must have depressed him. He motioned to our waitress he'd like another.

"Janice has always been very helpful when I've asked for information," said Meg. "Am I missing something?"

Dorian pursed his lips. Was he trying to decide if he should divulge something?

"We're not the police," I said quickly. "Even rumors can be helpful. After all, the Librarian of Congress and Maeve Dixon wanted us to investigate." I hoped my prodding would encourage Dorian to spill what was on his mind.

Before he could speak, we were interrupted by a familiar twang. "Well, snap my garters! If it isn't Miss Detective of Capitol Hill."

I turned around to the face of Grant Dawson, the head of the United States Botanic Garden.

"Mr. Dawson," I said, extending my hand. "What a pleasure."

Grant Dawson had been embroiled in our last murder mystery. He'd proven a particularly colorful character, full of southern musings and expressions. In the end, he'd been quite helpful in pointing me in the right direction of the guilty party.

"I see you know my friend Dorian. You really do get around." Then he turned toward Dorian. "They're both as pretty as a peach, but don't underestimate them. These gals mean business." He followed up his comment with a wicked cackle.

Dorian's glass had been refilled, and he seemed especially grateful for it.

"That's fair warning, Grant."

"How do you two know each other?" asked Meg. "I don't see too much connection between plants and old books."

"Well, it's as plain as a pig on a sofa," said Grant. "There's a legislative branch working group who gets together and discusses how to promote our Capitol Hill events."

"I didn't know that," said Meg.

"Let me tell you, little missy, there's much more to the legislative branch than Congress," said Dawson.

Factually correct, although wasn't that like saying there was more to the executive branch than the President? Or more to the judicial branch than the Supreme Court? All true statements, but somehow not exactly right, either. Congress ruled Capitol Hill and everyone knew it.

"We're still learning," I said. "Since Maeve Dixon became the chair of the oversight committee."

"That's right," said Dawson. "You're like royalty these days." Then he looked at Dorian and back at me and Meg. "Wait a second. This here is no coincidence." He shook his finger at us. "You're talking about the murder at the Library of Congress. I read about it online this afternoon."

"We're just having a friendly discussion," I said. "Don't read into it."

Dawson smirked. "Congress's junior Miss Marple is on the prowl again," he said. "That killer should be worried. Y'all are more tenacious than flies on. . ." He paused. "Well, I won't say."

"We were talking about Janice Jackson," said Meg. "Do you know her?"

I shot Meg daggers. Why was she egging Grant Dawson on? Besides, there was no need to discuss the investigation with outsiders.

Grant waved his hand dismissively. "That dog don't hunt," he said. "Janice Jackson is as straight as an arrow. Besides, why would she want to kill someone and steal from the Library of Congress? That's where her buns are buttered." He laughed at his own joke.

Dorian looked at Grant with an amused look on his face. "Well, if we knew the answer to that question, we wouldn't be drinking bargain whiskey at happy hour."

Grant Dawson stared at Dorian for several seconds and then burst into laughter. "Ladies, watch out. This one's slicker than snot and smashed bananas. I'd better get back to my table. They'll be wondering what happened to me. Holler if you need me!" With that, Grant Dawson disappeared into the now crowded bar area, sashaying his way back to his undoubtedly rapt entourage of plant-loving friends.

"That guy is too much," said Meg.

"He's certainly one of the livelier characters we've met in our travels," I said. "There's no forgetting Grant Dawson."

"Or Janice Jackson," said Meg. "We were just about to discuss her when Grant stopped by our table. Were you going to say something, Dorian?"

"I doubt it's significant," said Dorian. "But there was certainly friction between Gustav Gaffney and Janice."

"Can you tell us more?" I prodded.

Dorian sighed. "Gustav thought she could maintain a broader network within Congress. At times, he was highly critical of her."

"It sounds like Gaffney was really popular." The sarcasm dripped from Meg's voice. "Did anyone like him?"

"Miriam Dunlap did," he said immediately. "I always got along with him, too. He really had to keep the trains running and hold people accountable. It wasn't an easy job."

"Understood," I said. Dorian's comments were consistent with what I'd heard from the Librarian earlier today. "But Janice Jackson could have simply murdered Gustav. She didn't need to steal anything from the safe."

Dorian finished his second drink. "Sounds like you both have your work cut out for you." He threw down a twenty-dollar bill. "I need to get back to work. Give me a ring if you'd like to talk again."

I gave Meg some cash towards the check, and as she settled up with the waitress, I glanced at my phone. Darn. I'd missed several text messages during happy hour, including one from my brother.

Are you and Doug free to have dinner w/ me and Lisa tonight? I'll bring pizza.

I immediately texted Doug, who told me he'd left work as early as possible. He was already at home, enjoying a glass of vino and relaxing by our gas "faux" fireplace. He was happy to meet Sebastian's new girlfriend, and even more delighted that the deal included pizza.

I responded in the affirmative to my brother and turned to Meg. "Time to go home. Sebastian is bringing Lisa Reddy over, the new girlfriend."

We left the bar and picked up the pace down Pennsylvania Avenue to avoid the cold walk back to the Cannon Building. "Your brother isn't wasting any time. He must really like her," said Meg.

"I ran into Lisa today at the Library of Congress," I said. "She was there to secure the building after the crime had been reported to the police. I'm sure she told Sebastian about it."

"Sort of an awkward first meeting," said Meg. She imitated my voice. "Hello, my brother is dating you. And by the way, my husband is being questioned by your boss about the murder that just occurred upstairs!"

Meg had a way of funny way of making the mundane seem hilarious. "Well, it didn't quite happen that way. But I'm sure it was confusing, especially for her."

"I'm at my stop," said Meg, pointing to the Hawk 'n' Dove bar.

"What are you doing tonight?" We were several blocks away from the Metro station.

"Clay is meeting up with some other G-O-P chiefs of staff," said Meg. "He invited me to join them."

What a romantic night. While the H&D had certainly upped its game in the past several years with major renovation and improved menu, it didn't really qualify as a venue for a hot date. I'd best keep my mouth shut. Meg needed to sort this love triangle out on her own.

I forced a smile. "Have fun." I couldn't resist adding a dig. "On your group date."

Meg rolled her eyes. "Kit, don't be so conventional." With that rejoinder, she flipped her bob, opened the heavy door, and strutted into the bar.

There's a fine line between convention and self-respect. On the other hand, who was I to judge? My husband and I were excited at the prospect of someone providing us with free pizza for dinner. We weren't exactly on the *Washingtonian* party circuit.

Thirty minutes later, I pulled our Prius into the garage underneath our condo building in Arlington. If we moved to a house in a far-flung suburb, I was going to miss these relatively short commutes home.

After I parked the car, a text message was waiting for me from Doug.

Lisa & Sebastian brought a guest.

Maybe group dates were en vogue these days. Had they brought a friend of Lisa's? It seemed strange to invite someone else when meeting the sibling of your significant other.

I braced myself before entering our condo, ready for Clarence's usual exuberant greeting. After turning the knob, I slowly pushed the door open, waiting for the inevitable attempted escape. This time, Clarence was nowhere to be found.

I peeked around the door and immediately knew why Clarence had neglected his usual antics. Inside the living room, a large black Labrador sat directly opposite Clarence. Our mystery guest was Lisa's police dog.

"I see that Clarence has met Murphy," I said.

Doug smiled from our overstuffed armchair, wine glass in hand. "It's not exactly a friendship made in heaven. At least yet."

Clarence was eying Murphy warily, especially as Sebastian rubbed the other dog's neck. Clarence thought Sebastian was *his* special friend. I'm not sure how well Clarence understood the notion of sharing, particularly when it came to a favorite human's attention.

Lisa emerged from our kitchen, glass of wine also in hand. Her auburn hair remained in a ponytail, but she'd ditched the police uniform for boot cut jeans and a comfy grey cable knit sweater. Sebastian stood up and put his arm around Lisa's slim waist.

"Lisa tells me you ran into each other earlier today," said my brother. "At the scene of a murder."

"I'm afraid so. Not exactly the ideal circumstances," I said. "Maybe we should start over. You've already met Doug. I'm Kit, Sebastian's older sister." I extended my hand to Lisa, who accepted it and shook my hand lightly.

"Pleased to meet you," she said. "You met Murphy, but since he's not working now, you can pet him all you want."

I reached down to pat Murphy's head, aware of Clarence's burning gaze. After a couple of scratches, Clarence had enough. He let out a soft whine and placed his paw on my hand.

"Sorry, Clarence," I said. "I should have greeted you first." Upon hearing his name, Clarence sat up straight and gazed triumphantly at Murphy.

"Everyone has a drink already," said Doug. "And the pizzas are in the kitchen. We should sit down and eat while it's hot."

"Where did you get the pizza from?" I asked.

Sebastian grinned. "Pupatella. You're in for a real treat."

A small restaurant a few miles away, Pupatella had won many accolades for its Neapolitan style pizza made fresh in an Italian oven filled with volcanic ash from Mount Vesuvius outside Naples. Due to its popularity, it was notoriously difficult to find a seat during the dinner rush. With no delivery service, takeout was usually the only option.

Lisa listed off the pies. "We brought four different pizzas. Pepperoni, meatball, prosciutto, and Margherita."

"Lisa doesn't eat meat," said Sebastian. "So, we had to get one with just cheese."

We served ourselves slices from the various pies and sat down at our dining room table. "Lisa, how long have you been a police officer at the Capitol?" asked Doug.

"Only a year," she said. "I completed my criminal justice degree and worked as a patrol officer in Fairfax County for a few years." She wiped the oozing buffalo mozzarella cheese from her mouth before continuing. "Then I earned my certification from the Police Canine Association to work as a K-9 officer. I started looking around for available positions and got the job with the Capitol Hill police force."

"You were teamed up with Murphy when you joined the Capitol Hill police team?" I asked.

Lisa nodded, her mouth full of pizza. "Murphy is a scent dog focused on explosives. He's perfect for work in government buildings. Any time there's a threat, Murphy is there to make sure nothing smells dangerous."

"And Murphy stays with you at home?" I asked.

Lisa smiled as she patted Murphy, who sat attentively next to her. I noticed he didn't seem interested in the pizza. On the other side of the table, Doug was shoveling small pieces of pepperoni to Clarence so we'd avoid a scene. Clarence might be able to handle Sebastian petting another dog, but he drew the line at pepperoni.

"Most K-9 officers keep their police dog partners at home," she said. "When I searched for an apartment in Arlington, I only looked for dog-friendly rentals. It's good for Murphy and me to spend as much time together as possible."

"Sebastian, I don't think you ever told me how you and Lisa met," I said. A tech guy for a non-profit and a left-wing political activist in his spare time, Sebastian didn't exactly interact with law enforcement social circles on a daily basis. Unless the cops were threatening to arrest him at a protest.

"We met online," said Sebastian proudly. "There's a new dating app for socially conscious singles."

I groaned inwardly but forced a smile. "How nice. And Lisa, you would classify yourself as socially conscious?"

Lisa's face brightened. "Of course. Mostly, I'm involved with rescue organizations for dogs. Murphy is a rescue dog. Police departments are starting to use shelter dogs more and more. It saves a lot of money and many of the dogs are highly trainable."

"Clarence is a rescue dog," said Doug proudly. "Although I'm not sure he would have made it as a police dog. Maybe if the police department rewarded him with pepperoni."

Clarence heard his name and "pepperoni" in the same sentence. He issued an excited bark, and we all laughed.

"Lisa and I were compatible on a wide variety of factors and measures," said Sebastian. "Big data has really improved to increase the likelihood of success."

"Now you definitely sound like a techie," I said.

"I grew tired of getting set up by friends and hanging out at bars," said Lisa. "Between my job and volunteering for dog rescue organizations, I don't have a lot of time to spend on dates that lead nowhere."

"Well, it sounds like a very appropriate match," said Doug. "Kit, can I ask if you found out anything this afternoon about Gustav's murder and the theft?"

I caught Doug, Sebastian, and Lisa up on the case, recounting my conversation with Miriam Dunlap, Sergeant O'Halloran, and Dorian Jones.

"I'm still a suspect," said Doug glumly.

I reached over to pat his hand gently. "I'm afraid so, dear. But don't worry. We'll find whomever is responsible soon enough."

"I hope so." Doug twisted his wedding ring nervously. "It wasn't the best afternoon at work."

"What happened?" asked Sebastian as he helped himself to a slice of meatball pizza. I was partial to the prosciutto and pondered whether I should indulge in another piece. I did have to keep my strength up the next couple of days. Sleuthing was hard work. I snagged a slice and after one bite, I knew I'd made the right choice.

"Everyone was looking at me funny," said Doug. "Word travels fast. The staff knows the police are investigating and I'm a person of interest."

Doug was fairly new in his position. That couldn't be a good sign.

"I know the police are consulting with federal investigators," said Lisa. "They tend to think a professional criminal might be behind this."

"Not someone affiliated with the Library of Congress?" I asked.

"Perhaps someone on the inside helped by providing information," said Lisa. "Either on purpose or unwittingly."

"I'm not sure that's the right approach," I said.

"They'll examine all the places where the stolen items could show up," said Lisa. "And then work backwards from there."

"Would the thief really be that stupid to try to sell the contents of Lincoln's pockets?" asked Sebastian. "You're begging to get caught, even on he black market."

Lisa shrugged. "I don't specialize in these types of thefts. But what I heard is that thieves often sell the stolen treasure at a fraction of its value, since the dealer buying it knows it's stolen. But then after the item has changed hands several times, the price goes up."

"It seems like a risky proposition," I said.

"Yet, the theft of antiquities happens with some frequency," said Doug. "And they don't always catch the guilty parties. When I was growing up, everyone knew about the theft at the Isabella Stewart Gardner Museum in Boston. Thieves dressed up like police officers and conned their way into the museum in the middle of the night. They tied up the security guards and walked out with five hundred million dollars worth of paintings. Those works of art are still at large."

"They must have found a buyer for them," said Sebastian.

"Or maybe the thieves just like art," said Lisa. "You'd only get caught if you tried to sell the paintings."

I snapped my fingers. "That's Congressman Henry Chang. He's obsessed with Abraham Lincoln and has his own collection. I could see him keeping the stolen items and not trying to sell them."

"Sounds like someone worth investigating," said Sebastian, in between bites.

"The problem is that the police don't want to touch him since he's a member of Congress," I said. "Too politically sensitive. But that's where I come in."

Doug raised his eyebrows. "Be careful, Kit. I don't want you risking your job to investigate."

I waved my hand. "Not to worry. I'll check with Maeve Dixon tomorrow morning before doing anything."

Doug sighed. "I'd rather you didn't have to spend your time running around Capitol Hill chasing a diabolical criminal. But every day that those items remain missing, I worry that it's going to become harder and harder to recover them."

"Exactly," I said. "Let's not forget you're a suspect until we find the person or persons responsible."

Our conversation was interrupted by a soft canine whimper. We swiveled our heads to the direction of the sound. Clarence was sitting next to his dog bed, currently occupied by Murphy, who had decided our conversation was sufficiently boring and laid down to take a nap. Clarence placed one of his paws on Murphy's head in an apparent attempt to get him to move. Murphy completely ignored Clarence's overture and continued to snooze happily.

"Clarence is used to top billing around here," I said. "Sharing isn't in his vocabulary."

"No problem," said Lisa. "Murphy, come!"

Murphy instantly arose from his nap and ran to Lisa's side, sitting next to her at attention.

"Impressive!" exclaimed Doug. "Clarence would never move that fast."

Upon Murphy's departure, Clarence assumed control of his doggie bed, curling up in a tight circle and sporting a smug look of canine triumph.

"I'm not so sure about that, Doug," I said.

I reached over to the almost empty pizza box. Luckily, there was one slice left. I grabbed a piece of pepperoni off it.

"You just need to know which words our dog understands. CLARENCE!" I yelled. "PEPPERONI! PEPPERONI OVER HERE!"

In two seconds flat, Clarence was by my side, sitting at attention. I gave him his treat and he licked his lips.

"Let that be a lesson to all of you," I said.

"And what lesson is that, Kit?" asked Sebastian.

"With proper motivation, you can teach an old dog new tricks."

Everyone laughed. Thirty minutes later, our guests had departed. Doug and I stood side by side in our kitchen, placing dirty plates in the dishwasher and cleaning up any remnants of our delicious pizza feast.

"I really like Lisa," said Doug. "Your brother seems particularly happy."

I had to agree. The smile on Sebastian's face hadn't disappeared the entire evening. "He's finally settling into Washington. He's has a good job and now he has someone to share it with. Besides us, of course."

He chuckled. "We should not be the extent of your brother's social circle."

I turned to face Doug. "How are *you* doing? After all, discovering a dead body is not pleasant." I spoke from experience.

Doug shivered. "I'm okay, I guess. I feel responsible for Gustav's death."

"What do you mean?" I asked. "Please, Doug. Don't say that to the police."

He sighed. "Of course not, Kit. I'm not stupid. But if I hadn't been so eager to run off to my office last night, maybe Gustav wouldn't be dead. Perhaps I would have deterred the thief."

"Or the thief would have decided to kill two people instead of just one!" I exclaimed. "Doug, you can't hold yourself responsible. You didn't kill anyone. The guilty party is the person who murdered Gaffney and stole the Library's treasures."

Doug threw the dishtowel he was holding onto the counter. "I'd rather not talk about this anymore. Maybe the police will find the culprit tomorrow and all of this will be behind us."

"You heard Lisa. The feds have taken over the strategy on this one. They're looking for an art or antiquities thief. I could be wrong, but I think they're barking up the wrong tree." I bent down and scratched Clarence's head. "Right, buddy?" Clarence neither affirmed nor denied my proposition.

"If that's the case, then this investigation is going to drag out much longer than I'd like," said Doug.

"Not if I have anything to do about it." I gave Doug a gentle kiss. "Remember, I'm your secret weapon."

"Just as long as you don't become a target for the killer," said Doug. "If this person was willing to murder a high-ranking government official to get his or her hands on Lincoln memorabilia, there won't be any hesitation in hurting another person if *she* gets in the way."

I understood Doug's point. I'd been in too many sticky situations. I couldn't deny the risk involved with investigating nefarious business.

"Don't worry. That's why I'm working with the police. I'll turn any leads I have over to them." I crossed my heart with my index finger.

"Right, like I haven't heard *that* before." Doug's phone, which was sitting on our small dining room table, buzzed. He walked out of the kitchen and picked it up. After reading the message, his face brightened.

"That's Jonathan," he said with excitement in his voice.

I clenched my jaw. Jonathan was our realtor. I liked him enough, but today's events now occupied the bandwidth I reserved for house hunting.

"He has a house he wants us to see this week," said Doug. "A real steal in Falls Church. This is a new listing and it's even better than the others he wanted us to see."

Falls Church was the affluent suburb next to Arlington. It was a fine place to live, except that it was more suburban than urban and increased the commute. However, it provided a steady supply of modestly sized single-family homes with correspondingly-sized, fenced-in backyards. In other words, Doug's dream residence.

Doug passed me his phone, and I scrolled through the photos from the listing Jonathan had sent. It was a 1970s style split entry with a garage. Be still my beating heart.

"Really nice," I lied, giving the phone back to him. "But given the murder and theft, don't we have a lot on our plate right now? Maybe we should tell Jonathan we'll get back in touch with him in a few weeks, when things have settled down."

"A house at this price in Falls Church is going to have offers this week-end, Kit. We can't delay," said Doug in a rushed tone.

"Well, I really don't know what tomorrow is going to bring, especially if I can speak to Representative Chang. I'll have to rely on Maeve Dixon to set that up for me." I was telling the truth. It was difficult to set up meetings with members of Congress, so I needed to keep my schedule open.

"How about Friday?" asked Doug.

I grabbed my phone and looked at my schedule. I'd had a lunch sched-uled with a fellow chief of staff, but she'd canceled earlier in the week. "Noon on Friday is possible," I said slowly. "It needs to be brief, though, so we can both return to work."

Doug gave me the "thumbs up" sign and grabbed his phone to text Jonathan. After exchanging a few messages, Doug grinned. "We're all set for Friday!"

Although I wasn't sure about the house, agreeing to the viewing was worth the happy expression on Doug's face. After all, he'd had a terrible day. "I'm glad that Jonathan can make you forget today's unpleasantness. At least for a minute."

Doug's smile vanished as quickly as it had appeared. "Do you really think I'm in trouble, Kit?"

"The person who discovers the body usually comes under suspicion at first. The problem is that someone is planting seeds with the police about your conflict with the victim."

"You mean Gordon Endicott," said Doug.

"That's my guess. When I talked with Sergeant O'Halloran before leav-ing the office for the day, he mentioned you were still under suspicion. Someone has to be fueling the rumors about your supposed dispute with Gaffney."

"I'll try to see what I can find out tomorrow at work," said Doug.

"You should be careful." I put my arms around his neck and pulled him closer. "If Endicott is behind this and he figures out you're onto him, he won't hesitate to eliminate you, too."

"Enough talk about murder," said Doug, leading me down the hallway to our bedroom.

For once, I agreed to the moratorium.

Chapter Eight

———⟞⟞———

I WAS SLOW TO rise the next morning, the exhausting trials and tribulations
of the previous day keeping me in bed for an extra thirty minutes. Finally,
I threw off the covers and decided that despite the cold weather, a jog
outdoors for Clarence might wake us both up. Clarence initially resisted
the idea and buried his head underneath the blanket. But after I jingled
his leash and harness, he changed his mind and ran to the door, his butt
wiggling in excitement. Ten minutes later, we cruised along Fairfax Drive,
moving at a good clip so that the heat from our bodies could overcome the
outdoor chill.

As we trotted past Central Library, I wondered if my days living in
Arlington were numbered. A lull in the housing market had made it an
auspicious time to buy. If we wanted to trade in our condo for something
more spacious, this was the time to do it. Otherwise, we risked facing stiff
competition, escalating purchase clauses, and inevitable disappointment.

After crossing I-66, Clarence and I left the roadways for the Custis
Trail, a popular urban bike and running path. Although it was built
alongside the interstate, tall concrete barriers prevented traffic noise from
ruining the tranquility of the experience. Clarence enjoyed the smells of
the plethora of dogs who traversed the trail each day. If we moved away
from Arlington, Clarence and I would both miss our morning runs on
the Custis.

Of course, relocation was out of the question if Doug was awaiting
trial for the homicide of Gustav Gaffney. As we exited the trail in the
Virginia Square neighborhood and turned toward the closure of our jog-
ging loop, my mind drifted to weightier matters than real estate, namely

murder. Gordon Endicott was at the top of my list, although I'd have to figure out how I'd manage to orchestrate an encounter with him. I wasn't on staff at the Library of Congress and marching into the office of the chief Rare Books curator seemed brazen, even for me. Besides, if I appeared too eager, I'd likely cast suspicion back on Doug. That was the last thing I wanted to do.

It would be easier to start with Congressman Henry Chang. I'd ask to speak with Maeve Dixon first thing this morning and see if she could get me a few minutes with her esteemed colleague. Sergeant O'Halloran had made it abundantly clear he wasn't touching Chang with a ten-foot pole. What if he was the guilty party? There was no way I was going to let Chang pin this whole sordid mess on Doug or another innocent person simply because he was an elected official. Wasn't Lady Justice often depicted wearing a blindfold, depicting impartiality in judgment without regard to status, wealth, or privilege? I vaguely remembered such a detail from my college art history course. Who would have known? A liberal arts education was valuable after all.

I'd had no time yesterday to speak with Janice Jackson, the head of the congressional relations office. Meg mentioned she should be kept on the suspect list. Since Meg worked closely with Janice, maybe my B.F.F. could help broker an opportunity for the three of us to talk.

That left Lea Rutherford, the wealthy donor who was allegedly having an affair with Joe Malden, the Library's lawyer. I definitely didn't run in the same circles as her. That might prove the most difficult nut to crack. When I mentioned her name to Malden, he'd clammed up faster than a Trappist monk. I'd have better luck getting Clarence to talk to me. I'd better stew on that one.

We arrived back at the condo and soon found ourselves in the warm comfort of our kitchen. A few minutes later, Clarence had eaten his breakfast and I was enjoying a freshly brewed latte, which I'd made with the assistance of our industrial strength espresso machine. Doug was sitting at the kitchen table, enjoying his own cafe and reading the *Washington Post* on his iPad.

"Gustav's death and the theft made the front page of the paper," said Doug glumly.

"With good reason. It's not every day in Washington a leader of a cultural institution gets bashed over the head and a priceless treasure has gone missing."

"Well, when you put it that way, Kit." Doug eked out a tight smile.

"Does the *Post* say if the police have any suspects in mind?" I looked over his head to get a glimpse of the article on his tablet.

"There was some mumbo-gumbo about the police pursuing several promising leads," said Doug. "Just a flak making up stuff to cover up the fact that law enforcement has no idea what happened."

I massaged Doug's shoulders. "Don't worry. The authorities may not have a clue about what's going on, but I have a few ideas up my sleeve."

Doug looked at my arm. "Right now, all you have up your sleeve is a doggie cleanup bag for Clarence."

I looked at the bulge on my right arm. Doug was right. I often stuffed bags up my sleeve so I'd be ready if Clarence did number two on our jogs.

I shook my finger. "That's because I haven't put my sleuthing hat on. But once I do, I'll have a lot more in store."

Doug chuckled and returned his gaze to reading the news. "I have no doubt, Kit."

I dashed into the shower and pondered what to wear for the day. I had no idea what I might confront. Would the day be spent fulfilling my traditional duties as a chief of staff or would I focus more on solving the murder? In the end, I'd do what my boss wanted me to do.

Given the uncertainty, there was only one option. I veered toward a section of our walk-in closet saved for my black suits. There was only one outfit for women which pretty much covered all possible engagements or situations, and that was the black pantsuit. Most industries were leaning toward more casual work clothes, yet Capitol Hill was largely immune to such changes. Ann Taylor and Tahari were doing just fine in Washington. Over the years, I'd purchased a number of black suits in a variety of styles. All could be accessorized, either with a flashy or conservative top or appropriate jewelry. For today, I picked out a fitted two-button jacket, pants with a bit of stretch, and a pretty red popover blouse. No matter what happened, at least I'd be dressed appropriately and comfortably.

Doug was heading into the shower as I was leaving. Given that I had no idea how late I'd be tonight, I told him he was stuck with the Metro because I was taking the Prius. Unfortunately, traffic on a Thursday morning when Congress and the rest of the federal government was operating full tilt was never a pleasant experience. I opted for the scenic Memorial Bridge ride into the District of Columbia since I preferred the monuments to the concrete of I-395. But the blasted work on the historic bridge continued, making the ride move at a snail's pace. Literally. Clarence and I were slow joggers, and I knew we could have made it across the bridge faster.

Thirty minutes later, I parked my car underneath the congressional office buildings and reported for duty soon thereafter. I never beat Maeve Dixon to work. Her military habits stuck with her. She was early to appear at the office and even earlier to the gym. In particular, her exercise regimen had served her well. It was partially through the relationships she made at the congressional gym that she became a committee chair so quickly. Politics was dominated by men, and Maeve Dixon knew where to find them, namely trying to do pull-ups and master the bench press. I never saw her in action during these workout sessions, but I imagined she played her cards right. Just athletic enough to gain respect from her peers but stopping short of showing powerful people (of the masculine variety) they were comparatively out of shape. It was a good recipe for success in our nation's capital.

I sat down at my desk and logged onto my computer. Over a hundred email messages awaited my reply. This was always the problem when I had to focus on crime solving inside the United States Capitol. My *real* job didn't stop. As best as I could, I worked my way through the pile of inquiries. Most messages were forwarded to Meg or other Dixon staffers. Curious enough, there was an email from Library of Congress lawyer and baseball aficionado Joe Malden. I clicked on it and learned that Joe wanted that later today, perhaps around eleven. Without a second thought, I hit reply and told him I'd be there. I wasn't sure if Joe qualified as a suspect, but his connection to Lea Rutherford could be critical.

It was almost nine o'clock. All congressional offices would be open for business, so it was an appropriate time to bug Maeve Dixon about getting me an appointment with Henry Chang.

Patsy sat at her desk, staring at the computer screen with a pained expression.

"If you look too long like that, your face will freeze," I said lightly to our scheduler.

Patsy jumped and grabbed her glasses before they fell off her face. "Kit, you startled me."

"Sorry," I said. "But you seemed in such anguish. I had to interrupt it."

"Oh, that." Patsy waved aimlessly at her computer monitor. "As usual, Congresswoman Dixon has to be in three places at once this afternoon. I'm trying to figure out how to make it happen."

"You can work magic better than Hermione Granger," I said. "I'm sure it will work out." Patsy was a big fan of the J.K. Rowling books and Hermione was her favorite, a preference we shared.

Patsy blushed. "You're too kind. What can I help you with this morning?"

"I need to see Maeve," I said. "The sooner, the better."

"Go right on in. She's not on the phone and her first appointment doesn't start for another thirty minutes."

That was easy. Even though I was Dixon's chief of staff, since she became a committee chair, it was harder and harder to secure one-on-one time with her, especially if it wasn't scheduled ahead. The casual days of nonchalance had ended.

Dixon was sitting behind her desk, reading on her computer. She liked to peruse the *Washington Post* and *New York Times* in the morning, along with the local papers *Politico* and *Roll Call*. If she had enough time, she'd move onto the *Wall Street Journal*. I couldn't tell immediately how far she'd gotten this morning, but I had a feeling her reading had been unusually focused on the crime pages.

"Good morning, Madame Chair," I said politely.

"Kit, I'm glad you stopped by." She motioned to the chair in front of her desk. "Do you have any news to report about the Library of Congress?" She looked me straight in the eye.

"Yes, we know a few more facts. Gustav Gaffney was killed the night before, not yesterday morning when his body was discovered."

"By your husband, correct?" she asked.

"Yes, that's right." No point in masking the truth.

"I suppose the police will chase down alibis. Anything else to report?"

"I'm learning more about the people who attended the preview the night Gaffney died. I learned yesterday that the rare books librarian might have the connections necessary to move such valuable stolen items."

Maeve's countenance brightened. "Check him out today. See if he had a reason to engage in a major theft."

"I can try," I said. "I also learned that the Library's top lawyer is having an affair with one of their most generous donors. They were both at the event I attended the night Gaffney died."

Maeve pursed her lips. "It might be relevant, if one of them persuaded the other to do it. Is that all?"

"There's one other suspect I'd like to discuss with you ma'am, but it's sensitive."

Dixon straightened in her high-backed office chair. "What is it? Or rather, who is it?"

"Henry Chang," I said.

"As in the member of Congress?" asked Dixon, her eyes widening.

"Yes, that's him. He was at the event on Tuesday night and apparently he's quite an aficionado of all things historical."

Maeve's forehead wrinkled. "Why was Henry at the event on Tuesday when we had an invitation-only showing the next day, arranged especially for Congress?"

"I believe someone said he had a conflict with the Wednesday morning time, ma'am. But I intend to ask him that question, amongst others."

Maeve sighed. "I suppose it's not unprecedented to question an elected official about involvement in a crime. I can have Patsy patch me through to him. I'll insist he make time to meet with you. Is this morning convenient?"

"The sooner, the better," I said. "I have an appointment to chat with the Library of Congress chief lawyer at eleven."

"The one who's having an affair with the rich woman?" she asked.

"Yes, although I think they're both unattached, so it's really not an affair. I shouldn't have characterized it that way."

"Maybe I should start hanging out at the Library of Congress," said Maeve. "Apparently, it's the place for romance."

I chuckled. My boss was attractive and single. That combination was not exceedingly rare in Washington. But the amount of time she spent on her job in Congress meant she had almost no opportunity for a social life. Success didn't happen without tradeoffs, although I suspected Maeve could fit in romance if she really wanted to do so.

I had just gotten up to leave when Maeve called back. "Kit, before you go, don't forget to keep Miriam Dunlap apprised of the situation."

I nodded. "I'll try to fit in a meeting with her later today. Hopefully, I'll have something worthwhile to report."

It was time to do the rounds and talk to everyone on Team Dixon. If running *for* office was a sprint, then running *an* office was a marathon. New challenges and obstacles presented themselves on a daily basis. To that end, we'd assembled a competent team who tried their hardest for the people in North Carolina our boss had been elected to represent. All in all, I couldn't ask for much more.

I was going to start with Meg, but I didn't quite make it to her cubicle. Instead, our press secretary intercepted my path. Given the narrowness of the aisles in our office space, it wasn't difficult for him to prevent my forward progress.

"I need to speak with you," he said.

"I can see that, Kyle." I motioned toward his workspace. "Please have a seat and tell me what's going on."

In his mid-twenties, Kyle had a bright future ahead of him as a communications professional in Washington, D.C. Like many flacks, he tended toward the high-strung end of the spectrum. His mood literally depended on the press cycle, and every word uttered about Maeve Dixon that didn't meet his standards was a disaster of epic proportions. Kyle would eventually calm down after a few more years of seasoned experience. Unfortunately, by the time he did, he'd probably already have moved on to a more lucrative position outside Congress. Our salaries couldn't compete with K Street, so we had to rely upon talent who believed in public service.

Kyle did as he was told, straightening his skinny tie as he sat down in his ergonomically correct office chair. Millennials were no slouches, pun intended.

"This murder business at the Library of Congress is a real press nightmare," he said, motioning toward his iPhone. "We're trying to move Dixon's legislative agenda at the beginning of the year and instead, I'm answering questions about when and how this bureaucrat Gus was killed."

"Let's get a few facts straight, Kyle." I tried to keep my voice calm. "His name was Gustav Gaffney, not Gus. He was the Assistant Librarian of Congress, and I doubt he'd be too concerned that his murder is a press problem for you."

Kyle's face turned red. "Sorry," he said quickly. "I shouldn't have been so insensitive."

"It's okay. Consider it a valuable lesson learned."

He cleared his throat. "Keeping in mind there was a loss of life, I'm worried about the press on this."

"Understood," I said. "Please tell me about it."

"Of course, all the major news outlets are covering it, given the location and the theft associated with the murder," he explained. "But the Capitol Hill papers are getting at the congressional angle."

"Which ones?" I asked. "*Roll Call*? *The Hill*?" No wonder Maeve had been glued to her computer monitor.

"Yes, and more." He consulted his phone. "*Capitol Hill Times*, *Washingtonian*, *Washington Examiner*, and *Hill Rag*. I'm not even telling you about the blogs."

"I guess it makes sense. It's the biggest crime to occur on Capitol Hill since…" I paused.

"You mean since the last murder you were involved in."

"Yeah, right. I hope that's not getting into the press." It was never a good sign when Capitol Hill staff made headlines.

"Not yet, but Maeve Dixon's connection to this crime is a direct one given her position as chair of the relevant committee," he said. "Right now, everyone is focused on the salacious details of the murder itself. But if this goes unsolved, pretty soon reporters are going to need to advance the story, and an obvious place to start would be Maeve Dixon and what she's doing to make sure the guilty party is caught."

"Of course. I'm running point for her on this, serving as a liaison between the Librarian of Congress and the investigating sergeant from the police. Does that help?"

"For now, that's sufficient. If I start getting questions, I can offer up a statement about Dixon getting daily reports on the progress. But that will only satisfy them for so long. Understand?"

I got Kyle's point. Monitoring a situation was an acceptable answer for a news cycle or two. It wouldn't work if this dragged on and no one was apprehended.

"Listen, I'm making some inquiries today about the murder, so let's hope it will get solved quickly. I'll let you know if there's a big break in the case."

Kyle nodded. "Be careful, Kit."

I heard that phrase so often I should just give in and have it tattooed on my forehead. I managed a weak smile. "Thanks, Kyle. I will."

I'd turned the corner to talk to our legislative team when I heard Meg's voice. "Kit, is that you?"

"Yes," I said, appearing inside Meg's cubicle. "Here I am."

Very few congressional staff had private offices on Capitol Hill. The quarters were so tight, even more senior aides like Meg typically worked inside partially enclosed workspaces. Given Meg's position as legislative director, she had a larger space than most. She'd chosen to decorate it tastefully, adding a small lamp, colorful accessories, and modular organizing bins. A limited number of photos were tacked to the side wall, including pictures of Meg with myself, Trevor, and of course, Clay Donovan. Meg's indecision over her love life had spilled into her cubicle decor.

"How was your dinner last night with Sebastian's police officer girlfriend?" she asked, tilting her head to the side.

"How was your happy hour with Clay and friends?" I countered.

We stared at each other in a mini-standoff. After a few seconds, we both laughed. "You go first," said Meg.

"Okay. Lisa seems really great. They brought over pizza for dinner."

Meg interrupted. "From where?" Leave it to Meg and her penchant for foodie details.

"Pupatella."

"Oooh!" Meg's eyes almost turned green with envy. "I heard it's delicious."

"It was. We talked about the murder. Lisa said that the police are working with federal investigators. They seem to think a professional art thief is behind the crimes."

Meg frowned. "Who just happened to know the contents of Lincoln's pockets were being shown to a small group of people that evening?"

"They seem to think the thief might have an accomplice who works at the Library of Congress or has an affiliation with it."

"I suppose it's possible. Where does that leave the investigation?"

"They're going to focus on trying to see if the stolen items show up for sale underground. If so, the investigators can trace the goods back to the seller."

Meg grimaced. "That'll take forever. If I just stole precious treasures from the Library of Congress, the last thing I'm going to do is to try to sell them immediately. I'd wait for a while, until the trail goes cold."

"I agree, Meg," I said. "In the meantime, the crimes go unsolved. Did you overhear my conversation with Kyle?"

"There's no conversation I don't overhear, Kit." She motioned toward her pseudo wall, which was only six feet tall.

"Then you know that our boss has some serious skin in the game, too."

"What's your next move?" asked Meg.

Just as I was about to answer, Patsy interrupted us. She must have something important to say. Patsy rarely left her desk outside Dixon's office.

"Maeve was able to secure an appointment with Henry Chang," she said. "But you need to head over to his office now. He has a tight window before other commitments. I've emailed you his office location."

"Got it," I said. "Meg, we'll have to catch up later. I'll text you."

"Good luck, Kit," said Meg as I grabbed my purse and dashed out our office suite. Patsy's email said that Representative Henry Chang's office was located on the fourth floor of the Longworth Building. It was a typical freshman office, far away from the action. Ten minutes later, I arrived at the correct location, opened the glass door, and walked inside.

Members of Congress have considerable latitude concerning their office decorations. Most elected legislators choose to highlight the districts they represent. They hang framed posters featuring tourist attractions or scenic highlights. Others, who might be considered more self-promotional, displayed photographs of themselves with other important people. Many offices choose a mix between the two or even combine them. For example, an image of the member of Congress hiking a section of the Appalachian Trail in her district would be a perfect addition to the office decor.

Representative Henry Chang had taken a much different approach. His small waiting area was completely decked out with facsimile images featuring famous documents, photographs, and artifacts in American history. He had the Declaration of Independence, the Gettysburg Address, the Bill of Rights, Civil War tintype portraits, political cartoons, noteworthy newspaper headlines, and Revolutionary War maps. To his credit, Henry Chang appeared not to care much about himself. There was not one picture of him, his family, or even his dog. Instead, I felt as if I'd walked into a miniature museum. Even though nothing was authentic, the message was quite clear. Henry Chang cared a great deal about American history, and he chose to surround himself with it as much as humanly possible.

The young staff assistant behind the desk smiled. "Welcome to Congressman Chang's office. Can I help you?"

I explained who I was and that Chairwoman Maeve Dixon (it was always good to use her official title in these circumstances) had called for an appointment.

"Yes, our chief of staff explained you'd stop by. Please have a seat," he said in a friendly tone. "Or feel free to peruse our collection of American memorabilia." He waved his arm across the expanse of the waiting area, almost like Vanna White revealing a correct letter on "Wheel of Fortune."

"Thank you," I said in my most polite voice. "It's quite a display. Very different from other House of Representative office suites."

"Certainly," said the staff assistant eagerly. He leaned forward in his chair and ignored the buzz indicating he had a phone call. "Representative Chang is a big fan of American historical artifacts. He can't get enough of it."

No kidding. That's why I'm here. The question is whether he'd kill for it.

The staff assistant was awfully chatty. Maybe he could serve as a source of information. "Why does Congressman Chang have such a fascination with history?" I asked innocently.

"It's his passion," said my verbose friend. "He's a politician these days, but I think he wished he'd become a historian or curator."

"Being in politics is an odd alternative to choose," I said, almost under my breath.

The staff assistant must have heard me. "I think Representative Chang decided he wanted to become part of history. So he ran for Congress."

He'll get his wish if he was responsible for one of the most infamous heists in American history.

The staff assistant turned his attention back to his computer. "Oh, you can go back now." He pointed toward the door that led to the office area.

"Thank you. This conversation has been. . ." I paused for a beat to choose the right word. "Illuminating."

My young friend beamed. It wasn't every day he received such high praise; his job was pretty much a "no-thanks" gig. In other words, he received a lot of the blame and none of the credit.

After I opened the door to the suite, I realized the front-desk guy hadn't told me which way to turn for Chang's office. In a flash, a slim Asian woman was at my side. "Are you Kit Marshall?"

"Yes, ma'am," I said. "That's been my name for my entire life."

She didn't laugh at my humorous overture. "Right this way." She walked swiftly down the short hallway and opened the door to Representative Chang's private office.

Given what I'd just seen inside his foyer, I shouldn't have been surprised, but I was. Every wall of Chang's office boasted framed posters or other historical memorabilia. I couldn't examine everything with a magnifying glass, but I had the distinct feeling this display included items from the Congressman's private collection. While facsimiles adorned the waiting area, his inner sanctum boasted the real McCoy.

Representative Chang was seated behind his stately oak desk. He rose and offered his hand, although he avoided direct eye contact. He cleared his throat before speaking. "Ms. Marshall, I understand Chairwoman Dixon asked us to meet." He sat back down in his chair and motioned for me to sit opposite him. "Briefly, that is."

I suppressed an audible sigh. What a peach I'd picked off the tree.

"Thank you, Congressman. I cannot tell you how much Chairwoman Dixon appreciates your cooperation in this matter." I could feel the rigidness in my upper body intensifying. This conversation was already reminiscent of a post-Halloween visit to the dentist.

Chang reclined in his chair and folded his hands in a triangle. "I'm waiting, Ms. Marshall. What would you like to talk about?"

No sense in beating around the bush. "I'm here to speak to you about the murder of Gustav Gaffney."

"Are you referencing the crime at the Library of Congress?"

"Yes. Gustav Gaffney was the Assistant Librarian, and he was murdered on Tuesday evening. Not long after our viewing inside the Librarian's ceremonial office."

Chang shook his head slowly. "A terrible tragedy. The items from the

Lincoln assassination are priceless." He added. "And of course, the death of a Library of Congress employee."

"Where did you go after the preview ended?" I was pretty sure Chang was at the Library when I left to go to dinner with Sebastian and Meg. The last I remembered, Janice Jackson had scuttled off to find his coat.

"I chatted with the rare books curator for a while," said Chang.

"You mean Gordon Endicott."

"I think that was his name. I've spoken with him before at previous events."

"Then what did you do?" I prodded.

"As I recall, Gaffney put the items back in the safe and secured it," he said. "At that point, it was evident the evening had concluded. I put on my coat and came back here to work for a few more hours."

"Burning the midnight oil?" I asked, my eyebrows raised.

"We're in session this week for a reason, Ms. Marshall," he said curtly. "As I'm sure you know, Congress is usually adjourned this week to celebrate President's Day. But the Speaker of the House canceled the recess so we could work on several important bills."

Chang was right. It was unusual for Congress to work in Washington, D.C. this holiday week. It was probably why the Library of Congress decided to make such a big deal of the Lincoln treasures. It wasn't often that members of Congress were in town during the week of the President's Day holiday.

"Were you alone, or was your staff also working late?" I asked.

"I don't require my staff to remain at the office with me after hours," he said. "When I'm here by myself, I accomplish much more."

Chang didn't have an alibi. He could have easily put on his coat as if he was leaving, hid in the shadows of the Jefferson Building, waited for everyone to leave, and committed the crime.

The Congressman's phone buzzed. He raised his finger in the air to indicate he needed to take the call. After picking up the receiver, he said, "I understand, Daphne. I will be right out."

Chang stood. "Ms. Marshall, I'm afraid I have an important guest from my district who asked to speak with me personally. We'll have to end our meeting early."

I didn't budge. I had more questions for Chang and something told me I needed to take advantage of the situation and ask them. After all, the police were hesitant to treat him as a suspect. If he was involved in the murder and theft, it would be up to me to figure it out.

"I'm not in a big rush this morning," I said. "I'm happy to wait."

Chang folded his arms across his chest. "Perhaps it would be better if we rescheduled."

"I'll have to tell Chairwoman Dixon, if that's the case. I'm keeping her informed about the investigation. She'll want to know why we didn't finish our conversation." I tapped my foot while waiting for his response.

Chang stared at me for several moments as he weighed his options. "Very well, then. I will return in a few minutes." He dashed out of the office and closed the door behind him.

Whew. Sometimes it paid to be stubborn. I looked around Chang's office. Everything was as neat as a pin. My gaze drifted to his stately desk. I glanced back at the door. How long would it take to greet a needy constituent? From experience, it really depended on the level of neediness. I gulped, got up from my chair, and walked to the other side of the desk.

There wasn't much on the top of his desk besides his computer monitor, a daily American history calendar with a "fun fact" for each date, and exactly three pens. I'd have to try a drawer. I could hear Chang's voice outside the office, obviously in the throes of glad-handing his VIP visitor.

As carefully as possible so not to cause any noise, I opened the top drawer of the desk. Much like the surface of his desk, everything inside the drawer was in its proper place. A stapler, post-it notes, paper clips, and a small pad of paper were lined up perfectly next to each other. I was about to close the drawer when I noticed a business card wedged between the package of post-its and the box of paper clips. The voices outside the office seemed reasonably far away, so I grabbed the card and turned it over. It was a card for a dealer specializing in rare books, manuscripts, letter, and other historical memorabilia.

All of a sudden, I heard footsteps approaching. I slammed the drawer shut and in three swift steps, I was seated across the desk again. The problem was that I had the business card in my hand as the door opened. I shoved it inside my purse just as Henry Chang walked in.

If he thought I'd left my seat when he was gone, he didn't show it. He strode to his desk and sat down again. "Thank you for waiting, Ms. Marshall. Shall we resume our conversation?"

"Yes," I croaked. That had been too close for comfort. It was one thing to ask questions of a member of Congress under the orders of a committee chair. It was another altogether to get caught snooping inside the personal belongings of an elected official.

He tapped his fingers impatiently on the desk. "I'm waiting."

"I'm sorry," I said quickly. "Let's go back to Tuesday night at the Library of Congress. Why did you attend the event that evening instead of the V-I-P event that was scheduled the next day?"

"Two reasons, Ms. Marshall," he said. "First, I had a constituent breakfast which conflicted. Yes, I could have rescheduled it, but voters tend not to like it when you cancel meetings with them in Washington." He took a deep breath. "Second, I knew the event on Tuesday night would have fewer people in attendance. It was a better opportunity to see the contents of Lincoln's pockets up close. If I had come to the congressional event, I would have been one of many members of Congress in attendance. Tuesday night was much more preferable."

"How did you know about it?" I asked.

"Janice Jackson told me," he said immediately. "She knew I wouldn't want to miss the display and that I'd prefer the lower key event."

"Did she also tell you that Gustav Gaffney's fingerprints opened the safe?"

"You mean which fingerprints were linked to the safe's biometrics?" he repeated.

"Yes. Were you aware that Gaffney's prints were only one of two sets that could be used to gain access to it?"

"She might have mentioned it to me," said Chang, rubbing his chin. "I can't be sure. Janice provides me with copious amounts of information about the Library of Congress."

"And that's because you ask a lot questions, right?"

Chang threw his shoulders back, straightening in his chair. "As you can probably figure out, I thoroughly enjoy American history." His arm swept around the room.

"It's impressive. Are these items originals?" I asked.

"Some are," he said. He gestured to a framed poster to his right. "For example, this lithograph of Abraham Lincoln's 1861 inauguration is authentic."

It featured small portraits of each president from George Washington through Lincoln in an oval circle. "How did you acquire it?" I asked.

"Here and there, Ms. Marshall. I'm acquainted with quite a few sellers. I know when a good deal comes on the market."

That likely explained the business card I found in the drawer. It certainly reinforced the notion that Henry Chang would have the connections to unload rare items, perhaps even stolen ones.

I couldn't think of any more questions to ask, so I stood up to leave and extended my hand. "You've been generous with your time. I will be sure to tell my boss."

Chang exhaled. "I would appreciate that. Most members of Congress don't actively seek service on Chairwoman Dixon's committee. But I did."

"Because the committee oversees federal cultural institutions."

Chang nodded. "Given my interest in antiquities, I knew it would be a good fit."

"My colleague tells me you attend every event," I said.

His eyes gleamed. "Absolutely. You can ask Chairwoman Dixon. I'm a very conscientious member of the committee."

"I'll be sure to tell her about your. . ." I stammered before my brain found the right word. "Enthusiasm."

After leaving the suite, I checked my phone. It was quarter to eleven. There was no time to return to the Dixon office before heading over to the Library of Congress for my appointment with Joe Malden. As I weaved through the hallways, I considered my conversation with Congressman Chang. Meg's observation was accurate; he was definitely an odd duck. He seemed to care more about history and collectibles than about politics and policy. He certainly had the connections in that world to make a heist plausible. But something didn't add up. Why would Chang want to steal the contents of Lincoln's pockets? If he was guilty of anything, it was caring *too much* about history. He didn't seem like the type who would want such an important piece of Americana to fall into the wrong hands. However, it was possible that he stole the items so he could possess them as part of his own collection. I could picture Chang taking great delight in keeping it in some top-secret location where he could indulge himself in private viewings anytime he wanted.

I was so deep in thought, I almost collided with Sergeant O'Halloran inside the tunnel linking the Library of Congress to the Cannon House Office Building.

"Ms. Marshall, you should watch where you're going," said O'Halloran as he gracefully sidestepped me. I noticed the buttons on his white dress shirt were straining. Maybe walking back and forth underground to the Library of Congress would be good exercise for him.

"I apologize. But I had a good reason for my preoccupation. I was thinking about the conversation I just had with Representative Henry Chang."

O'Halloran raised both his eyebrows. "You decided he was worth the political risk."

"It was less risky than you might think. Remember, Chang is on a committee chaired by my boss. He's pretty eager to keep her happy with him."

"So, did you find anything out?" O'Halloran took two steps closer to me. I could tell he was eager to know whether Chang could be a suspect.

I explained to him that Chang had no alibi and certainly had the connections to move stolen high-priced items. But it didn't necessarily jive with his obvious reverence for American history.

O'Halloran listened and then inhaled deeply. He reached into his pocket and produced an unwrapped candy bar. He proceeded to peel away the wrapping and caught me eying him.

"Want a piece?" He extended his hand with a square of chocolate in it. Although it was a little gross that he'd pulled the candy from his pocket, it had been wrapped. Furthermore, breakfast seemed like a long time ago.

"Sure." I accepted the chocolate and popped it in my mouth. "Thank you."

"You shared with me, so I'm sharing with you. Isn't that how this partnership is supposed to work?" asked O'Halloran in a teasing tone.

"Sharing chocolate snacks is not exactly what I had in mind," I said. "Do you have any leads on the case?"

"I was over at the Library of Congress this morning, asking about everyone's whereabouts during the approximate time of the murder." He whipped out his trusty notebook and flipped it open. "I've worked a lot of cases, and everyone always has an alibi. It's my job to figure out who's lying."

In my limited experience solving homicides, I had to agree with O'Halloran. Determining "means" and "opportunity" to commit a crime were important. We already knew everyone who attended the preview event on Tuesday night had the means to kill Gustav. They had access to the building and knew the bust of Thomas Jefferson could serve as a convenient weapon. But alibis could cast doubt on whether all the attendees truly had the "opportunity" to murder Gustav and steal the safe's valuable contents.

"Does everyone have an alibi for the time of Gustav's death?" I asked.

"You see, Ms. Marshall, that's the interesting thing with this case." O'Halloran took the pencil out of his breast pocket and scratched the thin layer of hair on his head. "So far, I haven't come across a solid one."

"Such as?" I asked.

"Well, your hubby is a good example."

I bit my lip. "He was working. I went out to dinner with Meg, Trevor, and my brother Sebastian. Doug couldn't join us because he had to catch up on paperwork."

"What a *convenient* excuse," said O'Halloran. "Everyone loves doing paperwork at eight o'clock in the evening. Especially when the alternative is going out to dinner and throwing back a few cold ones."

"It might be hard for you to believe, but Doug's idea of a good time doesn't involve drinks with me and my friends."

O'Halloran glanced at his watch. "I believe you on that one. Especially blondie. She's a bit much to take these days, flitting around Capitol Hill with Trevor and that other chief of staff guy."

"How did you know that Meg was dating two men at one time?" I asked.

"Ms. Marshall, I didn't get promoted for nothing." He pressed his thumb into the middle of his chest. "I know what's going on around here."

Impressive. Nonetheless, I didn't want him to forget the larger point. "Doug may not have anyone to corroborate his alibi, but it makes perfect sense that he decided to return to his office to finish his work."

"Yeah, yeah," said O'Halloran. "I have to keep him on the suspect list, although to tell you the truth, I can't see the good professor bashing someone over the head with a statue of Jefferson. It's too messy for him."

"Well, that makes two of us, Sergeant. What's your next move?"

"I gotta get back to the office to meet the federal agents who are investigating this case. They'll have me so tied up in red tape, I won't be able to unwind myself for a week."

So much for empowering local law enforcement. They'll be focused on running fingerprints through every global criminal syndicate database from here to Europe and back. I had a distinct feeling it was up to me to investigate the home team.

"Good luck with that," I said as we parted ways.

O'Halloran yelled over his shoulder. "Keep me informed, Ms. Marshall. That's a direct order!"

"Yes, Sergeant O'Halloran." Why did I suddenly have the feeling I'd been drafted into service without a release date in sight?

Chapter Nine

⸻

I CONTINUED DOWN THE long corridor linking the House of Representatives offices to the Library of Congress's James Madison Building. Doug worked in the historic Thomas Jefferson Building, so I was less familiar with the floor plan of Madison. But I did know my way to the cafeteria, and Joe Malden said his office was nearby.

After taking the elevator to the sixth floor of the building, I followed the signs to the General Counsel's office. The main door was locked, and I had to use a buzzer to speak to the receptionist.

"My name is Kit Marshall. I'm here to see Joe Malden," I said loudly.

"Ma'am, you don't need to continue to hold the button when you speak," said the female voice. "It continues to buzz in my ear when you do that."

"Oh, I'm sorry." I took my finger off the button. Why aren't instructions provided with complex machinery?

"I'm letting you in now," said the voice.

The door made a clicking sound, and I pulled it open. Inside the foyer, the same voice greeted me. "Hello, Ms. Marshall. Joe's office is in the back of the suite." She pointed behind her.

I headed in the designated direction and found the office with Joe's name on it. The door was open, but I knocked softly before entering.

Joe was at his desk, reading a document. When he saw me, he smiled and motioned with his hand. "Please come in, Kit."

I took a seat across his desk and looked around. Joe's office was roomy, probably three times the size of my work space. He'd decorated it with a smattering of Boston Red Sox paraphernalia. There was a framed jersey, a 2018 poster of the World Series team, a fancy photograph of Fenway Park, and even a baseball bat with signatures on it. On top of all this, there was also a picturesque view of the iconic Jefferson Building dome. Although not quite as grand as the United States Capitol's world-famous structure, the Jefferson dome was no slouch. Doug had told me its architecture and design had been based on the Paris Opera House.

"This is an impressive workspace, Joe. I'm trying to hide my jealousy," I said.

Joe's face turned pink. "I try to remind myself how lucky I am. Sometimes I take it for granted. It is a beautiful office with a spectacular background."

"And you've surrounded yourself with your baseball memorabilia," I said, pointing to the bat resting against the wall.

"That's a Mookie Betts signed bat from 2018," he said proudly. "He was the league MVP that year."

"Quite a treasure," I said. "Why do you keep it at work?"

"I don't usually," said Joe. "A few people wanted to see it, so I brought it in. Quite frankly, I kind of like having it around. It makes me happy."

I understood. Having Clarence at work made me happy, at least when he wasn't stealing ice cream cones from toddlers visiting Congresswoman Dixon's office. That actually happened. I never needed to exaggerate when it came to Clarence's antics.

"Staff must still be quite unsettled about what happened yesterday," I said.

Joe chuckled. "That's an understatement. This is the Library of Congress, the largest repository of human knowledge in the world. People don't *die* here. This is where they come to *learn*."

"Fair point. In fact, I think Miriam Dunlap said something similar to me. Does anyone have an idea of who might be behind this?"

He leaned back in his chair. "Obviously, it's an outsider. A professional who gained access to the building and waited for his opportunity to strike."

Joe hadn't changed his tune from yesterday. I'd have to alter my approach or this was going to be Groundhog Day all over again.

"Wouldn't that person need some help?" I asked. "Even if the staff member providing the help had been manipulated?"

Joe thought about my question before answering. "I suppose it's possible. Someone might have provided information without knowing they were doing something wrong."

"Certainly," I said enthusiastically. At least now Joe was talking. "Maybe Lea Rutherford. She certainly knows a great deal about the Library of Congress and its operations."

"Due to her status as a top donor?" asked Joe.

"Yes," I said slowly. "And also due to the fact that the two of you are involved in a romantic relationship."

Joe shifted in his chair. "I'm not going to deny it. Who told you?"

"I have my sources." Ironically, a good detective never kisses and tells.

"Obviously. Not that many people know about it." Malden sighed. "But I don't see how my relationship with Lea has any bear on this case."

"Gustav Gaffney didn't approve of it. Now he's dead," I said. "From what I understand, Miriam Dunlap is much more understanding when it comes to love. Now, you and Lea are in the clear."

Joe crossed his arms across his chest. "Neither of us would kill Gustav simply because he didn't like the fact that we're involved romantically."

"You don't think that's a motive?" I asked. "From my perspective, it looks like a pretty substantial one, especially if it's getting serious between you and Ms. Rutherford. Maybe you'd like to take the relationship to the next level, but Gaffney stood in the way."

Joe shook his head. "I don't see how my relationship with Lea has any bearing on this case."

I had to concede to him there. "Regardless, I'd really like to speak with Ms. Rutherford. Given that she's one of the wealthiest women in the United States, it's hard for me to drop in. Is there any way you could help me set up a time to chat with her?"

Joe pressed his lips together. "If memory serves me correctly, she's at the D.C. Public Library today. She's a big contributor there, as well." He grabbed his phone and furiously texted for several seconds. After a brief pause, he placed it back on his desk. "You're in luck. She has some time later this afternoon if you'd like to swing by."

"She's at the new main branch building?"

"Yes, of course," said Malden, his chin jutted out. "She paid for an entire wing."

I should have known. "How nice. I appreciate you doing that for me. I'll be sure to let the Librarian of Congress know how helpful you've been."

"Please do," he said. "Your romantic musings aside, I don't have plans to quit my day job any time soon."

"Understood," I said. "But you were the one to email me today. Did you have something you wanted to discuss with me?"

"I thought you might have questions about the murder," he said. "I guessed that you might try to point the finger at me, especially since your husband is a prime suspect."

I clenched my jaw. "That's an exaggeration. The police are investigating plenty of other angles."

"I heard Doug was alone in his office after the event broke up." Malden tilted his head. "It doesn't sound good for him."

Now the Library's top lawyer had officially ticked me off. Two could play at this game. "Where were you after the display ended?"

"I went back to my office to work, but then Lea came to see me." His face turned pink. "She persuaded me to join her at her penthouse briefly. We were together until midnight or so, when I returned home." He folded his hands and placed them on the desk. I had the distinct feeling that Joe Malden wanted me to ask about his whereabouts during the time of the murder so he could provide me with his alibi. A bit too convenient, at least for my highly skeptical intuition.

"Did anyone see you?" I pressed. "A doorman, perhaps?"

"Lea's apartment has a private entrance," said Malden. "I suppose there's security footage somewhere, if the police needed to see it."

"Unless it's only saved for twenty-four hours," I said.

"It doesn't really matter, because we were together," said Joe, with a degree of confidence in his voice. "You can ask Lea this afternoon, if you like."

"I'll be sure to do that. Is there anything else you'd like to tell me, perhaps about the others who were at the event and had access to the office and safe?"

Joe shook his head slowly. "My colleagues are above reproach. I can't imagine anyone who would kill the Assistant Librarian and then steal a national treasure like the contents of Lincoln's pockets. It doesn't make any sense."

For the first time this morning, I felt like Joe Malden was telling me the truth. He'd offered his alibi in an obvious attempt to cross himself and Lea Rutherford off the suspect list. On the other hand, I didn't get the sense he thought anyone else associated with the Library of Congress could have committed the crime.

"I'll agree with you on that," I said. "It *doesn't* make any sense."

Joe stood up and so did I. He picked up his Red Sox bat and tapped his fingers on it. "I'll level with you. Gustav wasn't my favorite person, and he didn't exactly win popularity contests around here. But I can honestly say the disagreements weren't motivation for murder." He paused for a second. "At least anything I knew about."

"I'll keep digging," I said. "Sometimes, the dirty laundry is buried."

Malden laughed. "I hope you have a sturdy shovel."

I exited Joe Malden's office and decided to gather my thoughts over a cup of coffee inside the cafeteria. It was right around the corner, so I hustled down the hallway. Janice Jackson, the head of congressional relations, was headed in the opposite direction.

"Janice," I called out, waving my hand. "It's Kit Marshall from Maeve Dixon's office."

The congressional relations director spotted me and turned on her heels. "So good to see you at the Library of Congress," she said in a rushed clip. "Can I help you with anything?"

"No, I was just visiting Joe Malden. I don't know if you heard, but the Librarian of Congress asked me to assist the police in their investigation of Gustav Gaffney's murder and the theft. Chairwoman Dixon agreed, so here I am."

Janice ran her hand through her short, brown hair. "I did not know that. But I'm not surprised. I'm always the last to know *anything*."

That seemed odd to me. Wouldn't you want to tell your congressional relations person *everything*?

"It's really not a big deal. I've helped out with other Capitol Hill crimes before," I said.

Janice adjusted her dark green skirt and matching suit jacket. "Good luck. Every member of Congress is suddenly interested in the Library. I've got more congressional inquiries than I can handle. They're coming in via email, telephone, social media. Pretty soon, a carrier pigeon is going to arrive with a question."

"That makes sense to me." Members of Congress liked to follow fire whistles. A theft of this proportion on Capitol Hill, coupled with a murder, was a three-alarm affair.

"If that wasn't enough, we're hosting a small congressional reception this morning for a congressman who loves comic books." She sighed, and then her face brightened. "Would you like to see our display? The reception won't begin for another thirty minutes, but I think our curators have everything already assembled."

I glanced at my iPhone. "Sure. I had no idea the Library of Congress owns comic books." I always thought of the Library as a place for scholars who liked to search through old books and dusty letters. Doug loved it here, and that's what he did.

Janice motioned with her hand for me to follow her. "Come on. You're in for a treat."

I didn't have much time, but this seemed more interesting than getting a cup of stale coffee and reading email. It was the least I could do to help Janice out. Her job was to introduce the Library of Congress and its resources to elected officials and their staffs. By agreeing to view her display, I was handing her a nice win. It seemed like she needed it.

After a few turns, we eventually walked into a multipurpose room that had three long tables set up with Library of Congress staff standing behind them.

"Everyone, this is Kit Marshall, who works for Maeve Dixon," she announced. "I'm sure you all know that Congresswoman Dixon is the chair of our congressional oversight committee in the House of Representatives."

Her pronouncement had the intended effect. Everyone snapped to attention and put smiles on their faces.

Janice continued. "I met her in the hallway by chance and invited her to take a look at our comic book display this morning before our guest of honor shows up with his constituents."

"Thanks, everyone," I said. "Don't worry about me. I'll just take a speedy look and be on my way."

A woman in her early thirties manned the first table. Sporting funky cat's eye glasses with her dark hair pulled back into a sleek ponytail, she wore a black cardigan trimmed in a white ivory scallop, a button-down red blouse, a puffy grey skirt, black tights, and Mary Jane shoes with a chunky heel.

"Good morning," I said, feeling instantly frumpy in my plain black pantsuit. Maybe I should pay more attention to fashion? But when would I fit that in? Between murders? There never seemed to be enough hours in the day.

"Hello," she said brightly. "Let me know if you have any questions."

I didn't know much about comic books, having never read them as a kid or adult. The first one caught my eye. The title read "Wonder Woman for President." I pointed to it.

"What year was this one published?" I asked.

"That's 1943 from DC Comics," said the curator. "It was ahead of its time."

"Sort of," I said, pointing to the cover. "The sign at Wonder Woman's campaign rally says '1000 Years in the Future.'"

"Let's hope it's not a thousand years before we have a woman as president. You might also like to see this one." She pointed toward another comic. "It's Supergirl number one, published in 1972." As I examined the cover, she provided more background. "If you don't know, Supergirl is

Superman's cousin."

I smiled. "I did not know that. I feel like I could learn something new every day here." I moved to the end of the table, where there was a familiar face on a cover, or at least a masked face. "Spider Man," I said, pointing. "I know him."

"That's an important issue. It's the first one introducing the character Dr. Octopus. I believe the publication date is 1963. We also have the comic featuring the debut of Spider Man, but it's not on display today." She lowered her voice, "Too valuable. A lot of people remain shaken about the theft earlier in the week."

I leaned closer, careful not to touch the comics on the table. "What do you think happened?"

Her posture stiffened. "I have no idea. But we need to get those items back, and the police need to figure out who did this. If we have a thief in our midst, everything in our collection is vulnerable."

"Absolutely right," I said. "There's a lot of variety here. Quite frankly, I had no idea the Library of Congress even had comic books in its collection. I thought this place was for researchers only."

The well-dressed curator laughed. "We're for everyone who is curious and wants to learn, but we actually get a fair number of researchers who ask to read or examine our comic books. We also have collectors who want to examine verified copies before making a purchase."

"How many comics do you have?"

"We have the largest collection in the world," she said. "Well over a hundred thousand items."

A similarly aged man wearing a cardigan sweater and a skinny tie chimed in. "And that collection grew larger recently with a big acquisition in this area. A private collector donated his comics to us." He motioned toward his table display. "I have a few items from his gift over here. The donation included an original storyboard of a Mickey Mouse cartoon. We believe it was drawn in 1928."

I bent down to examine the pencil drawing of the world's most famous rodent. "I know nothing about comics or cartoons, and even I know this is really impressive."

The curator laughed. "Comics are a wholly American art form. We invented them. It makes sense we should trace the history of their publication here at the Library of Congress."

I shook both curators' hands and walked to the back of the room where Janice Jackson was standing. She was furiously typing on her iPhone but stopped when I approached.

"Did you enjoy seeing the display?" she asked.

"Loved it," I said. "Meg usually accompanies our boss when she visits legislative branch agencies under the committee's jurisdiction. But I might need to insist on joining her on these trips."

"You'll never be disappointed if you do," said Jackson. "Excuse me, but the member of Congress and his expected guests have arrived, and I need to meet them near the entrance to guide them here. The Members Room was already booked today so we put the display inside this room."

"The Members Room?" I asked. "What's that?"

Janice hurried out of the room and motioned for me to follow. "It's inside the Jefferson Building, not far from where we were on Tuesday night for the Lincoln display. It used to be the reading room for House members, but now it's a multi-purpose room we reserve for congressional events. I can show it to you sometime if you've never been inside it."

I had no more time with Janice right now, but suddenly I had an idea. "Do you have any time later in the day? I feel as though we haven't really had a chance to get to know one another. Would you be free for a drink after work?"

She pressed her lips together and answered slowly. "Sure, I think so. Let me check my schedule." She consulted her phone. "I'm free around five o'clock this evening. If you meet me inside the Great Hall, I can show you the Members Room and then we can walk down the street for a cocktail."

It wasn't the most enthusiastic response, but I'd take it. "Thanks, Janice. I'm looking forward to it."

I waved goodbye and retraced my steps back to the cafeteria, my original destination. The comic books were a real treat, but more importantly, the diversion had enabled me to schedule a time to chat privately with Janice. Her connection to the murder wasn't clear, but she had known about the safe. Meg had also mentioned that Gaffney had pressured Jackson to drum up more congressional support for the Library of Congress. That was easier said than done. Elected officials often found themselves pulled in a thousand directions and it was hard to get their attention for very long.

Inside the cafeteria, I triaged my email and sent important messages to our Dixon staff members. They knew the drill when I was working on a mystery with the congresswoman's blessing. Everyone else had to pitch in to make sure we kept all our balls in the air.

I'd had to cut my conversation with Meg short today, which was unfortunate. A bright idea popped into my head. I fired off a text to her.

Do you have a few hours free this afternoon?

Three dots appeared, indicating that she was writing back.

2 hour window at noon.

Oh, good. Maybe my plan would work.

Do you want to have lunch at the Portrait Gallery?

I could almost hear Meg squeal with delight. Trying out new lunch spots was a bonafide hobby for her.

Meet u there in 20.

Precisely twenty-three minutes later, I opened the door to the National Portrait Gallery, cleared security, and looked around. I must have arrived before Meg. Then I felt a tap on my shoulder.

"What took you so long?" asked Meg. She had on a stylish red pea coat with a matching knit tossed hat and gloves.

"I came as fast as I could," I said. "You have to switch Metro lines."

Meg waved her hand at me. "I caught a ride share here. It was four dollars and took seventeen minutes."

I raised my hands in defeat. "You got me there. A much better option." Transportation and combating the city's traffic was a perennial conversation amongst Washingtonians. No one had any good solutions, but that didn't stop the endless exchange of complaints and helpful tips.

We walked in the direction of the indoor courtyard where the cafe was located. "Why did you want to have lunch here?" asked Meg.

If we had the time to leave our office building for a meal, we usually patronized one of the eating establishments on nearby Pennsylvania Avenue. The National Portrait Gallery was north of the National Mall, in the vibrant Penn Quarter neighborhood. We rarely ventured so far away from Capitol Hill on a typical work day.

"If you're up for it, I arranged a meeting with Lea Rutherford at D.C. Public Library this afternoon," I explained. "The Portrait Gallery is nearby, and I remembered you liked the courtyard cafe here."

Meg beamed. "That was thoughtful of you, Kit." She touched my arm. "How is Doug holding up?"

"Thanks for asking. He's in good spirits. And hopeful that we find the person who did this soon so he can get back to his regular business. It's a major disruption at work."

Meg shook her head. "This isn't going away anytime soon. I heard there's going to be hearings. Several members of Congress want to make sure the Library has the best security systems in place to prevent another theft." Then she added, "Murder, too, of course."

Poor Gustav. He hadn't been forgotten, but his death was definitely playing second fiddle to the Lincoln theft.

As we walked inside the Portrait gallery's interior courtyard, my mood instantly brightened. Although inviting Meg to lunch had been a good reason to come here, my ulterior motive had been personal. With the sun streaming through the glass ceiling, there was no better place for a break, particularly when winter weather prohibited dining al fresco.

"This place is amazing." I tilted my head upward. The undulating glass canopy was reminiscent of natural cloud cover, enabling a pseudo outdoor experience during the dead of winter. Because today was sunny, the roof's steel lattice had cast a spiderweb of shadows on the exterior walls of the museum surrounding the spacious courtyard.

"They had a competition to redesign the courtyard and a British architecture firm won," said Meg. "Before that, it was open air, which meant it was empty for about half of the year."

"I like it this way," I said. "It's modern but somehow totally matches the older architecture of the museum building."

Meg headed towards the café, and I followed her. Architecture was considerably less important than food.

We both studied the options. The artisan cheese box sampler called my name, but I remembered last night's Puppatella feast. Who knew what the rest of the day would bring? Instead, I went for the roast turkey sandwich. Meg, however, never had any reservations about eating exactly what she wanted. She ordered a prosciutto sandwich with chips.

We carried our food to an open table next to a planter filled with flowers. After a few minutes of munching, Meg put her sandwich down. "Kit, I want to apologize."

I flinched. This didn't sound good.

"What for?"

"I know I've been distracted lately," she said. "It has a lot to do with my personal situation."

"You mean Trevor and Clay?"

"Of course, Kit. What else would it be?" Meg nibbled on a chip, staring vacantly at the half-full sunlit courtyard.

"People do have other problems than having two boyfriends," I said in a teasing voice.

Meg ignored my comment. "I know I need to make a decision soon. Or it will be made for me."

"Trevor doesn't think that three's company?" I tried to lighten the mood.

"He does not," said Meg. I noticed she'd only eaten half of her prosciutto sandwich. She had to be really upset if her appetite was affected.

"What about Clay?"

"He doesn't seem to mind as much," she said absently.

"As much or at all?" I asked pointedly.

"He hasn't complained about it. Clay is more laid back than Trevor. He's not in a rush. But he does get annoyed when I spend time with Trevor instead of him."

"Trevor's in a much different situation in his life," I said. "Sebastian had some wise advice when we went to Bullfeathers. You need to figure out which stage *you're* in."

Meg picked up her sandwich and took a big bite. Maybe she wasn't as upset as I thought. Just as likely, she wanted to avoid my difficult question.

While she was munching, I kept talking. "Don't think that I have all the answers. Relationships aren't easy." I told her about Doug's desire to find a house, which likely meant moving out of Arlington and further away from the city.

"I'd stand your ground on that one," she said, shaking her finger. "You don't want to become a *suburbanite*. It's bad enough you live in Arlington." Meg lived in a hip part of town and often gave me a hard time for living outside the urban walls of the District.

"We won't be moving anywhere if the authorities arrest Doug for murder and grand larceny," I said. "I might be wrong, but I'd think it would be a bad career move for a historian to get charged with stealing precious items of American antiquity."

Meg laughed. "That doesn't sound like something you'd put on your LinkedIn profile."

"Definitely not. Even if Doug wasn't a suspect, I'd feel like I need to figure who did this. It's bad enough when Maeve Dixon is counting on me. But now I have the Librarian of Congress, too."

Meg picked at her manicured nail. "Yeah, I wouldn't want her angry at me. Don't you think she has the power to ban you from all the libraries in the country?"

I narrowed my eyes. "I seriously doubt that, Meg. She's not a book czar."

"I don't know," she said. "Miriam Dunlap is pretty powerful. I wouldn't mess with it."

"Thanks for the warning." I crumpled up my sandwich wrapper and then proceeded to tell Meg about my meeting with Congressman Henry Chang.

She listened intently. "I'm telling you, that guy is weird. It's almost like he ran for Congress so he could have access to historical materials."

"That's not the usual *modus operandi,* for sure. Did he enter politics as a means to commit grand larceny?"

Meg polished off her prosciutto sandwich and licked her fingers for good measure. "That might be a little far-fetched. But he might have come up with the plot after he was elected to Congress."

"That does make better sense," I said. "Much more plausible."

"And he spends so much time with Janice Jackson," said Meg. "She certainly could have mentioned the details about the safe holding the Lincoln memorabilia."

"By the way, I ran into Janice before I texted you about lunch. She's going to show me the Members Room inside the Jefferson Building at five o'clock. Then, if she has enough time, we're going to grab a drink. Want to join?"

Meg grimaced. "Tonight is Trevor time. Would you mind if we invited him for the drink?"

"Of course not," I said. "He's perceptive, after all."

Meg sighed. "He's super smart and has it all together. Sometimes I wonder why he wants to date me."

I was almost at a loss for words, but not quite. "Meg, what do you mean? Trevor is the one who is lucky to be dating you!"

Meg shrugged. "I guess so. But he's so accomplished. He worked as a big-time lobbyist, wrote a book, and now has an office inside the Capitol Building."

I grabbed Meg's hand and squeezed it. "It's an impressive resume. But you shouldn't compare yourself to him. It's not a contest. That being said, you're successful, too."

Meg sighed. "Thanks, Kit. Sometimes it helps to have a cheerleader."

"Well, I was never a cheerleader. But I am your best friend."

A smile appeared on Meg's lips. "Even better."

Chapter Ten

―――∞―――

AFTER MEG UPDATED me on office gossip and Maeve Dixon's latest legislative endeavor, I checked the time. It was half past one. An email from Joe Malden explained that Lea Rutherford would expect us at the D.C. Public Library in about an hour.

"Should we get a cup of coffee from the cafe and check our emails?" I asked. "We have some time to kill. No pun intended."

"Kit, we're at the National Portrait Gallery. Why would we check our email if we have free time? Let's go see the presidential exhibit."

"Is that like the Hall of Presidents?"

Meg rolled her eyes. "This isn't Disney World. It's a permanent exhibit here. Every President and First Lady's portrait is on display." She raised her eyebrows. "Don't tell me you've never seen it."

I'd been to my share of Washington museums with Doug, but we tended to go to history museums rather than art galleries. "I really can't remember."

Meg tugged at my sleeve. "It's funny that you know the place to eat lunch but not the most famous exhibit. Come on."

I stood and followed Meg out of the bright courtyard. We trudged up a curved flight of stairs and followed the signs to the "America's Presidents" exhibit. The directions were unnecessary because it seemed as though every person in the museum was headed in the same direction.

Before we turned the corner, I caught sight of four familiar faces. Right outside the presidential gallery was a massive painting of the female Supreme Court justices: Sandra Day O'Connor, Ruth Bader Ginsberg, Sonia Sotomayor, and Elena Kagan.

"This is amazing. I need a photo to show Doug." I pulled out my phone and snapped away as a wave of tourists streamed by us. The painter, Nelson Shanks, had depicted the justices in their black robes inside a Supreme Court office near an interior courtyard.

"Popular place, huh?" I asked.

"You'll soon understand why." Meg made a right turn.

Directly before us stood George Washington. Well, not the actual George Washington. But one of the most well-known artistic likenesses of our first President.

"Wait a second," I said. "I know that painting."

"That's just the point, Kit," said Meg, laughing. "The National Portrait Gallery has the most famous portraits of every president on display."

"Cool," I muttered. I read the label on the Washington portrait. Gilbert Stuart had painted it in 1796. Washington looked regal, with a red velvet chair behind him and scarlet coverings on the table next to him. Sure enough, Stuart had based the painting on a common pose and background reserved for European kings. Washington wasn't a king, but Stuart had made him look like one. George III had nothing on our George, for sure.

Every president had at least one portrait in the gallery. We skipped a few of the lesser known chief executives and walked into the next room, which featured Abraham Lincoln. The portrait of Lincoln depicted him leaning forward, seated in a wooden high-back chair. His right hand held his head, and Lincoln's eyes were downcast, giving the appearance that our sixteenth president was deep in thought.

"I wish you could tell me who stole the contents of your pockets," I whispered under my breath. "Although maybe you don't care, given the fact you were assassinated that night."

"Are you talking to Lincoln?" asked Meg in a teasing voice.

"Sort of." I could feel my ears turn red with embarrassment. At least Meg and Doug wouldn't judge me. Anyone else would have taken it as a sign I was cracking up.

"Well, if that portrait isn't answering you, maybe one of these others will." Meg pointed to several other Lincoln likenesses in the exhibit. There were two life masks, a molding of his hands, and a cracked-plate photograph.

"You're right," I said. "There's a lot to see." I walked over to the glass case containing the life masks, which compared Lincoln's unwrinkled face in 1860 to his considerably aged face after the Civil War had taken its toll.

"Every museum or exhibit always has a lot of Lincoln related objects on display," said Meg. "Since Maeve Dixon became chair of the House Administration committee, I've seen more Lincoln artifacts than I can count."

Either Meg's comment or Abraham Lincoln's downcast stare caused my brain to light up. "You're exactly right, Meg. There's always more than one Lincoln artifact. Just like the display two nights ago at the Library of Congress."

Meg turned towards me. "What do you mean, Kit?"

"What did we see on display on Tuesday evening?"

"The contents of Lincoln's pockets the night he was assassinated." She placed her hands on her hips. "That's no big revelation."

"Yes, of course. But what was included in the display?"

"I remember the handkerchief with his name embroidered on it. And the confederate note, of course."

"There were also newspaper clippings, an ivory pocketknife, a watch fob, a button, a wallet, a case for his spectacles, a lens cleaner, and two pairs of glasses," I said.

"Do you have a photographic memory or something?" asked Meg.

"Not really. Doug was so excited about the big event scheduled for the next day recreating the discovery of the collection, he talked about it incessantly. That's how I remember what we saw."

"Why are we cataloguing everything in the collection, Kit?"

"Because it's curious that only two items were stolen out of all the objects. If you were a thief who went to the trouble of killing the Assistant Librarian of Congress to steal one of the greatest treasures in American history, why would you take the Confederate note and the handkerchief and leave the rest?"

Meg threw up her hands. "No idea. Maybe the thief was in a rush. After all, he or she had just committed murder."

"That's what I said initially," I said. "But that explanation doesn't make any sense. The person responsible had planned an incredibly risky crime. We know that no one was near the ceremonial office when Gustav was killed. Remember, Doug didn't discover his body until the next day. If there was an imminent threat, wouldn't a report for the crime been registered that night?"

"That's true," said Meg slowly. "If the thief was willing to bash someone over the head to open the safe, then why not take the extra five seconds to empty it entirely?"

"Exactly," I said. "Something has been bothering me from the beginning. Now, I think I know what it is."

A tourist wearing a bright red "Make America Great Again" baseball hat stood next to us. I guided Meg away from the glass cases containing the Lincoln life masks. "Let's move somewhere less crowded."

We moved into the next room of the exhibit, which contained the portraits of Ulysses S. Grant, Rutherford B. Hayes, Chester Arthur, and James Garfield. Although I'm sure they did much more than what they got credit for, these presidents weren't exactly the most popular with visitors.

Meg crossed her arms across her chest. "Now tell me," she said in a low voice. "What's the great revelation?"

We huddled next to Benjamin Harrison, whose portrait depicted a peaceful president reading a book. "We've been thinking about this murder from the wrong perspective."

An older woman with a headset audio guide made her way towards us. We moved onto William McKinley, who was currently standing all by his lonesome. Meg smoothed her blonde bob. "What do you mean, Kit?"

"I don't think the killer's motive was stealing the Lincoln items. Instead, the murderer wanted Gustav Gaffney dead and used the theft as a cover up for the murder."

Meg narrowed her eyes. "You're saying that stealing the Lincoln treasures wasn't the motive?"

I nodded. "That's precisely what I'm saying. We've been thinking about this crime as a theft that resulted in a murder. Instead, we *should* consider it might have been a murder that included a theft."

Meg took a few steps back and inhaled deeply. "So, what does that mean for the investigation?"

"I'm not sure O'Halloran or the federal investigators are going to buy it," I said. "They're focused on recovering the stolen items from the Library of Congress collection. Nothing is going to deter them from that."

"But we could pursue leads from this angle," said Meg.

"That's what I think we should do." We started to walk again, past Teddy Roosevelt and into the portion of the exhibit featuring twentieth century presidents.

We strolled past the iconic paintings of Woodrow Wilson, Franklin Roosevelt, and Dwight Eisenhower and stopped between the two Bush presidents, separated by an unusual depiction of Bill Clinton. Instead of a traditional approach, the Clinton portrait was a modernist piece of art. The painting was divided into small squares, each with an abstract design. A close examination revealed the mosaic composition, but distance made it look like a conventional image.

"Bill Clinton is trying to tell you something." Meg didn't bother to hide a smirk.

"I'll play along. What wisdom is he imparting?"

"Studying something up close gives a much different impression than if you step back and get much-needed perspective," she said. "Everyone investigating this case is standing too close to the portrait. But if you step back and take a look at the big picture, then the result is much better."

I smiled. "Bill Clinton isn't imparting wisdom here. I'm lucky to have such a smart best friend."

Chapter Eleven

W E DECIDED WAITING in line for a selfie with Barack Obama's portrait wasn't on the agenda for today's visit to the National Portrait Gallery, although it was entertaining to watch excited tourists snap Twitter-ready photos in front of the striking painting. Ten minutes later, we crossed over Ninth Street and entered the Martin Luther King D.C. Public Library.

"This building is amazing," said Meg. The bright February sun shone brightly off the windows of the new construction. The library recently finished a three-year renovation costing over two hundred million dollars. It had been a long time for the main branch to remain closed, but the result had been well worth the wait.

"I read a detailed article in the *Washington Post* about the new design," I said as we opened the door. "They had dozens of community meetings before settling on the plans."

Full length glass windows made the entrance inviting, with an exposed brick sidewalk. After passing through the vestibule, we entered an open foyer area. Kids on a school field trip were gathered underneath a mural depicting the life of Dr. Martin Luther King, the namesake of the library. Meg and I strode toward the main visitors' desk, where I assumed we could ask about the whereabouts of Lea Rutherford.

An older woman with black hair fastened in a loose bun greeted us. "Hello, my name is Juanita. How can I help you?"

"It's a pleasure to meet you," I said. "My name is Kit Marshall and this is my colleague Meg Peters. We work in Congress, and we're supposed to meet Lea Rutherford at two-thirty."

Juanita checked the time on her watch. "You're about five minutes early. I'll call upstairs to the main office and check on the status."

We stepped away from the desk to allow Juanita to work her magic. She pulled a pencil nestled inside her bun and poked the phone keypad. A few moments later, she motioned with her hand for us to approach.

"Ms. Rutherford is expecting you," said Juanita. "She suggests that you meet in the cafe. Do you know where that is?"

We shook our heads, and Juanita gave us directions. Soon we found ourselves inside an airy space with open stacks and a full-service cafe.

"This is way better than Starbucks." Meg's eyes scanned the bright, inviting room. "You can have coffee and look at books."

"Yes, and the books don't cost anything as long as you have a library card," I said.

We heard the loud clack of heels behind us and turned around. Sure enough, Lea Rutherford had arrived. She didn't exactly look like the typical public library patron with her long sleeve red sheath dress accented with a matching designer paisley scarf expertly wrapped around her neck. The Jimmy Choo velvet high heels really gave it away.

I waved my hand, since I doubted she would remember me. "Ms. Rutherford."

She plastered a smile on her face and ran her manicured nails through her perfectly coiffed blonde hair as she approached us. No woman in her fifties had hair that color, but I had to admit it looked natural.

"Kit Marshall, it's a pleasure to see you again," she purred. "And who is this?"

"My colleague Meg Peters," I said.

Meg offered her hand, never taking her eyes off Lea's diamond necklace. "I love your jewelry."

Lea's hand touched the diamond circle pendant. "Thank you. It was a gift from my deceased husband. I still miss him," she said wistfully. "In fact, he was a great patron of the D.C. Public Library. That's why I support it."

"We appreciate you taking time out of your busy day to speak with us," I said.

"Not a problem," she replied. "It's such a shame what happened at the Library of Congress. I hope law enforcement is able to recover the Lincoln treasures that were stolen."

Once again, no mention of poor Gustav. Although there was no love lost between Lea Rutherford and Gaffney, as I recalled.

"Joe Malden might have explained to you that the Librarian of Congress has asked me to keep her informed about the progress of the investigation,"

I said. "So that's why we're here."

"Please, let's sit down so we can chat comfortably. Would you like a drink from the cafe?" Lea gestured to the coffee bar. "It's on the house."

When I followed her gaze, I understood why. The coffee bar was conveniently named "The Rutherford Cafe."

"You were the donor who built this cafe," I said.

"Actually, this entire wing. But I thought the cafe was a fitting place for the Rutherford name," she said. "My husband was on the board here for many years."

Meg and I agreed to split a sparkling water, while Lea ordered an organic tea the cafe kept in stock just for her. We took a seat near the windows and enjoyed our refreshments for a moment.

Lea folded her hands on the table. "Well, what would you like to know?"

I had the feeling that despite her graciousness, our time was growing short with the heiress. "Do you have any theories about the theft and murder?"

Lea thought about my question for several moments before answering. "There's very few people who could benefit from stealing those items from the Lincoln collection."

"What do you mean?" asked Meg. "They're priceless."

"Exactly my point. Either someone desperately wanted them for a private collection or had the connections to move them on the black market."

"Such as?" I pressed.

"Gordon Endicott might have those relationships. He knows everyone in the antiquities world." Lea took a sip of her organic tea. "Or me, of course."

Meg's eyes sparkled as much as the diamonds adoring Lea's neck. "You? Is this a confession?"

Lea smiled wryly. "Hardly, dear. But obviously I qualify as a collector who might have an interest. I certainly have the means to cover my tracks and hide the stolen items. That is, if I *wanted* to do it."

"And did you *want* to do it, Ms. Rutherford?" I asked.

Lea sat back in her chair. "Of course not, Ms. Marshall. But I can see why you wanted to question me about it."

"Where did you go after the event ended on Tuesday night?" asked Meg.

"As you already know, I spend time outside the office with Joe Malden. He wanted to go back to his office for work. I followed him and persuaded him to join me back at my apartment." She smiled mischievously.

This corroborated Joe's version of events, but I wanted to press her on the timeline. "So, there was a period of time between the end of the event and when you showed up at his office?"

Lea's smile disappeared. "I suppose so. But not for more than a few minutes. I went to the bathroom to freshen up my makeup. Then I decided I wasn't going to take no for an answer and walked over to Joe's office in the Madison Building. I used the tunnel that connects the two buildings."

Enough time to bop Gaffney on the head, open the safe, and grab the items.

"You didn't like Gustav Gaffney very much, did you? I couldn't help but overhear on Tuesday night that you'd had disputes with him recently," I said.

"He wasn't my favorite person," said Lea. "Everyone knew that."

"Gaffney didn't like your proposal to display recent rare books you purchased. You gave the collection to Yale instead. Even before that, you thought Joe should have been named Assistant Librarian instead of Gustav."

"By that logic, I would have been angry with Miriam Dunlap, not Gustav," she countered.

"Unless you believed that if you eliminated Gaffney, Joe Malden would ascend to the position," said Meg. "If that was the case, you'd have a real motive for the murder."

"That's ridiculous," said Lea. "Joe was passed over once for the promotion. Why would that change?"

"Who knows?" said Meg. "Maybe you'd throw around your weight as a donor this time and the outcome would be different."

"That's an insult to me and Miriam Dunlap," said Lea, her face tightening.

"You're probably right," I agreed. "But you understand we need to explore these motives."

"I thought Gustav was killed so that the murderer could steal the contents of Lincoln's pockets," said Rutherford.

"The police are exploring that avenue, but we're investigating a different scenario," I said.

"You think someone killed Gustav and then stole the Lincoln items as an afterthought?" Rutherford narrowed her eyes.

"Not exactly," I said. "We think the murder might have been the objective. The killer stole the items to create the illusion that theft was the motive."

Lea tapped her red nail against the side of her cheek. "It's a plausible scenario. Gustav wasn't exactly Mr. Popularity."

"We've heard. Can you think of anyone who might want him dead?" I asked.

"You know about my disagreements with him, plus Joe's." She raised her eyebrows. "As I recall, Gustav wanted Gordon Endicott to run the scholarly center at the Library of Congress, not your husband."

"That was settled months ago." I glared at Lea. "Why would Doug kill Gustav after he already had the position?"

Lea shrugged. "Animosity. Elimination of a rival. People have murdered for less. Don't you watch *Game of Thrones*?"

"No, I don't," I said through clenched teeth.

"*House of Cards*?" she countered.

"Never." Fictional depictions of Capitol Hill usually got it wrong. It was a pet peeve of mine.

Meg interrupted our repartee. "Anyone else with a motive, Ms. Rutherford?"

"Janice Jackson was there on Tuesday night, wasn't she?" asked Lea.

Meg nodded. "She was there because Congressman Henry Chang attended."

"I don't know all the details, but Janice and Gustav worked together here." She waved her arm in a circular motion.

"At the D.C. Public Library?" I asked.

"Yes, before either of them worked at the Library of Congress," said Lea. "I remember it from the days when my husband was board chairman. Janice left first, then Gustav followed years later for the Assistant Librarian position."

"We'll ask Janice about it," I said.

"That Congressman is a bit odd," said Lea. "Given my stature, I've met my share of politicians over the years. Many of them have been interested in American history. But no one like Henry Chang. He's over the top."

"I had that impression when I spoke to him earlier today," I said.

"He's joined at the hip with Janice Jackson," said Lea. "She makes sure he has access to the Library of Congress and sees the high-profile collections."

"I've certainly noticed that," said Meg. "Every time I've attended an event at the Library of Congress, he's been there. But she does that because he's on the committee which oversees the Library."

Lea shook her head. "If you're looking for strange behavior, it looks as though you found it with Congressman Chang. He strikes me as just the type who would steal something and then keep it in his desk drawer so only he could look at it."

Meg shuddered. "That's a creepy thought."

"But if he did it, then why did he only steal the Confederate note and the handkerchief?" I asked. "If he really wanted the items for his own personal enjoyment, then you'd think he would have stolen everything in the collection."

"That's true," said Lea. "Maybe you're back to the idea that Gustav's murder was the primary crime. If that's the case, I hope you're able to recover the missing items. The Librarian of Congress must be very upset."

"She is quite vexed, about both Gustav's death and the theft, as you can imagine. That's why she asked me to keep an eye on the progress of the case," I said.

Lea smiled. "I can see why she'd want you to perform that function. You seem on top of things. But be careful, Ms. Marshall. If someone was willing to kill the Assistant Librarian, no matter what the motive, I don't think that person will hesitate to hurt someone else if threatened."

I gulped. "You're right, Ms. Rutherford. The sooner this gets solved, the better for everyone involved."

Lea stood, indicating that our meeting was over. She thrust her hand in my direction. "A pleasure to make your acquaintance again. I hope the next time we meet, it will be under better circumstances." I shook her hand and so did Meg.

We exited the building and stopped to chat on the plaza outside the library. It was an unseasonably warm February afternoon, which was one of the advantages of living in Washington, D.C. Even though we had our share of cold days, we usually caught a few days of spring-like warmth in the midst of winter.

"I'll get us a ride back to Capitol Hill." Meg whipped out her phone. "Three minutes until the car arrives."

"Any thoughts about our conversation with Lea?" I asked.

"She's really smooth. And self-confident."

"Billions of dollars tend to have that effect. But was she trying too hard to convince us she didn't have a motive to kill Gustav?"

Our driver pulled up, and we climbed inside the car. "It seemed that way. So maybe she has something to hide," said Meg.

"It's curious she also thinks Henry Chang is too eager for a congressman," I said. "We're not imagining it."

"Definitely not." Meg turned back to her phone and scrolled through her emails. "Kit, check your messages. I think the Librarian of Congress might want to see you."

Sure enough, there was an email from Dorian Jones in my inbox. He requested that I stop by the Librarian's office to give her an afternoon update on the case.

I sighed as I put my phone inside my purse. "Miriam Dunlap wants me to brief her. I'm not sure I have that much to report."

We arrived in front of the Cannon House Office Building and climbed out of the car. "I'd better get back to the office to check on everything. You have a meeting with Janice Jackson later on?" asked Meg.

"She offered to show me the Members Room inside the Jefferson Building. If there's enough time, we're going to walk down the street for a drink. Are you able to join us? You have a good working relationship with her. Maybe she'd feel more comfortable opening up if you were there."

"If I can bring Trevor and combine it with our date this evening, then I'm in," said Meg. "Dating two men is exhausting. That's another reason I need to figure out my love life. I never have a minute to myself!"

I ignored Meg's self-pitying comment. Having too many dates was a better problem than having none.

"Like I said, Trevor always picks up important tidbits when we're investigating," I said. "Tell him to meet us inside the Library's Great Hall at five."

Meg wagged her fingers goodbye to me, and we parted ways on Independence Avenue. Five minutes later, I opened the glass doors to the Librarian's suite on the sixth floor of the Madison Building.

"Thank you for stopping by, Kit," said Dorian. "The Librarian is very eager for an update on the case."

"I can talk to her about it, but I'm afraid I don't have that much to report since we met for drinks last night," I said.

Dorian frowned. "She's certainly not going to like *that* message. You'd better figure out a way to make it sound more substantial."

I thought for a moment. "I could run a theory by her and get her reaction. It might be helpful."

Dorian's face brightened. "There you go. As a fellow chief of staff, you know how to play the game."

I certainly do. Sometimes, I played it too well for my own good.

Chapter Twelve

———

DORIAN ESCORTED ME to the Librarian's private office and excused himself after letting us know he had a budget planning meeting to attend. Miriam Dunlap sat on the other side of her desk, swiveling back and forth nervously in her leather chair.

"Ms. Marshall, I appreciate your time. Can you please tell me about your progress on the case?" She peered at me from the bottom half of her reading glasses.

"I don't have anything definitive to share," I said. The Librarian's face fell. "But I would like to discuss a theory with you."

Dunlap's eyes sparkled. "A theory about who murdered Gustav?"

"Not who, but why," I said. "The federal investigators believe that Gustav was murdered because of the theft. They are pursuing every lead to recover the stolen items from the Lincoln collection."

The Librarian nodded, her expression solemn. "That makes perfect sense."

"It does make sense for the feds to chase down that angle. They have the resources and connections to locate stolen antiquities that could surface for sale. But I'm looking at the case differently."

Dunlap narrowed her eyes, removed her glasses, and folded her hands. "Go on, Ms. Marshall."

"I know you don't think someone associated with the Library of Congress could have killed Gustav, but what if we're thinking about this crime in the wrong way?"

"Please continue," she said, a touch of impatience in her voice. I'd better cut to the chase.

"Perhaps someone wanted to kill Gustav Gaffney and then stole the items to make it look like a theft."

The Librarian pursed her lips. "You mean the theft wasn't the reason for Gustav's death?"

"Exactly," I said, a little too enthusiastically.

"What makes you think this, Ms. Marshall?" she asked. "Especially since our highly trained federal investigators are pursuing the opposite explanation."

"The killer only took two items from the safe. The handkerchief and the Confederate note. If the motive was theft, then why not steal the entire collection? It would be much more valuable."

"Perhaps the murderer was interrupted," said Dunlap. "Or was in a rush."

"Gustav was killed soon after the preview event ended," I explained. "There's no evidence to suggest anyone was near the ceremonial office when the crime occurred. No one has come forward to report seeing anyone suspicious or hearing the attack. I think the perpetrator was alone on that floor of the Jefferson Building with Gustav. If that's the case, he or she would have had enough time to clean out the safe."

Dunlap sat back in her chair and picked up her glasses. She chewed on the stem as she considered my argument. "I still find it hard to believe one of our own might have killed Gustav," she said slowly. "But I understand why you are pursuing this line of inquiry. If the federal investigators are going down another path, you might as well follow alternative leads."

"Thank you for understanding. You have my word that I won't jump to any rash conclusions."

"I know you won't. After all, you'd want your husband treated the same way," said Dunlap with a wry smile.

"Certainly. Doug remains a suspect until we bring the guilty party to justice. That's not lost on me."

The Librarian leaned forward. "Have you talked to the potential suspects on your list? Can I help you with anyone?"

"Actually, I've talked to most of the attendees at the preview display. But not Gordon Endicott from Rare Books."

Miriam Dunlap reached for her phone and asked her executive assistant if he would connect her to the Rare Books Reading Room. "That's easily remedied," she said, with her hand over the receiver. After waiting for a minute, Endicott must have come on the line.

"Gordon, this is Miriam," she said. He must have interrupted her. "Yes, Miriam Dunlap. The Librarian of Congress."

After a pause, she continued. "Absolutely, Gordon. We're trying to regain some degree of normalcy. I'd like to bring someone by to chat with you in ten minutes. Is that suitable?"

She listened for a few seconds, and then answered. "Perfect. We'll see you soon." She hung up the phone.

Dunlap moved from around the desk and gently guided me by the arm toward the door. "We can finish our conversation on the walk over to the Rare Books Reading Room."

I followed her lead and considered my audience. Would Endicott clam up because I was married to Doug? Maybe it would make sense if I had a buffer.

"I need a moment to text a friend," I said. "He might be helpful for this conversation."

I fired off a text to Trevor. If he was free, maybe he could join me.

"Where are we going again?" I asked Dunlap.

"Second floor of the Jefferson Building. Then follow the signs to the Rare Books Reading Room."

"Got it." I finished my text with the location.

The Librarian of Congress resumed our chat when we entered the underground tunnel connecting the Madison and Jefferson Buildings. "What are you hoping to achieve by questioning Gordon Endicott?"

"A fair question," I said. "I want to know if he might have had a motive to murder Gaffney."

Miriam Dunlap kept up our conversation despite greeting every staff member who passed us inside the tunnel. Her people skills were comparable to a senior member of Congress. Political acumen didn't only reside in elected politicians.

"I can't think of one," she said. "Gustav liked Gordon very much. I'm sure you know he supported Gordon's candidacy to run the scholarly center."

I gulped. "You endorsed Doug, though."

"Yes, I did and for good reasons. By the way, Gordon has never showed one ounce of resentment about my decision."

"Why do you think he wanted that position?" I asked. "Hasn't Gordon worked in the rare books world his entire life?"

"Yes, you're correct. He might have been interested in the elevated pay. The job your husband occupies has a higher salary." She furrowed her brow. "Dorian might have mentioned to me that Gordon has some financial difficulties." She shook her head. "I try not to embroil myself in such gossip."

My brain churned. Endicott certainly had the connections to move stolen items on the black market. Even if he couldn't fetch full price for something as hot as items from the Lincoln collection, the money could certainly help him with any financial shortfall he might have. Best not share this information with the Librarian of Congress at this point in time. After all, I had promised her I wouldn't accuse a Library staff member without having substantial evidence.

As we entered the elevator to take us to the second floor, Dunlap turned to face me. "We're almost at the reading room. Anything else, Ms. Marshall? I have another appointment and can't stay for your interrogation of Gordon."

I snapped my fingers. "One more thing. I spoke with Lea Rutherford this afternoon at the D.C. Public Library. She told me that Janice Jackson and Gustav Gaffney worked there together several years ago. Did you know that?"

Miriam Dunlap chuckled. "It doesn't surprise me. There are almost two hundred thousand librarians in the United States and many other support staff working in libraries. Nevertheless, it's a very tight knit community, particularly amongst those who assume senior positions. We all know each other and many of us have worked as colleagues in previous positions."

"I'm going to meet Janice later today, and I'll ask her about it," I said.

The elevator dinged, and we stepped out. "That woman is always in motion," said Dunlap. "Always running to and fro between the Library and the congressional buildings. I don't know how she does it."

Gustav hadn't shared Dunlap's enthusiasm for Janice, but since the Librarian stuck out her hand, I assumed our conversation was over and decided it wasn't time to press my luck.

I shook her hand lightly. "Thank you again. You've been very helpful."

She gave me directions to find the Rare Books Reading Room before pressing the button to go back down the elevator. "Keep me updated, Ms. Marshall. I like surprises when I'm doing research. I do not like surprises when it involves murder."

"Words to live by," I muttered, walking down the hallway. Unless it involved chocolate, wine, or presents, I didn't like surprises, either.

I came upon a door with the sign "Rare Book and Special Collections Reading Room" posted outside. I walked inside the room and immediately felt I'd been transported to a secret enclave from a different era. The lighting was kept at a low level despite the impressive chandelier that hung from the ceiling. Wooden tables with comb-back chairs were arranged in neat rows on each side of the room. Was I inside a contemporary Diogenes

Club? I half-expected Mycroft Holmes to turn the corner and ask if I fancied a glass of sherry.

A younger woman with fashionable glasses and a dark brown ponytail stood behind the desk. "Can I help you? Do you have an appointment?"

"The answer to both questions is yes, but not to view materials," I explained. "I'm here to speak with Gordon Endicott. The Librarian of Congress called him a few minutes earlier to let him know about it."

"Of course," she said. "I believe your friend has already arrived for the meeting."

"Friend?" I asked, puzzled.

Then I heard a familiar voice as a man with brown hair turned around in one of the fancy chairs. "Did you forget that you invited me to join you?" asked Trevor.

"No, of course not," I said. "I'm surprised you beat me here. That's all."

"An invitation to our nation's preeminent rare books reading room is quite infrequent." He walked toward us. "I did not hesitate."

Trevor had the uncanny ability of appearing and disappearing in a flash. I'd hoped that Meg could figure out how he did it since she started dating him. So far, she was none the wiser. Or, if she knew, she wasn't sharing the secret with me.

"Well, thank you for joining me," I said. "Would you like us to wait here for Gordon?" I asked the librarian.

"I'll phone to let him know you've arrived." After she did so, she asked whether we'd visited the Rare Books Reading Room before.

"I haven't," I said.

"Once before," said Trevor. "Not too long ago, I briefly considered writing a book on detective stories published in the 1800s. The Library of Congress has quite a collection of these so-called dime store novels."

"Yes," said the librarian, her face flush with excitement. "Did you find what you were looking for?"

"Certainly," said Trevor. "But I decided against writing the book so I could focus on. . ." He paused briefly. "Other pursuits."

I had no doubt he meant Meg. If that was the case, he'd made the right choice.

"This reading room is modeled after Independence Hall in Philadelphia," she said proudly. "Do you recognize the similarities?"

"Now that you mention it, I can see the resemblance," I said.

"We're the division who is responsible for Thomas Jefferson's collection of books, which formed the basis of the Library of Congress's collection over two hundred years ago," she said.

"You must have a lot of books from the founding era," I said.

"We do, but we also have collections you might not know about," she said. "Do you know we have Houdini's magic library?"

"Just make sure you have it under lock and key," I said. "You wouldn't want it to *disappear*." I laughed at my one-liner as Trevor rolled his eyes.

"It might not be an appropriate time to joke about items disappearing from our collection," said a deep voice.

Gordon Endicott approached us. "Please come join me in my office where we'll have more privacy." He gave a curt nod to the librarian at the front desk.

Not exactly a barrel of laughs. I suppose my witticism had been in poor taste, but I hadn't meant it that way.

We sat down in Endicott's office, which was sparsely decorated. Almost nothing was visible on his desk, and every paper had been filed neatly in alphabetized folders sitting upright on a shelf. Of course, he was a rare books librarian, so I suppose it wasn't too surprising he seemed more organized and meticulous than Adrian Monk.

"Thank you for taking the time to speak with us, Mr. Endicott," I said. "You may have met my colleague Trevor at the viewing on Tuesday night."

"We are acquainted," he said.

"We also have a friend in common," said Trevor. "Professor James Mansfield from Yale University, a historian of the highest caliber. I understand you know him quite well."

Trevor had been doing his homework. We met Professor Mansfield last spring when Doug and I attended a history conference at the legendary Continental Club while solving a double murder. He'd been quite helpful as we identified the likely suspects and exposed the killer.

"James and I have known each other for many years. In the early part of my career, I worked at the Beinecke." Endicott must have seen the blank look on my face. "That's the rare book and manuscript library at Yale. It's one of the largest libraries of its kind in the world."

I slid down in my chair. Trying to keep up with this conversation was like trying to out-tweet a certain President. There was no way to keep up.

Trevor continued. "Professor Mansfield swears you are one of the most connected curators in the rare book world."

Endicott tilted his chin upward. "That's a very generous statement from James."

Now I knew where Trevor was going with this line of conversation. "If that's the case, then you must know how someone could move valuable items quickly," I said. "Even if they were stolen."

Endicott inhaled deeply. "I can assure you, Ms. Marshall, that I have no information about the missing contents of Lincoln's pockets or their whereabouts."

I wasn't about to let him off the hook that easily. "But you know that world inside and out. You can't deny it."

"And I shall not deny it," said Endicott. "That doesn't mean I had anything to do with the theft."

"Let's try a different approach," I said. "Is there a way to move stolen goods similar to what was taken from the Library of Congress?"

"It would be immensely difficult," he said. "Not impossible, but everyone knows about this theft. It's been covered by all major newspapers in the world. If a shady dealer buys the items, how will he resell them when everyone knows the provenance? It's a big risk. Consequently, the dealer would not pay anywhere near the estimated value."

"Still, a few hundred thousand bucks goes a long way, doesn't it?" I asked slyly.

"I suppose so, but not nearly equivalent to the risk undertaken," he said. "Not to mention the thief also committed murder."

"What did you do after the event ended that night?" I asked.

"After making sure the collection was secure inside the safe, I went home," he said. "I took the Metro, as I always do."

"Did anyone see you leave the Library of Congress?" asked Trevor.

"I'm sure people did see me leave, but I doubt anyone could verify my alibi, if that's what you're inquiring about. However, I do have my Metro card." Endicott took out his wallet and produced his subway pass.

"And that's your alibi?" I raised my eyebrows.

"Precisely. Metro can verify that I used this pass to travel home to Maryland on Tuesday evening. They track all activity in case there's a payment dispute," he said, with more than a hint of smugness in his answer.

I started to reply, but then caught myself. No need to show all my cards, so to speak. Metro could verify that a passenger used that particular subway card to travel from Capitol Hill to suburban Maryland on Tuesday night. That person may or may not have been Gordon Endicott. A partner in crime could have made the trip, giving Endicott a legitimate alibi.

Motive was still elusive. I needed to figure out if Endicott needed the money from stealing valuable treasures. There wasn't an obviously subtle way to find out. I rubbed my hand down my pant leg and went for it.

"I'm sorry to ask you this," I said. "But I heard through the grapevine you might have some financial troubles. Is that true?"

Endicott's lip curled. "What concern is it of yours?"

I was prepared for that question. "I know you wanted Doug's job, but I don't know why, especially since you've worked in the rare books and antiquities field for your whole career. I figured you might have wanted the higher salary."

Trevor shifted in his chair and averted his eyes. Even he was uncomfortable with my line of questioning. Short of asking Sergeant O'Halloran to examine Endicott's banking and tax statements, this approach was the only way to get a direct answer about motive.

Endicott's voice wavered. "There's no crime in changing career direction, Ms. Marshall."

"Certainly not," I said. "I simply thought it might be motivated by financial concerns, since I'd heard rumors."

Endicott rocked backwards in his chair and formed a steeple with his two hands. "For argument's sake, let's say money pushed me to want a promotion. I don't understand why you're asking me about it."

I didn't particularly want to spell it out for him, but he left me no choice. "Since you didn't get the job, perhaps you had to engage in criminal activities to secure additional income."

Endicott's nostrils flared. "That's absurd. I just finished telling you those items would be difficult to move on the black market."

"Difficult, but not impossible," said Trevor. "Especially coming from a man with your professional relationships. Professor Mansfield assured me you know everyone in the business."

Endicott rose. "He is correct that I know legitimate people, not thieves or murderers. I must return to my work, so please do not think it rude when I ask you to leave."

We stood up and said our farewells abruptly. When we were outside the reading room, Trevor turned to me. "I usually don't mind a business-like demeanor, but you were rather accusatory, Kit."

"Besides the fact that he's a suspect for this crime and may have a motive, he's also trying to cast suspicion on Doug." My voice quivered. "Perhaps I was a little harsh. But every day this murder goes unsolved, my husband's reputation suffers."

Trevor never dwelled on emotional misfires for too long. "What's done is done. Endicott certainly could have killed Gaffney. That Metro card alibi doesn't hold water. It's flimsy, at best."

"I agree. But I think Endicott was telling the truth about trying to sell the stolen items for money. He might have the network to do it, but I don't know if our other suspects do."

"Where does that leave us?" asked Trevor.

"Either Gordon Endicott is the guilty party, likely with an accomplice. Or the real motive for killing Gustav Gaffney wasn't theft, but something else entirely."

Chapter Thirteen

~~~

A FTER PARTING WAYS with Trevor and confirming I'd see him soon for the
meeting with Janice Jackson, I realized that although I'd spent the better
part of the day at the Library of Congress, I hadn't seen or heard from
Doug. I hoped he was able to manage the stress. I pulled out my phone and
sent him a text.

I'm @ LOC. Are you free???

A minute later, my phone dinged.

Busy. Let's plan for dinner.

I sent Doug a "happy face" emoticon so he would know I agreed with
his reply. No sense in letting him know I'd run into O'Halloran this morning and he was still on the suspect list. Telling someone the police and
federal authorities were investigating him for murder wasn't best delivered
via text message.

A check on the time confirmed that I had forty-five minutes before meeting Janice Jackson, Meg, and Trevor inside the Great Hall. Walking back to our
office would be a supreme waste of time. Instead, I got on the elevator, exited
on the ground floor, and walked down the dimly lit hallway. Did someone
forget to pay the electric bill at the Library of Congress? Or perhaps the cav-
ernous passageways were supposed to be reminiscent of the oldest libraries in
the world, like the famous Trinity College Library in Ireland, the Bodleian at
Oxford, or even the fictitious Restricted Section at Hogwarts.

The intricate design of the architecture and ceilings were so impressive, I almost walked into a signpost, which read "Main Reading Room

Entrance." I'd glanced inside the beautiful main reading room a few times from the top balcony, but never walked inside. Why not? Like Meg said, didn't it make sense to take advantage of these impressive locations when we visited them for work? Sleuthing wasn't *technically* my job, but it was close enough.

I walked inside and spotted the entrance of the reading room at the end of a short hallway. At the very least, I could sit quietly inside and check my emails while I waited for five o'clock to roll around. I was just about to enter when a woman's voice interrupted me.

"Excuse me, miss, but I need to see your identification."

A gray-haired woman wearing a comfy-looking cardigan motioned for me to walk over to her desk. She peered at me above her reading glasses. I'd seen that look before. It was exactly how Giles stared at Buffy the Vampire Slayer when she interrupted his reading to ask about a particularly dangerous demon.

"Do you mean this?" I pulled out my congressional identification from my purse.

The librarian pursed her lips. "That'll do. Since you're a congressional staffer, you don't need a reader's card like the rest of the public."

"Okay, thanks," I said tentatively. I suppose they had to put someone who would guard the entrance with a sharp eye and tongue.

I walked inside the reading room and was immediately overwhelmed by the beauty and splendor that surrounded me.

"Wow." It wasn't a particularly articulate reaction to my surroundings, but it was all I could muster at the moment. The partial view from the top balcony didn't do the Main Reading Room justice. I shuffled forward a few steps, my neck craned upwards so I could take in the full effect of the structure.

A librarian behind the round desk in the center of the room must have noticed my stumbling. He emerged from behind the wooden barrier and stood next to me.

"Can I help you?" he whispered.

"I've never actually been inside this room before," I explained. "I guess I'm in awe of it."

He smiled. "That's a common response. Would you like me to tell you about it?"

"Sure," I said. "But I don't want to take you away from your work."

"I'm a general reference librarian, but since I work inside this space, I spend a considerable amount of time answering questions about our surroundings." He waved his arm around. "You can understand why."

I nodded, and he motioned for us to sit down behind a desk a safe distance away from researchers so we wouldn't disturb them.

"There's a lot of symbolic meaning inside this room. Eight marble columns on the circular edges of the room provide the framing. Each one signifies a different field of inquiry. There's religion, art, philosophy, history, commerce, science, poetry, and law." His finger rotated around the room. "At the top of each of these columns is two bronze statues. For example, Beethoven and Michelangelo represent art while Shakespeare and Homer signify poetry." He grinned. "You get the idea."

"What about those stained-glass windows?" I asked. "Are those the seals of the states?"

The eyes of my librarian turned tour guide sparkled. "Exactly! Those eight stained glass windows contain the seal of the United States in the middle. Each window has six state or territory seals. When this building was opened in 1897, Alaska and Hawaii did not have status as either a state or territory, so they were not included."

"It's hard to focus on research when you're inside such a beautiful building," I said. Nonetheless, there were dozens of researchers occupying the desks that encircled the room. Most had their heads buried in books or other Library of Congress materials.

"This is our point of entry for many users," said the librarian. "We have general reference librarians on staff to help navigate the collections. Many researchers will visit a specialized reading room eventually, but this is where most people start their knowledge journey." He smiled kindly. Certainly, this man had found the right job. It always made me feel good about government when I met someone who clearly enjoyed his or her work.

I looked around the room. "Where do the books come from? They're not on shelves here."

He laughed and pointed to the center of the room where the reference desk was located. "If you look closely, there's a door behind the desk," he explained. "That leads downstairs to a room where the books arrive. We have a tunnel system underneath the library buildings that serve as the delivery mechanism for books that are paged. Some materials are held offsite, and trucks bring those items several times a day."

"That's an amazing system," I said. "The door looks like where you might keep the Book of Secrets."

"That book doesn't exist, although a lot of fans of the *National Treasure* movies think it does," he said. "I assure you there are no secret books downstairs. But there are a lot of unique books that make up our collection. And some of them do contain secrets, if you look hard enough." His eyes sparkled. "You just need to engage our collections to find them."

I stuck out my hand. "You've been quite helpful. I don't have time to read anything today, but maybe someday I'll need a quiet place to think. I'll know exactly where to come."

He shook my hand with a firm grip. "My pleasure."

After I unabashedly snapped a selfie, I walked back through the corridor where I entered. After following the helpful directional signs, I eventually found myself inside the Great Hall. Janice Jackson had said she'd meet me here in fifteen minutes. Doug had told me this area resembled Grand Central Station during the day, with tourists, researchers, school groups, and distinguished visitors passing through. Right now, it was completely empty. I found a bench and sat down with my phone. The emails were too numerous to begin triaging. Instead, I texted Meg and asked if she was on her way. She replied and said she was, but Trevor might arrive a few minutes late. Since free moments were rare, I messaged Doug and asked him about dinner plans. Three dots appeared, so I awaited his reply.

Meet Sebastian @ Rocklands

Rocklands was a well-regarded barbecue place in Arlington. After letting Doug know I was fine with the plan, he texted back.

Will bring Clarence & Murphy

We would really test Clarence's inner angel by combining a new dog with one of his favorite foods. Since it was such an unseasonably warm day, we could sit outside with the dogs and enjoy our meal. Well, "enjoy" might be a stretch. Hopefully Clarence would be on his very best behavior. Our chubby beagle mutt loved barbecue almost as much as he loved pepperoni.

I was so engrossed with my digital conversation, I didn't see Janice Jackson arrive. My head jerked up from my phone when I heard my name.

"Kit, would you like to see the Members Room, as I promised?"

Janice Jackson was standing ten feet away. She motioned for me to follow her. We exited the Great Hall, walked past several glass display cases, and proceeded down a long, decorative hallway marked "No Entrance."

"Gosh, I feel like I'm getting the V-I-P tour," I said.

"You are," she said. "We don't show our everyday visitors the Members Room."

We turned to the right, and Janice pulled out a bulky set of keys. "Never know where my job might take me. Members of Congress request to see the darnedest places. I finally got a set of keys that made sure I wouldn't have to say no when someone important asked."

After she unlocked the door, we walked into a long, stately wood-paneled room, bookended by marble fireplaces. The United States flag and Library of Congress flag stood on either side of the entrance. With a red carpet and elaborate paintings on the ceiling, it looked like the American version of a throne room.

"This is almost as impressive as the Main Reading Room," I said. "I stopped in for a few minutes before meeting you."

"This was the first reading room for Congress," said Janice. "Now it serves as a gathering or function room. Members of Congress can hold constituent events, lunches, or other meetings here. As you might imagine, it's quite a popular venue."

"You said that members of Congress ask to see unusual places inside the building, right?" I walked toward the south fireplace so I could get a better look at the colorful mosaic above it.

Janice followed me. "This mosaic represents history. One wreath symbolizes peace, and the other signifies war. The central figure is holding a pen and book in her hand. Notice that behind her, the artist included an Egyptian pyramid, a Greek temple, and a Roman amphitheater."

"It's quite elaborate," I said. "Given what I've seen today at the Library of Congress, I can't imagine anything more fitting than a homage to the discipline of history."

"The mosaic was prepared in Venice and shipped here," said Janice. "And you're right. History is our business, and it's my job to make sure Capitol Hill knows it." She thrust her shoulders back as her chin jutted out.

It wasn't lost on me that Janice had avoided my earlier question. "Does Congressman Chang ask to see some of those unexpected places?"

Janice pursed her lips. "A good congressional relations liaison never tells her secrets."

"I wondered if he did," I said. "I don't know if I mentioned it this morning, but I visited his office earlier today."

"And why did you do that?" Janice plastered a smile on her face, but couldn't hide the edge to her voice.

"I wanted to talk to him about the theft and the murder," I said. "And find out why he came to the preview display the night before instead of waiting for the congressional event the next day."

"I told him about it," said Janice quickly. "Congressman Chang is new to elected office, but he's one of our strongest supporters. We like to make sure he's happy."

I was just about to ask Janice about her whereabouts on Tuesday night when Meg and Trevor walked in the room. "I didn't know we were expecting more visitors," she said.

I ignored the less than subtle dig. "Janice, you know Meg, and I believe you met Trevor at the Lincoln preview event."

She pressed her lips into a thin line. "Yes, of course. Delighted to see you again."

"In my position for the Chief Administrative Officer for the House, I visit many beautiful rooms inside the Capitol complex," he said. "I hadn't been inside the Members Room before, so thank you for allowing me to experience it."

Trevor knew how and when to turn on the charm. Janice appeared delighted to lap up Trevor's effusiveness. "Aren't you delightful?" she said, turning towards Meg. "You've really found a keeper."

Meg blushed. "Don't let us interrupt your conversation. We'll have a look around while you chat." With Janice's back turned, Meg gave me a thumbs up.

"I do have another question for you," I said. "Where did you go after the display wrapped up on Tuesday night?"

"I wanted to drop in on an important staffer who was working late. I made my way over to the Senate office buildings," she said. "The work of a congressional liaison is never over, you know."

"Who was the meeting with?" I asked. "I'm sure Sergeant O'Halloran will want to verify it."

Janice's face remained expressionless, but if I had to guess, she was working hard to keep her demeanor on an even keel. "It turned out she wasn't available. Long story short, I walked over to the Senate for nothing. By the time I returned to the Library, it was late."

"You didn't see anything or anyone in the vicinity of the Great Hall?" I asked. "You might have returned near the time of the murder."

She shook her head vigorously. "I bypassed the Jefferson Building. I walked back to the Madison Building directly."

"I see," I said. "Too bad."

"Of course, I told all of this to the police. You can check," she said confidently.

I nodded. "Do you have any idea who might have done this?"

"None whatsoever," she said. "That's what I've told everyone."

"I heard a rumor that you and Gustav Gaffney didn't get along. Was he pressing you to do more in your job? Was he dissatisfied with your work?"

She waved her hand dismissively. "That's par for the course in the field of congressional relations. Everyone expects miracles, when legislators these days are pulled in a million different directions. It's almost like I can wave my magic wand and secure unlimited funding and legislative fixes to every last problem."

I was sympathetic to Janice's point of view, but I still wanted to know if Gustav rubbed her the wrong way. "You'd known Gustav for a long time, hadn't you?"

"Yes." Her face was blank. "What does that matter?"

"At the D.C. Public Library, you were colleagues earlier in your career," I said.

"We were, but I don't see how that matters. I left that job for my current position at the Library of Congress."

"And then Gustav arrived here about a year ago," I said. "Is that right?"

"I suppose so," she said. "Time flies by, doesn't it?"

Trevor and Meg circled back to us. I wasn't getting anywhere with Janice on her relationship with Gustav Gaffney.

"Thank you again for letting us see this room," said Trevor. "We didn't mean to interrupt your conversation."

"We weren't talking about anything consequential," said Janice, glancing at her watch. "I'm afraid we should lock up this room now."

"Would you like to join us for a drink around the corner?" asked Meg. "Kit mentioned you might join us for happy hour."

"I'd love nothing more. But I need to finish some work in my office. I'll take a rain check." She hustled us out, shut the door firmly behind us, and locked it. We retraced our steps back to the Great Hall where we said our goodbyes.

"Would you like to join us, Kit?" asked Meg.

I glanced at my watch. "Sure, if it's speedy. I'm meeting Doug and Sebastian for dinner in Arlington tonight, and I don't want to keep them waiting too long."

Ten minutes later, we each had a libation in hand at the Pennsylvania Avenue wine bar Sonoma. Meg and I had ordered a glass of the Italian bubbly Prosecco, and Trevor opted for the bartender's recommended Cabernet Sauvignon.

After our first sips, Trevor leaned in. "Are you any closer in solving the case, Kit?"

I sighed. "This one is a puzzler. Everyone says they have an alibi, but their claims have more holes than Swiss cheese."

Meg giggled. "I prefer mozzarella."

I rolled my eyes. "Trevor, are you sure you're really in love with her?" I elbowed my best friend on the bar stool next to me.

"Guilty as charged," he said. "Pun very much intended."

I placed my flute on the bar and rubbed my temples. "I'm not sure how to move forward. On top of it all, Doug is *still* a suspect."

Meg placed her half-empty glass next to mine. "Don't get upset, Kit. It's always like this right before you solve the mystery. Let's go through it systematically. Person by person."

"Alright," I said slowly. "There's Joe Malden, the Library's top lawyer."

"What's his motive?" asked Trevor.

"He resented Gustav Gaffney for getting the number two spot," I said. "He's also romantically involved with Lea Rutherford, the rich donor."

"And Rutherford didn't like the victim, either. He didn't agree with Lea's ideas for future exhibits," added Meg.

"Is that really a motive for murder, though?" asked Trevor.

"They could be in it together," I said. "They're each other's alibis for the night in question. The two of them might have hatched this plot to get rid of Gustav once and for all."

"Even more importantly, he also didn't like their romantic relationship," said Meg. "He let Joe know he disapproved."

Trevor sipped his wine. "Okay, I'm convinced. Definitely enough there for motive. Let's move on."

Even though Trevor had mellowed since he started dating Meg, his bossy persona managed to surface from time to time. "Next is Gordon Endicott, the rare books director. He didn't have a beef with Gaffney, but he has the connections to move stolen goods," I said. "As you know, Professor Mansfield confirmed it."

"He certainly did," said Trevor. "He has an alibi, but it sounds like a potential setup to me. He was awfully eager to explain how Metro cards work."

"And while he didn't admit to being short on cash, he didn't deny it, either," I said.

"Wasn't he also trying to implicate Doug?" asked Meg.

"Joe Malden seemed to think so," I said. "But that could have been a diversion on Malden's part to cast suspicion elsewhere."

"Anyone else?" asked Trevor.

"Janice Jackson," said Meg. "She and Gustav weren't the best of pals. We learned earlier today that they worked together at the D.C. Public Library. There's a history there."

"I tried to ask her about her past and her work relationship with Gustav. She's definitely spent a lot of time with elected officials. She knows how to bypass the hard questions," I said.

"What about an alibi?" Meg took the last sip of her Prosecco.

"She dropped by a Senate office to see a staffer. She walked through the congressional tunnel, only to find out the person wasn't around," I said.

"Maybe O'Halloran could check her alibi for you," said Trevor. "Verify it or something."

"Good idea," I said. "I'll text him to ask about it."

"Last, but not least, is Congressman Henry Chang." I drained my flute and placed it next to Meg's empty glass. She motioned the bartender for a refill, but I waved him off. I needed to head back to Arlington for dinner and one drink was my limit.

"There's definitely something fishy about him," said Meg. "He's way too eager."

"Does he have an alibi?" asked Trevor.

"Not really," I said. "He claims he returned to his office and worked for a while. No staff were with him."

"Someone surely saw him walking through the corridors or tunnels," said Trevor. "Or the security cameras might have captured him."

"If he's telling the truth, I'm sure the police could either confirm or disprove his alibi," I said. "The problem is that Sergeant O'Halloran isn't authorized to investigate Chang. He's a member of Congress and he'd need solid evidence."

"And we don't have any," said Meg glumly.

"Well, we do have this." I reached into my purse and pulled out the business card I lifted from Chang's office. "When the Congressman left the room to meet with a constituent, I took a look around and found it."

"He's been talking to a dealer in rare collectible items," said Trevor, fingering the card.

"It's circumstantial," I admitted. "After all, his office is decorated with all kinds of historical memorabilia. He could be buying or selling something legitimately."

"Did you tell O'Halloran what you found in Chang's office?" asked Trevor.

I shook my head. "I thought about it but decided not to mention it. I don't think he would have liked the fact that I lifted something from a potential suspect's office. Especially since the office belongs to a United States congressman."

"Probably a good move," said Meg. "But if you truly suspect Chang, you're going to need O'Halloran's help to verify his whereabouts after the preview ended."

I threw a few bills on the bar for my drink. Meg had a good point. "I'd better update him about what we learned today. It confirms what he said earlier. Everyone claims to have an alibi, but they're all flimsy. Including Doug's, by the way."

"If we think of anything, we'll be in touch," said Meg.

"Tell Doug to hang in there," said Trevor. A man of uncomplicated emotions, Trevor rarely offered sympathetic words. Perhaps Meg was rubbing off on him.

I gave Meg a side hug. "Enjoy your evening."

I was a step away from leaving Sonoma when I heard a familiar voice behind me. "Kit Marshall, is that you?"

Although I was pretty sure I'd regret it, I turned on my heels and faced the music. "Clarissa Smythe?"

There was no mistaking Clarissa Smythe. One of the most sought after campaign fundraisers on the Hill, Clarissa cut an impressive figure. With wavy auburn hair and a Soul Cycle body, Clarissa drew attention wherever she went. Her track record as a fundraiser didn't hurt, either. When Clarissa signed up for a campaign, she always outraged her opponent. Her scorecard registered more wins than Tom Brady.

"Of course, it is, darling." She sashayed towards me and pecked my cheek.

"You must be gearing up for campaign season," I said. "Are you here to pick up new clients?"

"Maybe a few," she said slyly. "Do you have any prospects for me?"

Clarissa had been involved with a murder during Maeve Dixon's last close election. Since that episode, she'd been a reliable source of information. Maybe it was dumb luck she'd spotted me.

"As a matter of fact, what about Henry Chang?" I asked. "Have you been approached to help him with his reelection?"

Clarissa's perfectly red lips turned downwards in a frown. "That new congressman? He's an odd duck."

"So you do know him," I said.

"Of course I do," she said quickly. "There isn't a first-term member of the House who doesn't want me to work for them in their next cycle. But that guy gives me the creeps."

Clarissa didn't scare easily. "What's wrong with him?"

She shrugged her shoulders. "Nothing, really. I mean, he's a single guy in Congress who never held political office before. He likes reading books about history and collecting old souvenirs." She paused to take a sip of wine. "Kit, you have to understand. I'm a fundraiser. I need to sell my clients. How do I sell that?"

"You got me there," I said. "He's not married or attached?"

She shook her head. "Nope. He doesn't even own a dog. If he had a golden retriever or even a Labrador, then I could promote that. But there's *nada*. Just his dusty books or pictures or whatever they are."

"Don't worry, Clarissa," I said. "I'll keep my eyes and ears open for other opportunities for you."

She smiled, displaying her mouthful of perfectly white teeth. "Thanks, honey. Tell Maeve I'll see her soon for a meeting."

I wagged my fingers goodbye at her and walked out the door. I hadn't said anything to Clarissa, but I was unaware that my boss had a meeting with her on the schedule. Maeve usually included me during her political strategy sessions. I made a mental note to ask her about it after the murder had been resolved and life returned to normal.

Fifteen minutes later, I was headed toward the I-395 highway, heading home to Arlington. Sebastian was on his way to pick up Doug and Clarence. They'd meet me at Rocklands BBQ shortly. The temperature was holding in the mid-fifties. A little chilly for an outdoor meal, but you had to take what you could get in mid-February.

I decided to give Sergeant O'Halloran a call. When we bought the Prius a few years ago, we wisely invested in a hands-free dialing system. I thought I'd use it mostly for work calls during my commute, not following up on a murder investigation. It reminded me of a Christopher Walken quote I ran across a while ago: "At its best, life is completely unpredictable."

O'Halloran picked up after only one ring. "Sergeant, this is Kit Marshall. I wanted to check in with you about the Library of Congress investigation."

"Ah, yes. The larceny at the Library. As far as everyone is concerned, nothing else matters these days. Do you have any revelatory insights to share?"

I recapped my day, focusing on Congressman Chang's uncorroborated whereabouts on Tuesday night, Janice and Gustav's prior relationship at the D.C. Public Library, Endicott's possible financial concerns, Lea Rutherford's apparent dislike of Gustav Gaffney, and Joe Malden's all-too-convenient alibi.

"That's quite a load of information, Ms. Marshall," said Sergeant O'Halloran. "You covered a lot of ground today."

"I'm not sure it made a difference," I said in a somber voice. "I still don't know who killed the Assistant Librarian and stole the Lincoln items."

"Don't despair. This is likely a professional job. No way an amateur can crack this one. You might want to tell your boss and the Librarian of Congress that you're out of your depth."

I wasn't ready to give up, especially if Doug was still a suspect. "If the motive was theft, then why did the perpetrator only steal two items from the safe? It doesn't make sense."

"Our experts are working on it, Ms. Marshall. It might be the case those would be the easiest to move on the blood antiquities market."

It sounded like a weak excuse to me. "If it's just the same to you, I'm going to continue to pursue the notion this was a murder first and the theft was an afterthought."

O'Halloran sighed. "It's a free country, especially with your boss and the Librarian giving you the green light."

"Did you verify Janice Jackson's alibi for that evening?"

"I'm pretty sure we had someone look at all the Library of Congress employees on their security footage. Let me check my notes." I heard the shuffle of papers. O'Halloran was old school. He was pen and paper all the way. "Here it is. The security footage showed her exiting the Library and in the direction of the congressional buildings. At exactly the time she claimed."

That might be a dead end, but I wasn't giving up so easily. "I know you don't like investigating elected members of Congress, but do you think you could check on Henry Chang's alibi for me? I'm sure there would be security footage if he went through the underground tunnels back to his office."

O'Halloran paused a moment before answering. I suspected he didn't want to expend any resources on my hair-brained theory, but he also wanted to avoid blowback if I told Maeve Dixon or Miriam Dunlap he wasn't cooperating. I didn't like playing hardball, but with no other feasible options, I had to apply the leverage available to me.

"I might be able to assign someone to look back through the tapes for Chang," said O'Halloran. "But this is going to have to stay between us. I don't want anyone hearing about the investigation of a congressman. Get it?"

"Sounds fair to me. If I get any other concrete leads, I'll let you know."

"Later, Ms. Marshall." He paused for a beat and I heard the distinct crackle of a candy wrapper. *"Bleez weeb airfool."*

Luckily, I'd been around O'Halloran long enough to know that he routinely spoke with his mouth full.

"Yes, I'll be careful," I said, shaking my head. "Good night, Sergeant."

I clicked off my hands-free dialing system, pleased with my multi-tasking. I'd convinced O'Halloran to check out Chang's alibi and made it to the restaurant in record time. As I pulled into the parking lot, I recognized Sebastian's black Tesla Model 3 parked in the "electric car only" space. For a guy who came to D.C. as a self-avowed protester, my little brother had certainly acclimated to living inside the Beltway. Of course, Sebastian claimed his car investment was merely a reflection of his supercharged, socially conscious eco-friendly lifestyle.

Doug and Sebastian were already outside, sitting on a picnic table with beer bottles in tow. Clarence and Murphy were on opposite sides of the table, both with their black noses in the air.

I walked over and took a seat next to Doug, who gave me a kiss on the cheek. "Glad you made it, Kit. I didn't know if you wanted a beer."

"I stopped by Sonoma with Meg and Trevor earlier. I think I'm fine without." I gave Clarence a pat on the head and noticed he was wearing his blue bandana. "You dressed Clarence up for the occasion."

Doug smiled. "He hasn't worn it in so long, I decided to celebrate the warm weather."

"What a beautiful day. It reminds me of California," said Sebastian, with a small dose of wistfulness in his voice. "I'm watching Murphy for Lisa tonight. She needs to log some extra hours at work, but Murphy wasn't needed. I picked him up on Capitol Hill and then picked up Doug and Clarence."

Immediately, Clarence wiggled his butt. He loved to acknowledge his name in conversation. I reached down and patted his head. "These doggies are really excited about having barbecue."

"Don't worry. We ordered some extra chicken for them," said Doug.

With ribs and brisket on the table, I seriously doubted whether Murphy and Clarence would be satisfied with poultry. But I suppose chicken was better than nothing.

"What's new with you guys?" asked Sebastian.

"I'm sure Kit spent the day trying to convince the police and anyone who would listen that I didn't murder the Assistant Librarian of Congress two days ago," said Doug.

"You are correct," I said. "Unfortunately, I don't know who killed

Gaffney. You're not in the clear quite yet. But I'm working on it."

"That's why Lisa had to stay at work late tonight," said Sebastian. "All available police officers are tracking down leads."

We stopped chatting when a Rocklands waiter brought over our food. Doug and Sebastian had gone all out. The table was now filled with baby-back ribs, brisket, chicken, baked beans, and potato salad. I looked down at my feet. Clarence positioned himself at my feet and licked his lips.

After helping myself to a plate full of food, I picked up our conversation. "I hope Lisa is able to help figure out who did it and why. As far as I'm concerned, there's a lot of suspects, but I'm pretty short on clues."

"For what it's worth, everyone knows you're investigating," said Doug. "Several people mentioned it to me today at work."

I winced. "That might not be a good thing."

"You'd better be careful, sis." Sebastian wiped his mouth after polishing off a rib. "I know you're used to this stuff and you want to clear Doug's name, but this person means business. No one wants to get caught for murder *and* grand larceny."

"Maybe we should talk about something else," I said, polishing off a rib. "A topic that's more. . ." I searched for the right word. "Pleasant."

Doug immediately perked up. "How about real estate?"

I preferred murder, quite frankly.

"Are you still looking to buy a house?" asked Sebastian.

As if on cue, Clarence growled softly. Although I'm sure he was eager to have a backyard, his interjection was pure coincidence. Clarence's mind was on food. I noticed he eyed Murphy warily. Clarence had grown up as an only dog and didn't like to share, especially when it came to barbecue chicken. I tore off a piece and gave it to him, which spent less than one second on his lips before it disappeared.

"We're in the market. Our realtor Jonathan wants to show us a split-level in Falls Church tomorrow." Doug leaned forward, barely able to contain his excitement. "It has a fenced-in backyard."

Sebastian's eyes lit up. "That'll be great for Clarence and Murphy."

I could almost read Clarence's mind. *First, I have to share my chicken. Now you want me to share my backyard, too?*

"Nothing is settled yet," I said abruptly. "Quite frankly, we have a lot on our plate right now."

Doug lowered his head. "Of course not. But it's a very good deal."

Sebastian forged ahead, blissfully obvious to any tension the current conversation had fomented. "You should really consider an eco-friendly home," he said, shaking a half-eaten rib at us. "There's lot of options out there. Solar-powered, harvested rainwater, geothermal heating, compostable toilet."

My brother loved talking about the environment. He also detested Wall Street greed, corporate farming, our current immigration policy, and the military industrial complex. But the environment was his all-time favorite cause.

"I don't even want to know what a compostable toilet looks like inside a house," I said. "But thanks for making us aware of the green options out there."

"Or you could consider a tiny house," said Sebastian. "There's only two of you and Clarence. A tiny house might be a good choice for affordability and the environment." Sebastian ran his fingers through his dishwater blond hair. Now he was on a roll.

"Do they have those in the D.C. area?" I asked.

"They will soon," said Sebastian. "It would be perfect for me, Lisa, and Murphy."

Sebastian's last comment caught me off guard. "Wait a second. You haven't known Lisa that long. Don't you think you'd better take it slow before moving into a three hundred square foot house together?"

Sebastian drained his beer. "I don't second guess my feelings, big sister. Not everyone creates a twenty-step flowchart before making a decision." He winked his eye at Doug.

I crossed my arms in front of my chest. "That's not fair, Sebastian."

He reached across the table and patted my hand. "You're right, Kit. That's not fair. You don't always create a flowchart. Sometimes you build a spreadsheet instead."

Doug chuckled. "Very funny," I said. "There's nothing wrong with being deliberate or analytical." I tapped my fingers on the table. "Besides, I'm not afraid to act."

I'd given Doug an opening and he seized it. "In that case, we're on for the appointment with Jonathan tomorrow. Since you're a *woman of action.*"

"Fine. We'll go see the house at lunchtime." I stabbed a piece of potato salad with my fork and shoved it in my mouth.

"Terrific!" said Sebastian. I caught him smiling at Doug. I wondered if the two of them had cooked this up on the ride over to Rocklands from our condo. I wouldn't put it past them.

"It will have to be a fast viewing," said Doug. "We've rescheduled the big Lincoln congressional event for late tomorrow afternoon. We're going to display all the items, minus the two stolen pieces. To make up for the earlier cancellation, we're also going to show Lincoln's handwritten Second Inaugural Address."

"That's a big deal, right?" Try as I might, I couldn't always keep up with Doug's brain. There were only so many history factoids a mere mortal could commit to memory.

"Certainly. The text of the speech is engraved on a wall inside the Lincoln Memorial," said Doug. "You'd recognize the famous quotes from it, like 'with malice toward none and charity for all.' Many scholars argue it's Lincoln's greatest speech, even better than the Gettysburg Address."

"Are you expecting a lot of members of Congress? I bet Maeve Dixon will attend, although I wasn't at the office very much today."

"We are," said Doug. "In fact, since Congress might convene a rare Saturday session, all the House members and senators are staying in town on a Friday. Our event is supposed to be a nice break for them. I think the Speaker of the House is attending."

"In that case, I know Maeve Dixon will be there," I said. The Speaker hand-picked my boss for her current chairmanship. She was her own person but knew where her bread was buttered.

Doug sighed. "It's going to be chaotic tomorrow. With congressional leaders attending, there will be security sweeps before the event. Everything is shutting down around noon at the Library so the Capitol Hill police can do their thing."

Sebastian had been listening to our conversation intently. Still fairly new to the Washington, D.C. area, he found insider discussions about our government fascinating. "Do they do that all the time for Congress?"

"There's always security," I explained. "I suspect they're taking extra precautions tomorrow because the Speaker will be attending. She's third in line to the presidency, you know."

"Oh yeah," said Sebastian. "I totally forgot. I guess I could use a civics review."

Our plates were now mostly empty. We packed up the remaining chicken for Clarence and Murphy as leftovers and walked back to Sebastian's car.

"Doug, do you want to drive the Prius home?" I flipped him the key. "I wouldn't mind riding home with Sebastian." I planned to interrogate him about the seriousness of his relationship with Lisa.

"No problem," said Doug. "See you at home."

I was about to climb into the front seat when Sebastian motioned for me to stop.

"Kit, do you mind sitting in the back with Clarence and Murphy? They were a little rambunctious on the way here and it might be better if you sat back there with them." Sebastian didn't want to say it, but he was uber-protective of his Tesla. I doubted he wanted Clarence's slobber on the front seat.

"Not at all," I said. My suit would be a magnet for the dog hair, but a trip to the dry cleaner was on the schedule for this weekend. Besides, it was a real treat to snuggle with *two* dogs.

We were stopped at a red light on Washington Boulevard when Clarence's nose went up in the air. He sniffed several times, followed by a low growl.

"Clarence, what's wrong?" I massaged his ears. He responded by shaking his butt and nudging me.

I followed his gaze and realized he was staring at the doggy box of leftover chicken. It was on the other side of me. Noticeably closer to Murphy than Clarence. Uh-oh.

"Sorry, buddy. Do you want the chicken closer to you?" I asked.

"Kit, I wouldn't do that," said Sebastian. "As I recall, Clarence really can't restrain himself."

Sebastian's comment reminded me of an unfortunate incident with pepperoni pizza that happened a while back. Let's just say that Clarence distinguished himself that evening, and not in a particularly auspicious way.

Clarence growled again and pawed at my arm. "It's fine, Sebastian. He just doesn't want the leftovers closer to Murphy." Clarence was already wary of another dog taking over his territory. Food envy might throw him over the top.

I picked up the box and put it on the other side of me. Clarence wagged his tail and sat back down. "See? Problem solved."

Unfortunately, my little plan had failed to take Murphy into account. He apparently liked the leftover chicken right where it was. Murphy lunged across my lap in an attempt to return the box to its rightful place. Clarence was having none of that. He intercepted Murphy's head by grabbing it with both paws.

"Oh no! Dog fight!" I screamed.

Sebastian kept his eyes on the road. "What in the hell is going on back there?"

Murphy was undeterred by Clarence's attempt to box his ears. He wedged his muzzle next to my thigh, determined to reclaim the leftover container. Clarence burrowed his mouth in the same spot. In short order, they each grabbed a corner of the doggy box. I knew what was coming next, but there was no way to stop it. They both pulled backwards at precisely the same time. The container of barbecue exploded, leaving a half-pound of chicken right on my legs. Without missing a beat, Clarence and Murphy immediately dove on top of me, determined to make short work of the feast.

"Can someone help me?" I bellowed. "You might want to stop the car."

"We're almost at your place, Kit," said Sebastian. "No point in delaying."

The good news was that the feeding frenzy was over in ten seconds. My black suit pants were smeared with red sauce, and I smelled like I'd just stepped out of a Texas roadhouse. But at least there was no more chicken on my lap.

Sebastian pulled up next to our condo building. He got out and opened the door so I could crawl out of the backseat with Clarence, who was so busy licking his lips, he didn't realize we were home.

Sebastian took a closer look at my stained pantsuit. "Jeez, Kit. Sorry about all of that. I guess even though Murphy is a police dog, he can be rambunctious."

I mustered a smile. "Nothing my dry cleaner can't handle. And if not, then I have ten other black suits inside my closet." Due to the canine shenanigans, I'd neglected to ask him about his relationship with Lisa. It would have to wait until next time

Sebastian gave us a salute. "See you around." Before he put the car in gear, he honked the horn and motioned for me. I went back to the car and stuck my head inside the window.

"Is something wrong?" I asked. "In addition to the obvious fact that I'm covered in barbecue sauce."

"Please be careful, Kit," he said. "Not all messes can be cleaned up easily."

Little brothers can be annoying. As it turns out, every once in a while, they're dead right.

Chapter Fourteen

~~~

FRIDAY WAS USUALLY a delicious reprieve. Most of the time, members of Congress have already departed for a weekend of politicking back in the home district. That typically leaves Washington, D.C. staff with the entire day to catch up with emails, paperwork, and other administrative minutiae that no sane person can possibly stomach while engaged with actual legislative deal-making. However, in the spirit that there's no rest for the weary, this week offered no such respite. Not only did I have a murder to solve, but Congress had also decided to remain in legislative session. This meant Maeve Dixon was staying put, and it was business as usual. No one was happy about this development, including the entire staff and the Congresswoman herself.

It was half past seven, and I scanned my closet yet again. Fridays meant casual attire. With the House of Representatives in full operation, I couldn't get away with tan corduroys and a turtleneck. Luckily, hiding in the far corner I spotted my last clean black suit. I threw it on, thankful to find one final outfit to get me through the week. I was finishing my makeup when Doug walked into our bedroom.

"Let's ride to work together today," he said. "Then I can meet you at noon for our real estate appointment, and we can drive together."

I'd almost forgotten the meeting with Jonathan. What could possibly get me through the dreaded tour inside a split-level rambler in suburban Falls Church? Clarence nuzzled my leg as he frequently did when he saw me getting ready for work in the morning. An idea popped into my head.

"Let's take Clarence," I said. "He can come to work with me today. Maeve Dixon is in the office, but she won't mind. He can visit the open house with us and check out the backyard. Didn't you say it was fenced in?"

Doug nodded. "There's a pretty sizable yard. Even if he can't come inside the house, it's warm enough for him to run around outside."

"I hate leaving him alone on Fridays." I rubbed his ears. "Besides, I think Clarence should have a vote about where we live."

"I don't have a problem with that," said Doug. "He'll take one look at the outdoor play space and there won't be a question."

I gave Clarence a knowing look. Doug might think he had our beagle mutt in his pocket, but I knew otherwise. Clarence didn't cross the hand who filled his doggy bowl on a daily basis.

Less than an hour later, I dropped Doug off at the Library of Congress, parked my car, and entered the Cannon House Office Building. It always took twice as long to arrive at our suite when Clarence joined me. He had a habit of wagging his tail at anyone who paid the slightest bit of attention to him, so we inevitably stopped for several head scratches and belly rubs before reaching our final destination.

Patsy caught me on the way to my desk. "As soon as you get Clarence settled, the Congresswoman would like to see you."

I knew this wouldn't be the typical Friday, but I hadn't expected the craziness to start as soon as I walked through the door. Thankfully, Clarence knew the drill. After helping himself to a drink of water from his bowl, he curled up next to my desk on the cushion I kept for him. By the time I left my office, he was already snoring. A dog's life, indeed.

Maeve Dixon wasn't outfitted in her usual power suit with high heels. Instead, her shoulder-length brown hair was in a ponytail, which matched her workout capris and University of North Carolina t-shirt. She must have seen the curious look on my face. "I apologize for my casual attire. I slept in later than usual, so I'm running behind."

It was a nice reminder that even my ultra-disciplined boss was human. "This Friday schedule has everyone off schedule," I said.

She nodded as she sipped a smoothie from her eco-friendly water bottle. "Speaking of schedules, that's why I wanted to talk to you." She wiped a thin line of green liquid from her upper lip. Maeve Dixon swore by her daily kale shakes for breakfast. I shuddered, finding delicious comfort in my bagel and coffee ritual.

"The Librarian's office called me this morning." She put on her cheaters so she could read her scrawled handwriting. "Miriam Dunlap would like an update on the investigation. Unfortunately, she has a packed schedule today and only has a short window of availability this morning."

"That's perfectly fine," I said. "I have time to walk over to the Madison Building to meet her."

"That's the rub," said Maeve. "She's not on Capitol Hill this morning. She's at Ford's Theater. They'd planned an event about Lincoln for this week, and despite the theft, Ford's decided to forge ahead." She smiled. "So to speak."

I tried to hide my annoyance. Ford's wasn't too far away, but I hadn't necessarily budgeted for a morning trip off-site. "And you think it's necessary that I speak with her?"

Maeve took a long sip of her smoothie and sat down on the couch opposite me. "I think so, Kit. We're deep into this, at least until the bad guy or gal gets caught. If you don't have any more leads, then tell her. But she must stay informed."

"Sergeant O'Halloran is following up on a few alibis for me. Right now, I have a lot of possibilities but no real answers, I'm afraid."

"Something will break," she said. "Or law enforcement will figure out who did this. In the meantime, we have political responsibilities to fulfill."

In other words, I needed to get my butt to Ford's Theater. Pronto. After going over a few more details regarding today's legislative agenda on the floor, Maeve dismissed me and told me to get the details about Ford's from Patsy.

"I'll see you at the Library of Congress event later today, correct?" she asked.

I looked at her blankly.

"The rescheduled show-and-tell of the remaining Lincoln items from the night he was assassinated," she said. "You are going, aren't you?"

Of course, I was. It had completely slipped my mind. "Yes, I'll be there. By the way, I have a personal appointment at noon in Virginia. After I speak with the Librarian at Ford's, do you mind if I spend my lunch hour taking care of it?"

Maeve waved her hand dismissively. "Of course, Kit. I know you work all hours of the day at this job, whether or not you have a murder to solve. Please take the time you need, as long as you're back for the rescheduled event later in the afternoon at the Library."

"That won't be a problem," I said. Particularly since I had no plans to spend more than twenty minutes inside the house Jonathan was showing us.

On the way back to my desk, I asked Patsy for the details about Ford's Theater. I had some time before I had to leave. Clarence was curled up on his doggie bed. He barely opened an eye when I returned. I imagined what he must be thinking. *Working hard? Too bad you can't take a nap with me.*

I'd been forging my way through the hundreds of emails which had built up in my inbox when my phone dinged. Maybe Jonathan had contacted Doug and he couldn't make our real estate appointment. I grabbed my phone to check the message.

No such luck. The text was from Trevor.

Time for coffee? Breakfast?

There was a tone of desperation that was uncharacteristic for the composed, stoic Trevor I knew. My response was typical for Washington. I answered his question with my own question.

Is something wrong?

The three dots appeared immediately.

Would like to talk.

Somehow, I doubted this was about murder. However, I'd bet my coveted congressional parking spot that it was about another "M" word, namely Meg.

Longworth in 5?

Trevor responded in the affirmative, so I abandoned any hope at making a dent in my email responses and set off for the main House of Representatives cafeteria. Meg wasn't at her desk, so I couldn't check in with her before speaking to Trevor. I'd have to wing it.

As I entered the large eatery, the smells of breakfast greeted me and my stomach rumbled in response. If I had to spend my lunch hour touring a house with an over eager realtor and husband, I'd better fortify myself. Pancakes would do the trick. Topped with warm syrup, of course.

After paying for my meal, I spotted Trevor in the far corner of the cafeteria. I plunked my tray on the table and took the seat opposite him. My longtime friend didn't look so good. Almost to a fault, Trevor was always neatly dressed, well rested, and perfectly attired. This morning, there were dark circles under his eyes and his white dress shirt looked wrinkled. His normally coiffed hair seemed in immediate need of a trim. Something was up.

"Is everything okay, Trevor?" I opened my plastic container and dug into my pancakes.

"I've been better," he said in a flat voice. "But it is heartening to know that you continue to prefer to drown your breakfast food with that gelatinous, sugary liquid masquerading as maple syrup."

I was relieved. Trevor couldn't be too down and out if he was making fun of my unhealthy eating habits yet again. Ignoring his snark, I asked, "Well, what is it, then? Unfortunately, I don't have all day. I'm meeting the Librarian of Congress at Ford's Theater in less than an hour."

He swallowed hard. "I'm not sure you'll be of any help."

I put down my plastic fork and knife and wiped my sticky mouth. "Let me guess. You want Meg to decide who she wants to date exclusively."

He leaned across the table. "You know what's going on."

Men really could be clueless about female friendships. "Of course, I do, Trevor. I'm Meg's best friend."

His eyes glowed through his wire-rimmed glasses. "What do you think? What should I do?"

"Let's back up for a second," I said. "I haven't had much time to speak with Meg about this. Remember, we have a murder investigation going on and Doug is a prime suspect until it gets solved."

Trevor pursed his lips. "I know."

"But I think Meg knows she can't keep dating two men seriously forever."

Trevor rubbed the back of his neck nervously. "What do I do in the meantime? Just wait around for Meg to make a decision?"

"I know you don't like it, but you'd better give her time. She needs to figure out what she wants," I said. "You and Clay may seem similar on the surface, but I think the choice between the two of you is actually quite stark. Meg needs time to realize that."

"What do you mean?" Trevor's eyes blinked nervously.

"I don't think I should say too much more. This is really between you and Meg." I glanced at my phone. "Besides, I need to grab a ride to Ford's Theater for my meeting."

Trevor sank back in his chair. "Do you have any new leads? My boss wants to stay informed and law enforcement isn't saying much."

"I don't know too much more than when I saw you last night," I said. "O'Halloran is looking into Congressman Chang's whereabouts after the display ended. Don't spread that factoid around, though. He doesn't want anyone to know a member of Congress is a potential suspect."

"No update on anyone else?"

"Janice Jackson's alibi stands up. She showed up on a video camera leaving the Library of Congress at the right time, just like she claimed,"

I explained.

"Maybe the lawyer and Lea Rutherford did it," said Trevor. "They certainly each had a reason to dislike the victim. Or the rare books expert, if he needed the money from the theft."

"There's plenty of possibilities but nothing definitive. Which leaves us right back to where we started. With Doug as a suspect." I rubbed my temples. The pancakes had brightened my mood but Trevor's questions about the case had brought back the anxiety.

Trevor tapped his fingers on the table. "Something isn't right. I'm not sure what it is. If it comes to me, I'll be sure to let you know."

"Please do, Trevor." I stood. "I'll even take hunches at this point."

Trevor adjusted his glasses. "I would hope I could do better than a mere hunch." On this other matter we spoke about, I'll do as you say, as much as I'd like to give Meg a deadline to make a choice."

"Hang in there, Trevor." I waved goodbye and dashed out of the cafeteria.

Fifteen minutes later, I'd caught a ride share to the Penn Quarter neighborhood of the city, home of cultural institutions such as the Shakespeare Theatre, the National Building Museum, the Navy Memorial, and Ford's Theatre. Even though I knew the famous theater had been renovated several times, I got chills when visiting. This was the spot of our nation's most infamous murder. No matter how many times I walked inside, I mentally transported myself to that fateful night in 1865 when American history was forever altered by the assassination of our sixteenth president.

The lobby outside the theater, which also included the gift shop, was eerily empty when I walked inside. But then I heard voices from the direction of the theater, so I followed them inside the hallowed hall. I was instantly transported in time. The box where Lincoln was shot was on the right-hand side, decorated in exactly the same way it had been in 1865, with a framed picture of George Washington on the balcony.

Before I could appreciate my surroundings more fully, I heard a familiar voice. "Kit, so glad you could meet us here."

I swiveled my head and saw Dorian Jones approaching, the Librarian's chief of staff. I extended my hand. "Not a problem. We're lucky it could fit into my schedule."

He gestured toward the stage. "The program is almost over. This was a private event for archivists, historians, and other V-I-Ps." He lowered his voice and wiggled his eyebrows. "Donors."

I nodded. Anyone who was someone in Washington, D.C. knew the name of the game. It started with the letter "f" and ended in "g." And it wasn't a curse word, at least in the traditional sense. Yes, that's right. FUNDRAISING. It made the world go round. Whether it was political donors to a campaign or cultural philanthropists, nothing happened in our fair city without it.

Miriam Dunlap was on stage with a uniformed park ranger and a man in a suit, who was probably the executive director of Ford's. I whispered back to Dorian. "What's the program about?"

"A celebration of Lincoln's birthday event," he said. "Talking about the visitor experience at Ford's plus the Library's stellar Lincoln collection." His eyes narrowed. "Of course, there's been a lot of questions about the theft and murder."

It was sort of ironic. Lincoln had been murdered in this very theater. Now, the Librarian of Congress was talking about the subsequent theft and murder surrounding Lincoln's possessions of that fateful night. Somehow, we'd come full circle, hadn't we?

At that moment, the audience clapped politely as the participants removed their lavaliere microphones and exited the stage. Miriam Dunlap and the other panelists made their way to the back of the theater.

Dunlap made a beeline in my direction and immediately introduced me to the park ranger and the head honcho of Ford's. I exchanged pleasantries with everyone, mindful of the time.

"We have several members of Congress who are big supporters of this site," said the Ford's director enthusiastically.

"Such as Congressman Chang?" I kept my voice as innocent as possible. I had no dog in this flight, except to catch a murderer and thief.

"Of course," said the director, a smile plastered across his face. "He was here today."

Librarian Dunlap chimed in. "Congressman Chang is our biggest congressional supporter at the Library of Congress. He's practically joined at the hip with our congressional relations liaison." She looked pointedly at her chief of staff. "Isn't that right?"

Dorian nodded. "He's our number one fan."

I am your number one fan. Wasn't that the famous line from Stephen King's *Misery*? I'd read the book from the master suspense writer decades ago. The quote, spoken by Kathy Bates in the movie, had resonated with me. So-called number one fans had a way of becoming downright deadly. I suppressed a shudder while others buoyed their heads in sycophant approval.

Sure enough, Chang was walking up the center aisle of Ford's Theatre.

Didn't this man engage in any routine legislative activity? I made a mental note to make sure he'd seen "Schoolhouse Rock." Maybe Chang needed to learn how a lonely bill could become a law? After spotting us, he joined our group of conversationalists.

"As a member of our House oversight committee, I'm sure you know Kit Marshall from Chairwoman Dixon's staff," said the Librarian.

"Of course," said Chang. "We've met previously."

He'd consciously avoided that I'd questioned him about the theft and Gaffney's murder. I'd have done the same if I was in his situation.

"I thoroughly enjoyed your presentation today," said Dorian to the Ford's Theatre director. "The museum downstairs is a great addition, as well."

"We will need to pay careful attention to our artifacts," said the director solemnly. "In case there's someone who is hell bent on stealing more Lincoln paraphernalia."

I stole a glance at Congressman Chang. His face remained stoic. If he was our thief, he knew how to play it cool.

"What would be your most valuable item related to Lincoln?" I asked.

"Probably John Wilkes Booth's Deringer that he used to kill Lincoln," he said. "Quite a macabre item, but our visitors make a point of seeing it."

Dorian whispered to me. "I learned from the program today that it was a single shot pistol. If Booth had misfired, there would have been no opportunity to reload. He had one chance to murder Lincoln that evening."

"Sounds familiar," I murmured. I remained convinced that whomever killed the Assistant Librarian and stole the items knew it was an unusual opportunity for the crimes and acted that night because of it.

"I hope you are able to join us for the reception," said the Ford's director. "It's right this way." He ushered us out of the theater and back inside the lobby.

Miriam Dunlap spoke up. "I'll be there in a moment." She motioned for me to follow her inside the adjacent gift shop.

"Thank you for meeting me here, Kit," said the Librarian. "Between this morning event and now the rescheduled congressional show-and-tell this afternoon, I won't have another free moment today." She picked up a beer pint glass with Lincoln's likeness and the Ford's Theatre logo on it. "Seems like an odd gift, doesn't it?"

I giggled. "I'm not sure Abraham Lincoln would approve."

"I don't know about his shopping preferences, but I am *certain* he would not be pleased if he knew the items in his pockets at the time of his death had been stolen," said Dunlap. "Are we any closer to knowing what happened?"

"I'm tracking down everyone's whereabouts after the preview event concluded inside the ceremonial office. Sergeant O'Halloran is providing assistance." I lowered my voice and scanned the gift shop to make sure no one was listening to our conversation. "He's checking out Congressman Chang's alibi, but don't tell anyone. He could get serious blowback if his superiors found out he was investigating a sitting member of Congress. Even informal inquiries might get him in trouble with the higher-ups."

Dunlap's eyes widened. "I won't say a thing. Janice Jackson would be devastated if Congressman Chang is behind this." Her eyes twinkled. "Those two get along *really* well."

"More than a professional relationship?" I asked. "Is that why he spends so much time at the Library of Congress?"

"I have no idea," the Librarian said quickly. "I shouldn't engage in gossip like that."

Despite Dunlap's abrupt disavowal, my mind was already racing. Did Chang leverage a romantic relationship to uncover relevant details about the Lincoln collection and how to steal it? It was starting to make sense. The question was how to prove it. Hopefully the police could determine if Chang was telling the truth about retiring to his office after the event ended.

"It might be impolite to gossip, but you never know when pieces of information could be relevant to solving the crime," I said.

Dunlap seemed to consider my comment. "I appreciate that, Ms. Marshall. But as I've said before, Library staff are dedicated professionals. I can't see how one of them could be involved."

"And you haven't thought of another motive, besides theft, to kill Gustav?"

"I'm afraid I only worked with Gustav for less than a year," she said. "He had a long career beforehand. But he was relatively new to the Library of Congress. Quite frankly, I'm not sure he was around long enough to have created enemies."

"Oh, I wouldn't be so sure," I said. "It seems like Gustav had already ruffled a few feathers."

"Enough to kill him?" The Librarian's forehead wrinkled in despair.

"That's exactly what I'm trying to figure out," I said.

"Are you attending the event this afternoon with Chairwoman Dixon?" asked Dunlap.

"We'll be there," I said.

"I'd hoped that the missing items would have been returned by now," said Dunlap. "I suppose we'll have to simply proceed with what we have." She sighed as the worry lines on her forehead deepened.

"My boss is looking forward to it," I said, mostly wanting to mollify the Librarian's legitimate concerns.

"If you need anything regarding the event, be sure to contact Janice Jackson," said Dunlap. "That woman is always running between the Library and the congressional buildings. I told her she was allowed to wear tennis shoes to work."

I laughed. "Not a bad idea. Better for walking than these." I pointed to my high-heeled black boots.

"Take care, Ms. Marshall," said the Librarian. "Contact Dorian if there's a break in the case so he can keep me informed."

I rushed out of the gift shop and was about to exit the theater onto Tenth Street when a woman's voice called out my name. I spun around and found myself face to face with an old friend.

"Vivian Langsford," I said in a low voice, almost to myself.

The fifty-something bombshell grabbed my hands and gave me a hug. "I haven't seen you in ages," she said. "Since after Lyndon's murder."

Her late husband, Senator Lyndon Langsford, had been my first political boss in Congress. His murder was the first mystery I'd solved, and I'll never forget it since I was the primary suspect until I exposed the guilty party.

"What brings you to Ford's Theatre?" I asked. Vivian looked gorgeous, as always. She'd always liked me, but her affection toward me grew after I kept a personal secret of hers I'd uncovered while hunting her husband's killer.

"I'm a donor, of course," said Vivian. That made sense. She'd brought the money to the marriage and bankrolled her husband's numerous campaigns for political office.

She placed her hand on her shapely hip. "And why are you here, dear? You're still working on Capitol Hill, aren't you? For that southern woman?" Her eyes sparkled. Vivian Langsford was a lot of things, but feminist wasn't one of them.

"That's right." I took a deep breath. "I'm here to speak with the Librarian of Congress. About the murder and theft that happened earlier this week."

Vivian took a step back in her high heels. teetering a bit. "Oh my. I'm afraid you caught me off guard on that one." She blinked several times. "I suppose that makes sense. You've continued to solve murders after Lyndon's death." She gave me a tight smile. "I do read the newspapers, you know."

"Of course." An idea popped into my brain. It was a long shot, but worth a try. "Do you happen to know Lea Rutherford?" I had a hunch that Vivian might run in the same circles as her. In my experience, rich people tended to hang together, for better or worse.

Vivian tilted her heavily made up face to the side. "Yes, as a matter of fact, I do. Is she involved in this matter?"

I didn't want Vivian running to Lea after our conversation ended. "Indirectly," I said, careful to keep my voice casual. "She's a generous Library of Congress supporter and was inside the historic Jefferson Building for an event on the night of the murder."

Vivian tapped her long, red manicured nail against her cheek. "I see." Then she leaned closer. "Let me tell you about Lea. She's a tough customer. I would not underestimate her."

I could feel Vivian's breath against my cheek, which was a little too close for comfort. I leaned backwards. "I'm not, Mrs. Langsford. Believe me."

"Smart girl," said Vivian. "You'll have to excuse me. I need to find this reception. I used to think it was busy being a Senator's wife. But now that I've taken on a more philanthropic role, it's simply maddening."

Somehow, I doubted Vivian's life was too strenuous. "It was nice seeing you again. I'm really glad to know you're doing well."

Vivian grinned, exposing her perfectly capped white teeth. Despite the fake, superficial veneer she often exuded, her smile was genuine. She leaned across and gently grabbed my arm. "Every favor deserves a return. You once were discrete when confronted with an indiscretion of mine." She paused and looked me directly in the eye. "Pay attention to Lea Rutherford and watch your back, Ms. Marshall."

Chapter Fifteen

———∼∼∼———

A FTER RUSHING BACK to Capitol Hill and collecting Clarence, I pulled up in front of the Library's Jefferson Building in our Prius. Doug was waiting for us in front of Neptune's Fountain, but I could have seen the anguish on his face a mile away.

"We're going to be late for our appointment with Jonathan," he said as he climbed into the car. "And we can't stay too long because I need to be back here for the congressional event this afternoon."

"As do I, Doug. I promised the Librarian of Congress I'd attend with Maeve Dixon." I reached over and patted his hand as I made the turn onto the I-395 South freeway. "Don't worry. If we really like the house, I'm sure we can go back to see it again this weekend."

"It will probably have ten offers by then," grumbled Doug.

"Someone woke up on the wrong side of the bed." Perhaps he'd lighten up once Jonathan showed him this supposed dream house in Falls Church.

"There's a lot going on with the event being rescheduled. Plus, I'm still a suspect in Gustav's death." He shook his head. "I can't help but think that people are whispering about me when I walk into a room."

"You're likely imagining things, Doug. Even if you're not, once the killer is caught, everything will go back to normal." Then I caught myself. Doug needed an empathetic voice. "But I know this is a really difficult time."

"Any new leads?" Doug asked, gently biting his lip.

"Not much." I gripped the steering wheel tightly. "I ran into Vivian Langsford this morning after meeting briefly with Miriam Dunlap at Ford's Theatre. She advised that I pay attention to Lea Rutherford and not underestimate her."

Doug perked up. "That sounds like a potential lead. Did Vivian explain why?"

"I didn't have time to interrogate her about it. But if I had to guess, I think Vivian wanted to make sure I was listening to what Rutherford had told me."

Doug slumped back in his seat. "Vivian doesn't think Lea Rutherford is the murderer and thief?"

"I'm not sure," I said slowly. "But if Vivian thinks I should pay attention to what Rutherford has to say, I'll be sure to follow her advice."

Doug had been tracking our progress on a GPS app. "Take this exit and make a left."

I did as he instructed and followed his verbal directions until we pulled up in front of a ranch-style house on a quiet cul-de-sac. Sure enough, our realtor Jonathan was waiting for us in the driveway. I mentally braced myself for the hard sell that was sure to follow.

We parked the car and the three of us walked to meet Jonathan, who was waving his hands enthusiastically. "Doug and Kit, over here!" It wasn't really possible to miss him, but I guess Jonathan didn't want to take any chances.

"It's been ages since I saw you!" he exclaimed. "And look, you even brought your pup so he could check out the backyard. This is a doggie friendly house, for sure!"

Doug pumped Jonathan's hand up and down. "Thanks for showing it to us on short notice. We only have about twenty minutes, so if you can get us inside quickly, that would be great."

"Alrighty, then!" said Jonathan. "Follow me to the backyard, which is where we can start."

The rear of the property was enclosed by a wooden fence. Jonathan opened the gated entry door, and we stepped into a sizable yard with a patio near the corner. Once we were safely inside, I unclipped Clarence's leash, and he charged across the lawn, undoubtedly chasing an innocent, unsuspecting squirrel.

"It looks like he's ready to move right in," said Jonathan, a wide smile plastered across his face.

"Unfortunately, Clarence hasn't figured out how to negotiate a loan for a mortgage yet," I said. "So, it's not really his decision."

Jonathan stared at me for a few seconds and then burst into laughter. "You are so funny, Kit. I forgot how I enjoy your wit and humor. Come on, follow me around to the front and we can see the inside of the house."

As we walked toward the gate, Doug turned around and gave me the high sign. I'd better behave. After all, Doug was under a lot of stress lately and he was really looking forward to seeing this house. I checked out the surroundings as Jonathan finagled with the lockbox outside the front door. It seemed nice enough, with several cars parked alongside the tree-lined street. Front yards were littered with bicycles, landscaped flower gardens, and Adirondack chairs. Of course, there was no restaurant, store, or watering hole in sight. This was the heart of suburbia and there was nothing but sidewalks and houses for as far as the eye could see. Was this reality my immediate future? I swallowed hard and followed Jonathan and Doug inside the house.

A small but well adorned dining room with perfectly restored hardwood floors led us into the kitchen. Jonathan led the way. "Now, if I remember correctly, the two of you don't cook at home very often, but that might change if you buy this house!" He stepped aside to reveal a completely remodeled kitchen, complete with cobalt blue granite countertops, stainless steel appliances, and a country-style island.

"It is beautiful," I said. "But I'm afraid you're right. Other than to make coffee from our beloved espresso machine, I confess that I don't spend too much time in the kitchen."

"Not a problem," said Jonathan. "Let's go see the master bedroom. Even if you don't cook, I know you have to sleep!" He laughed at his own joke and charged down the hallway.

The main bedroom had been renovated and it showed. New paint, designer closets, and an attached "his and her" bathroom did strike me as enticing. If suburban living was less than thrilling, at least it could be done in comfort and style. French doors in the corner opened onto a small landing that was attached to the outdoor patio.

"Can I open the door?" I asked.

Delighted that I showed more than feigned interest, Jonathan's eyes brightened. "Of course, Kit. *Mi casa es su casa*." This wasn't really his house, but I kept my mouth shut.

I opened the door and stepped outside. This February had been rather mild. In a few months, spring would arrive and we'd have two or three weeks of pleasant weather before the onslaught of humidity and heat. Clarence would undoubtedly enjoy a backyard like this, especially as the warm days approached.

I scanned the expanse of the outdoor area and didn't see Clarence. He probably had investigated the line of bushes in the far corner of the yard and was busy digging a massive hole. Although he was a beagle rescue, he wasn't a purebred. I had a distinct feeling that Clarence had a grandparent who had been a terrier.

"Clarence! If you're digging over there, I'm going to be really angry."

I walked across the yard and looked between the bushes. Clarence wasn't there. I scanned left and right. No sign of our dog.

"Doug!" I screamed. "Clarence is gone!"

Had he somehow breached the gate? No such luck. It was latched securely. The fencing was over six feet. Clarence was spry, but no way could he jump that high.

Doug emerged from the house and joined me. "I'm sure he's here, Kit. He's just hiding."

I turned around. "Where? I already looked behind the bushes."

Doug spotted a small shed in the opposite corner. "He's probably inside there." He marched over to the shed and whipped open the door. After ten seconds, he emerged from the enclosed structure.

"Not there," he said quietly.

Jonathan came outside. "Is your doggie playing games?"

"I don't think so. He's not here, and I have no idea where he could have gone." I didn't bother to hide the frantic sound of my voice. I'd never been separated from Clarence. If he'd escaped, he would get lost in a strange neighborhood.

"Kit and Doug, you'd better take a look at this," said Jonathan, who was standing next to the patio table. His face had drained of all color.

We both hustled over to Jonathan, who now had a white unlined piece of paper in his hand. The scrawled handwriting delivered an ominous message: "IF YOU WANT TO SEE YOUR DOG AGAIN, BACK OFF!"

Chapter Sixteen

———— ~~~ ————

M Y HEART SANK like an anchor. I grabbed Doug's arm to steady myself. While I'd never fainted before, I felt as though I was on the precipice. Doug must have sensed my body sway. He grabbed me just before I hit the ground.

Luckily, I only wavered for a moment. Doug helped me stand straight again. "Jonathan, can you get Kit a glass of water from the kitchen?" Our realtor scampered off, likely relieved he could escape the tense situation.

"Are you okay, Kit?" Doug asked in a quaking voice.

I grabbed a patio chair to steady myself and sat down. "I think so. I can't believe Clarence has been taken."

"Whomever did this wants to intimidate you," he said. "You can stop pursuing this case and make it known to everyone involved. Then the guilty person will have no need to keep him."

Doug was a professor and always thought logically. The problem was that we were dealing with someone who was clearly deranged. "I don't know if a reasonable approach like that will get us Clarence back," I said.

Jonathan approached with the glass of water. "I'm only your realtor and maybe you don't want to answer a personal question. But I can't help wondering. Do you guys have mortal enemies or something?"

Doug started to answer. "It's nothing like that. Kit is investigating a murder and theft at the Library of Congress. . ."

Jonathan cut him off. "Did you say *murder*?"

"Yes," said Doug slowly. "Kit has solved several murders in the recent past. She's quite adept at it."

Jonathan put up his hand. "Listen, I really like you both. But I had no idea you were involved with killers, thieves, and dognappers."

"It's not like they're our friends, Jonathan," said Doug. "The Librarian of Congress asked Kit to help. . ."

"Enough said," said Jonathan. "I've read my share of Dan Brown. I know what's going on. Missing artifacts, the involvement of government officials, and dead bodies." He ticked each off with his finger. "I'm afraid I'm going to have to think about our professional relationship going forward. I simply cannot get caught up in your craziness." He motioned for us to follow him to the backyard gate.

"Are you kicking us out?" I asked. "After our dog was stolen from the house you want to sell us?"

"Quite frankly, nothing like this has ever happened to me before. They don't go over these scenarios when you take the exam for the realtor license. I don't know what to do when a crime occurs during a showing." He stood by the gate with his hands on his hips.

Doug grabbed the note from the patio table with one hand and took my arm with the other. "Let's go, Kit. There's no clues here about Clarence's whereabouts."

Jonathan slammed the fence door behind us. Doug and I stood outside the house on the sidewalk and looked at each other.

"What should I do?" I asked in small voice. The person who had taken Clarence had already brutally killed one person. Clarence's welfare wouldn't be a priority. His life was in danger.

"Call Sergeant O'Halloran," said Doug. "This is out of his jurisdiction, but let's find out if he's got any more information about solving these crimes. In the meantime, I'll call the local authorities to report Clarence as missing. You never know. The person who stole him might turn him loose unexpectedly."

I pulled out my phone and dialed O'Halloran while Doug made his call. Luckily, he picked up after the first ring.

"Sergeant, this is Kit Marshall." I tried to keep my voice steady. "I have disturbing news. Our dog Clarence has been taken." I proceeded to explain the circumstances and the note that was left at the scene.

O'Halloran didn't respond right away. I heard him take a deep breath. "Ms. Marshall, I am very sorry. This isn't in my jurisdiction, but if you send me a photo of your dog, I will alert all Capitol police about it, in case the culprit decides to bring him in the vicinity."

"I'll do that, Sergeant," I said. "This means, of course, that Gustav's killer isn't an antiquities thief who decided to steal the contents of Lincoln's

LARCENY AT THE LIBRARY

pockets. It's an insider." I took a deep breath. "Unless you think my husband stole our dog, it also eliminates him from the suspect list."

"Just as you alleged all along, Ms. Marshall," said the former detective. "The Library of Congress has that big congressional event scheduled for later today. I'm going to make sure we have enough officers there to watch everyone."

"Doug is going to deal with the local police. But I'm headed back to Capitol Hill soon. Were you able to check on Congressman Chang's alibi?" I asked.

"As a matter of fact, I did. Security cameras caught Chang walking into his office at exactly the time he claimed," said O'Halloran. "I grabbed a still image from the video feed with the time stamp. I'll email it to you."

"When did he leave his office?"

"We checked that, too," he said. "I thought he might have tried to establish an alibi before circling back to the Library of Congress to commit the crimes. But he stayed late in the office, just as he claimed. Until well after midnight, which would have been after the murder, according to the medical examiner."

So much for trying to pin this on Chang, unless he had some sort of secret tunnel from his office to the Library of Congress. Given his obsession with historical secrets, I couldn't completely discount the possibility. Maybe we were stuck in a bad Dan Brown novel.

I thanked O'Halloran again before ending the call. I consulted my phone, which had hundreds of pictures of Clarence. I emailed three of the most recent photos to the police sergeant so he could distribute them. I choked back tears as I looked at Clarence's adorable beagle face with his big, sheepish eyes. My stomach lurched at the thought of Clarence in the hands of a cold-blooded killer.

O'Halloran's picture of Chang had appeared in my email inbox. I clicked on the picture to make sure it was indeed Chang in the image. The black and white photo was grainy, but it was clearly the congressman's profile. I immediately recognized the overcoat he'd been wearing today at Ford's Theatre. Unless he had a certified doppelgänger out there, Chang had a tight alibi for the crimes. Nonetheless, something bugged me about the photograph, but I couldn't put my finger on it.

Doug had gotten off the phone and put his arm around me. "Don't worry, Kit. We'll get Clarence back. The Falls Church police are coming to take a statement. I can handle it."

"Won't you be late for the afternoon event?" I asked.

"It's fine," said Doug. "Once I've spoken with the police, I'll take an Uber back to the Library of Congress. Why don't you go return to the Hill and see if you can figure out who might have done this?"

I didn't like the idea of splitting up from Doug since quite frankly, I felt like I might fall apart at any given moment. Short of a miracle, there was no doubt I needed to solve this mystery before Clarence was gone too long. My dog's safety depended on it.

"Okay. I'll head back and try to sort this out," I said. "The good news is that the police won't suspect you anymore."

Doug must have noticed the quiver in my voice. He hugged me tight. "Kit, I promise I'll do everything I can to find Clarence. But you need to be careful, too. The killer took him so you'd back off." He waved the note around. "Don't become the next victim."

I grabbed the keys from Doug and jumped inside the Prius. With light midday traffic, I made it back to Capitol Hill in twenty minutes. I thought about checking in at the office but scrapped the idea. Maeve Dixon would need to hold down the fort herself today. Politics was important, but nowhere near as precious to me as bringing Clarence home.

After parking the car in the House of Representatives garage, I hustled through security and immediately proceeded to the underground tunnel system that connected the House office buildings with the Library of Congress. As I walked through the hallways, I thought about my next move. Who could I speak with who might be able to help? I decided to start with Dorian, the Librarian's chief of staff. Hopefully he'd be back from Ford's Theatre and could point me in the right direction.

The receptionist inside the Librarian's suite confirmed that Dorian had returned from this morning's event. A moment later, he emerged from his office.

"Kit, I didn't expect to see you again until the congressional event later this afternoon," he said.

I quickly explained what had happened to Clarence. He removed his glasses and rubbed his eyes.

"I can't believe this," he said. "This points to someone on the inside."

"I'm afraid so. Either someone who works here or is closely affiliated with the institution."

"The Librarian of Congress is not going to like this news," he said solemnly. "But I will be sure to tell her as soon as she's back in the office." He looked nervously at his watch. "I need to speak with Joe Malden."

"What's going on?" I hated to be nosy, but there was a lot on the line. The time for being polite had flown out the window when Clarence disappeared.

Dorian started to answer but was interrupted by the front office assistant. "Excuse me. Lea Rutherford is on the line. She needs to speak with you. Now."

Dorian rolled his eyes. "I don't know what else can go wrong today." He turned to me. "I'll be right back after I take this call." He disappeared into the rear of the office suite.

I grabbed my phone out of my purse. Sergeant O'Halloran had received my photos of Clarence and had dispatched them to all police units on the Hill. I hadn't heard from Doug. I hoped that meant the local police were proving helpful. I realized I hadn't let Meg know about today's developments. For some reason, I couldn't bring myself to text her about Clarence's disappearance. There were some things that just had to be communicated in person. My mind drifted back to the photograph of Congressman Chang. Something bothered me about it, yet I couldn't figure out what it might be. I decided to forward the image to Meg with a note asking her if she had any thoughts about it.

Just as I finished sending the email, Dorian reappeared. "Kit, can you join me in my office? There's something I need to talk to you about."

I followed Dorian back to his office, which wasn't much bigger than mine. I squeezed into a chair opposite his desk. "Lea Rutherford was trying to track you down."

"Me?" I tapped my finger to my chest. "Why?"

"She said that the two of you talked about Gustav Gaffney's work at the D.C. Public Library yesterday."

"We did," I said. "Lea's husband was a big donor to D-C-P-L so she had some background information on Gaffney and Jackson. It wasn't too revealing, as I recall."

"She must have decided to investigate the history," said Dorian. "She called because she wanted me to tell you that Janice Jackson and Gustav Gaffney did work at the D-C-P-L together. Apparently, they were both in senior positions during her husband's tenure as chairman."

"There's probably a lot of people here who worked together previously," I said. "I'm not sure why it's important she confirmed that piece of information." I tapped my fingers on the desk.

"It's important because Gaffney was Janice's boss, and he got her fired," said Dorian. "Lea remembered there was tension between them, but she wasn't sure what the story was. She went back through her husband's files, and sure enough, there was a record of Gustav's personnel action."

I sat back in the chair and rubbed my chin. "That is interesting. The problem is that Janice Jackson has an alibi for the murder. She's on the Library of Congress security cameras, headed to the tunnels so she could meet with a congressional staffer. Sergeant O'Halloran verified it for me."

"Ah," said Dorian. "Well, it was good of Lea to follow up, I guess."

"Before you were interrupted with the phone call, you were going to tell me about Joe Malden. You said you needed to see him. Is something the matter?"

Dorian sagged into his chair. "We have another problem. Joe's bat has gone missing."

"His bat?" I narrowed my eyes.

"You know, his baseball bat." Dorian waved his arms around like he was taking a major league swing. "The famous Red Sox outfielder Mookie Betts signed it."

I nodded. "He showed it to me when I visited him a few days ago in his office. I remember he said he kept it in the office because it made him happy."

Dorian frowned. "Not anymore. It's gone." He sighed heavily. "It makes me think we have a serious thief inside the Library of Congress. First, it was Abraham Lincoln artifacts. Now it's valuable sports memorabilia."

"At least Joe wasn't hurt," I said. "Better than what happened to poor Gustav."

Dorian stood up. "I'd better talk to him about it. Would you like to join me?"

Quite frankly, I didn't have any other leads. "Sure. Maybe Joe has thought of something about the murder."

Dorian motioned for me to lead the way. Two minutes later, we arrived at Joe's office. He was sitting at his desk, staring into space.

Dorian waved his hands in front of Joe's face. "Are you awake?"

Joe snapped to attention. "Oh, it's you." He turned his head and spotted me behind Dorian. His face fell. "And you."

"I wanted to talk to you about your baseball bat," said Dorian. "What happened?"

"Beats me," said Joe. "It was sitting here in my office this morning. I went to a meeting and when I got back to my desk, it was gone."

"Who knew you had the bat here?" I asked.

He rubbed his eyes. "Everyone. I showed it off to anyone who visited me."

"Gordon Endicott," I muttered. "Did he ever come to your office?"

"Yes, he was here at some time or the other," he said.

"If the two crimes are related, then maybe the thief tried to sell the Lincoln items but wasn't successful. If the motive is money, then he might be motivated to steal something else valuable. Your bat was an easy mark," I said.

"Not a bad theory," said Dorian. "It would certainly explain why one theft led to the other."

Joe looked pointedly at Dorian. "Maybe you should pay Endicott a visit. I really want my bat back. If he stole it, I doubt he had an opportunity to smuggle it out of the building yet."

"I shouldn't really accuse anyone" Dorian fidgeted with his tie.

"You could easily talk with him." Joe didn't bother to hide the desperation in his voice. "If I show up at his office, it's suspicious. But you're the chief of staff. Can't you speak with anyone who works here?"

Dorian blinked rapidly. "I suppose so I guess I could ask him if everything is in order for the congressional event later today."

Joe's face brightened. "Perfect." He got up from behind his desk and grabbed his coat off the hanger. "I think I need a cup of coffee."

I felt badly that Joe's bat was stolen, but he was much luckier than me. A baseball bat could be replaced. Clarence could not.

"By the way, were you here at the Library of Congress all day?" I asked.

"Of course, I was," said Joe. "Where else would I be? Anyone can tell you I didn't leave this building."

"You weren't the only person to have something stolen." I briefly told him about Clarence and studied his face. His eyes bulged as I spoke. He was either genuinely surprised about Clarence's dognapping or a very convincing liar.

"I'm sorry to hear this news," he said in a gentle tone. "I've been completely out of sorts about my baseball bat. What you've lost is much more precious."

"Thank you," I said. "You can understand why we need to figure out who killed Gustav. It's the only way we can have Clarence returned to us."

Dorian spoke up. "Lea Rutherford called me. Do you know where she is?"

I looked directly at Dorian, hoping my expression conveyed the gratitude I felt. It was a perfect question to ask.

"As a matter of fact, I do," said Joe. "She should be on her jet, headed to the west coast. The Getty has an exhibit opening in March for Women's History Month. She wanted a preview."

Such a specific alibi would be easy enough to verify. I doubted he was lying. After all, it would have been easy for Joe to abscond with his own baseball bat, thus diverting guilt and attention. Something told me that wasn't the case.

Joe put his jacket on. "If you don't have any more questions, I'm going to take that break and grab a cup of coffee. It's been a long day and we have a lot of important guests this afternoon for the preview."

All of a sudden, I felt like a ton of bricks had hit me.

"Wait a second," I said.

Joe turned around and looked and me and Dorian.

"What? Am I not allowed to have a cup of coffee?" he asked, his eyes narrowed.

I waved him off. "Where are you going for the coffee?"

"A block away on Independence Avenue." He pointed to his window. "It's winter time, Kit. That's why I need my coat."

"Exactly," I said. "You are one hundred percent correct, Joe."

I grabbed my phone out of my purse and fired off a text message to O'Halloran. Both Joe and Dorian stared at me as I rubbed my temples, waiting for his response.

"Kit, what's going on?" asked Dorian.

"I'm not sure," I murmured. "But I have a hunch about who killed Gustav."

"And it involves my cup of coffee?" asked Joe.

"No, but I wouldn't be surprised that if we find the killer, we'll also find the baseball bat," I said.

My phone dinged. Sergeant O'Halloran had responded. I glanced at my phone to see his reply.

"Dorian, I think we need to head over to the Jefferson Building now," I said.

"Why?" he asked.

"To find out if my intuition is right about who killed Gustav Gaffney and stole the contents of Lincoln's pockets."

Chapter Seventeen

———

I DIDN'T WAIT FOR Dorian to ask more questions. Instead, I hustled out of the office and was waiting by the elevator when he caught up.

"Are you going to tell me what's going on?" he asked, slightly out breath.

"I don't think I should right now," I said. "If I'm wrong, I wouldn't want to lessen your opinion of anyone."

He followed me into the elevator. I hit the button for the ground floor, which provided access to the Jefferson Building underground tunnel.

"Can you at least tell me what Joe Malden said that clued you in? One second we were talking about Lea Rutherford's whereabouts, and before I knew it, you'd run away."

"Actually, it has to do with this." We exited the elevator, and I pointed straight ahead.

"What?" Dorian followed my gaze. "The Jefferson tunnel?"

"Not exactly," I said. "But the tunnel system that connects the Library of Congress with the congressional complex."

We were deep inside the labyrinth maze of tunnels when my phone buzzed. Good to know I could get reception underground. It was Doug. He wanted to give me an update about Clarence. I hit the button to make a phone call, but it wouldn't go through. There was sufficient bandwidth inside the tunnel to send a text, but not enough to connect the call.

I sighed deeply. We hustled up two flights of steps and emerged inside the Great Hall, which now had a stage and chairs assembled for the congressional event.

"They already finished the set up for everything," said Dorian. "The security sweep went through a few hours ago."

"My husband wants to talk to me," I said. "Do you mind if I take this call inside the Members Room? It will be quiet there."

Dorian waved me off. "Sure, go ahead. I'm going to speak with our event staff to make sure there are no glitches." He rubbed his temples. "We need a flawless performance today after the week we've had. I'll meet you back here in ten minutes or so and maybe you can tell me what's going on." He shuffled towards an opposite hallway.

I walked into the alcove and down the hallway to the Members Room. The door was open, so I stepped inside. The beautiful salon had been decorated for a reception, likely scheduled to take place before or after the congressional show-and-tell. I glanced at my phone. Members of Congress wouldn't be arriving for another hour or so. Two bars were set up at opposite sides of the room, adorned with fancy cocktail and martini glasses. Empty tables awaited the smattering of hors d'oeuvres and tasty edibles that would accompany the libations. Today's event would be educational and then politicians would be able to unwind after a long week of hearings, votes, and meetings. No wonder the Library of Congress was such a popular place for Congress. It was literally an oasis of knowledge inside a capital city desert of hardscrabble politics, shameless tweets, and perennial backbiting.

I punched Doug's number and glanced around the room. Not a soul in sight. It was much better to have this conversation inside a private room rather than the Great Hall where anyone could eavesdrop. I walked to the corner of the Members Room by the fireplace and sat down in an ornate chair. Was everything inside this building built at the turn of the century? The decor certainly seemed like it.

"Kit, where are you?" I could hear the tension in Doug's voice.

"The Jefferson Building. Are you headed here now?" I asked.

"I am," he said. "The local police came to the house and I gave them Clarence's information. They're not too optimistic, though. People usually call to report a lost dog, not one that has been kidnapped."

I sighed. "I doubt Clarence is still in Falls Church. He's with the murderer."

"Are you any closer to figuring out who that is?"

I told Doug about Joe Malden's missing bat and the phone call to Dorian from Lea Rutherford.

"Are you sure this isn't a ploy by Lea and Joe to cast suspicion elsewhere?" asked Doug.

"I thought about that possibility, but I don't think that's the case. Besides,

Lea isn't in town today, and Joe didn't leave the office this morning."

"Any other info? I should arrive in about twenty minutes."

"There was something else." I told Doug my theory about who may have killed Gustav and stole the contents of Lincoln's pockets.

"If that's the case, Kit, then you'd better get out of there and find Sergeant O'Halloran," he said. "You shouldn't waste any time. You don't want any unfriendly encounters."

"Don't worry. I decided I'm going to tell Dorian about it. I thought there might be a way to spring a trap to see if my hunch is correct, but I'm fresh out of ideas on that front." I said. "Then we can contact O'Halloran. My number one priority is finding Clarence, after all. I don't want to waste any more time."

"Be careful," said Doug. "I'll be there soon."

"I know," I said. "I wouldn't be here if Clarence's life wasn't on the line."

"We'll bring him home," said my husband softly.

"I can't imagine life without him, Doug." I clicked off the phone and rubbed my eyes. I'd experienced other trying days in my life. Today was amongst the worst. Every time I took a second to breathe, I envisioned Clarence's pleading eyes, desperately hoping that either me or Doug would rescue him.

It was time to find Dorian and clue him in on my suspicions. If he had a bright idea, maybe the two of us could chase down my lead and figure out if I was correct.

I was about to stand up when I heard the slam of a door. I leaned to the left in the high back chair, looking over my shoulder to figure out what happened.

My stomach lurched. The door to the Members Room was now closed, and Janice Jackson was standing on the other side of it. She was holding a baseball bat in her right hand, and it was pointed directly at me.

Chapter Eighteen

⁓

"**P**LEASE, DON'T GET up on my account," said Janice. "Although I was fascinated by your conversation."

I stood and braced myself. Countless times in my life, I'd been wrong when I jumped to conclusions. As Alanis Morissette professed, isn't it ironic the one time I put two and two together and got four, I was dealing with a psychopathic killer?

"Eavesdropping isn't very polite." I forced my voice to remain steady.

Janice walked towards me, holding the bat in her right hand. Now she was tapping the end of it with her left hand, probably quite similar to how Mookie Betts approached the plate before slamming the next pitch for a home run. Except Janice Jackson didn't want to blow the cover off a baseball. Instead, I was the target.

I moved to left, positioning myself in front of one of the decorated bars. "Don't be ridiculous. Dorian walked over with me to the Jefferson Building. He'll call in the cavalry when he figures out I disappeared."

"Lies, lies, lies," said Janice. She tapped the bat. "It's pathetic, really."

I scanned the bar. There had to be a weapon I could grab and use to defend myself against Janice's attack. To my dismay, all I saw was fancy glassware and a corkscrew. The bottles of wine and liquor were way out of reach. If there were knives to cut the lemons and limes, they were safely stowed behind the countertop.

"I'm actually telling the truth," I said in my most sincere voice. "If you kill me, you're going to prison. Doug is headed this way, too."

"I was careful not to contaminate this bat with fingerprints." Both of her hands were covered with black leather gloves. "It's cold outside, so it wasn't hard to mask the evidence. These were inside my coat pocket."

"Doug will tell the police what I told him," I said. "You can't get away with this."

"It's hearsay," she said. "And who says that Doug won't have an unfortunate accident on his way home from work later today? Perhaps he'll be so distraught over your death, he'll decide to end his own life. Seems like the perfect ending to a charming love story." She flashed her teeth, her smile resembling the Joker's maniacal grin.

"You're completely deranged," I said. "But I suppose your insanity makes sense, given what's happened. Gustav knew you were unhinged when he worked with you at the D.C. Public Library. He fired you. Somehow, you made your way to the Library of Congress."

"Gustav was a close-minded man," sneered Janice. "He never understood you have to break a few eggs to get what you want in life." She tapped the bat against her left hand again. "He got rid of me at D.C. Public when he found out I'd arranged modest compensation for a few city council members who had helped us out. Did he think that everything in life comes for free? He was a naive man who never belonged in a position of power, especially in this city."

"But then your paths crossed again." The longer I could keep Janice talking, the higher my chances of survival. Dorian would eventually wander down the hallway when I didn't show at our meeting point.

"It took years of consulting and freelance work to reverse the damage he'd had on my career," said Janice. "After I fought my way back to a worthwhile position at the Library of Congress, he showed up as the new Assistant Librarian. He had it in for me from the start."

"I'm guessing that Gustav threatened to remove you from your current post in congressional relations. You couldn't have it, correct?" I edged my way to the right, trying to make sure I positioned myself directly opposite the door. Maybe I could make a run for it before Janice attacked me with the bat.

"He did exactly that," said Janice. "I'd worked hard to establish myself in this role. Gustav couldn't let the past go. He refused to see me in a new light."

"So, you decided to kill him," I said. "It was easier said than done. You had to wait for the right opportunity."

"I needed to come up with a legitimate motive to cast suspicion elsewhere. There were a lot of people who disliked him," she said. "But nothing that could justify murder."

"Until you heard about the preview display of the Lincoln collection. A theft could mask your true intentions," I said.

Janice inched closer. "I have to admit, the one thing I didn't account for was you. If I'd known Miriam Dunlap was going to unleash Capitol Hill's favorite bloodhound on the case, it might have changed my calculus."

The word "bloodhound" made me think of Clarence. "By the way, where's my dog?" I kept moving to the right, scanning the room for a makeshift weapon to hold Janice off.

"He's somewhere safe," she said. "Don't worry. I wouldn't hurt a dog. I'm not heartless. A pity that it doesn't matter, though. Neither you or your husband will see him again." She took a long step in my direction.

"Not so fast, Janice," I said. "You've got to catch me."

"Actually, I don't have to catch you," she said. "This bat will do the trick."

With that threatening pronouncement, she swung the bat in my direction. I sidestepped her lunging attempt and moved toward the opposite corner of the room. Much to my chagrin, she repositioned herself to block the room's only exit.

"Don't try to make a break for it, Kit." She reached inside her blazer pocket and pulled out a mammoth set of keys. "I locked us in. There's no way you're getting out." She paused for a beat. "Unless it's in a body bag, of course." She took another big step toward me.

Janice was now perilously close, and I'd wedged myself in a corner. Even though her previous swing of the Mookie Betts bat had missed, I didn't know how long I could evade her attack. My eyes darted around the room. It was filled with breathtaking artwork and framed with intricate wooden paneling. With all its fancy bling, there wasn't a damn weapon to save my precious hide. Whomever decorated the Members Room had certainly forgotten the all-important balance between aesthetics and functionality. If I survived, I'd have to bring up this observation with the Librarian of Congress.

Janice swung the bat again and this time, it missed connecting by inches. That was way too close for comfort. Then I spotted it. Against the far wall, only about ten feet away, was the light blue Library of Congress flag, standing upright in its decorative iron holder. Someone had probably moved the United States flag to the viewing stage inside the Great Hall but had left the agency's pennant inside the Members Room for the reception.

"What about Congressman Chang?" I asked. "Was he in on it? Everyone knows you two are buddies. Or maybe more." I took two steps sideways to the right.

"That's what got Gustav killed. He thought I was bribing Chang." She inched closer.

"The Assistant Librarian knew you were up to your old tricks." I took a few more baby steps toward the flagpole.

"He couldn't believe that I could develop a close working relationship with a politician without a *quid pro quo*," she said. "Gustav didn't have any evidence, but he said he was going to move me out of my position into some worthless job where it wouldn't matter if I showed up to work."

"And you couldn't stomach that," I said. "You had to take action."

"I had no choice. He was going to ruin my career." She shook her head. "Yet again. Lightning doesn't strike twice, Kit. At least on my watch."

"This might surprise you, but I actually agree," I said.

Janice chuckled. "You agree with my decision to kill Gustav?"

"Not exactly." Then I lunged and grabbed the flagpole out of its holder. It was heavy, but I could probably muster one strong counter-attack with it. "Strong women need to take action when threatened."

With all my might, I swung the pole as hard as I could in Janice's direction. Much longer than a baseball bat, the pole hit Janice across the mid-section of her body. She stumbled and fell to the floor. I sprinted to the door and pulled at the knob. Janice hadn't lied. It was locked. In desperation, I banged on the wooden door.

"Dorian, I'm inside the Members Room! Help!" I screamed as loud as I could.

My blow had caught Janice off guard but hadn't seriously harmed her. In a matter of seconds, she managed to get back on her feet, baseball bat in hand.

"Now I really am going to kill you," she growled.

She swung the bat harder this time, and it would have surely knocked me into next week. Luckily, I was one step ahead of her. Assuming a defensive posture, I used the flagpole to block the blow, which caused Janice to fall backwards.

That's when I heard a familiar sound. It wasn't Dorian's voice, as I'd hoped. In fact, it was better. A deep "woof" was followed by the familiar scamper of paws on a marble floor. Clarence had found me!

As Janice tried to regain her balance, I banged on the door again.

"I'm locked inside the Members Room!" I screamed. After all, Clarence had brought backup, right?

Janice steadied herself again and moved closer to me. The flagpole wouldn't be able to prevent the next swing of the bat.

"Help!" I screamed. "She's going to kill me!"

Janice cocked the bat, just like mighty Casey stepping up to the plate. Then she unleashed a swing headed directly for my head. With no way to stop it, I dove out of the way to the ground. The bat hit the heavy wooden door, which was evidently made of sturdy wood that could withstand a nuclear bomb. She flew backwards again, this time landing squarely on her butt. At that exact moment, the handle jiggled and the door flew open.

Clarence led the way. As soon as he spotted me, he sprinted over and licked my face. Doug was a few steps behind, followed by Dorian, Lisa, and Murphy.

"Kit, are you hurt?" Doug bent down to look at me.

"No, I'm okay," I said breathlessly. "Lisa, make sure you don't let that woman out of your sight." I pointed to Janice. "She confessed to Gustav's murder and then tried to kill me."

Janice scrambled to her feet and made a fast move towards the door. Caught off-balance, Lisa couldn't stop her. Janice was just about to exit the Members Room and dash down the hallway when Murphy caught up with her, positioning himself directly in in her path. The large black canine squared to face her, standing tall with the hair on the back of his neck raised, his ears pinned back, and his teeth slightly bared.

Janice stopped in her tracks. "Capitol Hill police dogs don't attack people," she muttered.

She took one step forward. Murphy responded with a growl, his tail at attention.

Lisa was now directly behind Janice. "If I was you, I wouldn't take that chance. By the way, you're under arrest for the murder of Gustav Gaffney and the attempted murder of Kit Marshall."

Janice stopped dead in her tracks. Caught between a highly trained canine's menacing stare and Lisa's apprehension, she decided retreat was the better option. Janice stepped backwards, which gave Lisa the opportunity to slap cuffs on her.

The situation sufficiently diffused, a relaxed Murphy ran towards Clarence, sniffing his ears and then giving him a big kiss. Clarence raised his front paw and gave Murphy a half hug, his tongue lolling to the side in a happy grin.

Lisa marched down the hallway with Janice in tow. Doug helped me up and put his arms around me. "I'm so glad everyone is safe and sound," he said, his voice muffled by his tight embrace.

I pulled back and stared into Doug's eyes. "Me, too. Hey, don't you have some rare Abraham Lincoln materials to display?"

"President Lincoln would have something to say about this whole episode." He put his arm around me as we walked out of the room, with Murphy and Clarence trailing behind us.

"What might that be?" I asked.

"You can fool some of the people all the time and all of the people some of the time, but you cannot fool all of the people all of the time," he said.

I smiled. "I'm glad Mr. Lincoln got the final word on the matter."

Chapter Nineteen

A S IT TURNED out, the story did not end with Abraham Lincoln or his insightful quote. After a restful weekend, the Librarian of Congress invited everyone involved in solving the mystery to her sixth floor Madison Building office for a late afternoon champagne toast.

Dorian stood between me and Congresswoman Dixon. "This is the type of event we'd normally host inside the ceremonial," he said in a hushed tone. "We thought it was too soon after the murder."

"I agree," said Maeve. "Give it some time and perhaps think about a makeover for that space." She added, "Of course, within historical standards appropriate for the building."

"Absolutely, ma'am," said Dorian.

For the past couple of days, Doug and I resolved not to speak much about what had transpired. The hours we spent not knowing Clarence's whereabouts had affected us deeply, only adding to the stress of Doug's status as a murder suspect for several days. The weekend had given us much needed time to process the apprehensiveness of the entire ordeal. While I still hadn't dealt fully with the emotional turmoil, now I was ready for some answers. I certainly had a long list of questions.

"When will the Librarian give the toast?" I asked Dorian.

He looked at his watch. "Probably in about twenty minutes or so. Are you on a tight schedule? We want to make sure you can hear it. After all, it's been a difficult week for you and Doug."

"Not at all," I said. "But I do want to find out exactly what happened on Friday." Sergeant O'Halloran had just arrived, with Lisa and Murphy in tow.

"Take all the time you need," said Dorian. "After all, Janice might have gotten away with everything if you weren't involved."

I smiled in response to Dorian and made a beeline across the room. Doug saw where I was headed and followed with Clarence, who had received a special dispensation to attend the festivities inside the Library of Congress today. Non-working dogs weren't permitted inside the Library, and Clarence seemed to know he was enjoying special status. He strutted behind Doug and sat down politely next to Murphy, who promptly issued a greeting lick.

"Good afternoon, Sergeant O'Halloran." I extended my hand.

O'Halloran grinned. "Really, Ms. Marshall. At this point in our relationship, I would think we've progressed beyond a handshake." He extended his arms and embraced me in a quick, tight hug. I squeezed him back.

A Library employee who had been pressed into hosting service offered us a drink. "Prosecco? Sparkling grape juice?"

"Grape juice for me," said O'Halloran. "Technically, I'm on duty."

"Thank goodness I'm not." I grabbed a plastic flute of the bubbly.

"The Librarian bought Prosecco because she heard it was your favorite," said the helpful staffer.

"She was correct," I said. "Meg and I have a philosophy, and it's quite simple. Life is better with Prosecco."

O'Halloran shook his head. "It's amazing you two manage to solve murders and pass legislation. Wonders may never cease."

"Sergeant, I need your help on this one," I said. "I had a pretty good hunch that Janice was behind the murder and the theft. But she revealed herself to me when she tried to smash me with the Red Sox bat inside the Members Room."

"When someone's chasing you around a locked room with a weapon, you tend to conclude that person is a homicidal maniac," said O'Halloran, his eyebrows raised.

"I get it, but I have a few lingering questions." I linked arms with Doug. "Over the weekend, I thought about the investigation and there's some loose ends. I'd like some answers, especially since Doug was a suspect."

"Ms. Marshall, even in cases resulting in a conviction, there are loose ends." He sighed. "But I suppose you've both earned the right to ask your questions. Fire away."

"We heard the stolen Lincoln items were recovered," I said. "Can you confirm that?"

O'Halloran nodded. "Of course. Janice Jackson is as crazy as they come, but she didn't kill Gaffney to steal the contents of Lincoln's pockets."

He pursed his lips. "At least, we don't *think* she did."

"You sound hesitant, Sergeant," said Doug.

"Janice had two reasons for the theft." O'Halloran paused to put several pieces of cheese on his plate, along with tall stack of crackers. "First and foremost, she wanted to divert suspicion away from herself for the murder. She created her own red herring, so to speak." Then he stuffed a piece of cheddar into his mouth, along with a wheat Triscuit.

While O'Halloran chewed, I finished his thought. "Let me guess. The second motive involves Congressman Chang."

O'Halloran swallowed and wiped the remaining crumbs off his face. "Bingo."

"Was Chang in on it?" I leaned closer to O'Halloran and lowered my voice. "That would be a major scandal, Sergeant."

"We have no evidence to substantiate such a theory. It's not clear what Janice was going to do with the stolen items. She mentioned during one of our interrogations that she thought about asking Chang if he'd want to take possession of them if he promised to support the Library of Congress in ways Janice saw fit," said O'Halloran.

"But Chang denies it," said Doug.

"He contends he had no knowledge of the theft and swears he would have run to the police or federal investigators if Janice had approached him with such an offer," said O'Halloran.

I studied O'Halloran's face. I'd know the cop for several years now and could tell when he was feeding me a line. "But you're not sure he's telling the truth."

"I'll tell you what I'm going to tell the Librarian. I wouldn't leave Chang alone in a room with a bunch of fancy books from the Library's collection," he said. "Or anything else that isn't nailed down."

"I'll keep that in mind the next time I work on a congressional display," said Doug.

Clarence squirmed and whimpered softly. I grabbed two pieces of cheese and slipped them to Clarence and Murphy. O'Halloran raised his eyebrows but said nothing.

"From what I gather, you fingered Janice before she tried to kill you," said O'Halloran.

Doug nodded. "I talked to Kit on the phone, and she told me her suspicions. Not a minute later, Lisa called to say that she'd located Clarence. I told her to head to the Jefferson Building to find Kit."

Lisa, who had been standing quietly with Murphy, spoke up. "It's not entirely accurate to say that I located Clarence. It was really Murphy's doing."

"Police dog at work," said O'Halloran. "I'm not surprised." He patted Murphy gently on the head.

"When I heard Clarence had gone missing, I wondered if the person who took him had brought him to Capitol Hill. Almost all the suspects work here," explained Lisa. "I let Murphy sniff Clarence's blue bandana. It was in the back of Sebastian's car after their tussle over the barbecue. Then we took off for our regular rounds. Sure enough, Murphy went bananas outside of a congressional office in the Rayburn Building."

"How did the pooch end up there?" asked O'Halloran as he munched on a sizable chuck of gouda.

"Janice needed to get back to Capitol Hill quickly after she stalked Kit and Doug and dognapped Clarence. There was nowhere to stash him inside the Library of Congress, so she took him to a congressional office where she knew the chief of staff well." Lisa paused to take a breath. "Janice told her a fabricated story about dog sitting for a friend in a pinch. The chief said she'd be happy to watch Clarence for the day. He was eating a biscuit when Murphy and I showed up on the scene."

"That chief of staff must have flipped out when the Capitol Hill police showed up in her office, looking for a stolen dog," I said.

"She didn't believe me until I showed the all-points bulletin and photograph that Sergeant O'Halloran issued about Clarence's disappearance," said Lisa.

Clarence's ears shifted backward. Even he knew an APB was a big deal. I wondered if any other dog had ever received that designation before on Capitol Hill.

I gave O'Halloran a gentle punch on his right shoulder. "You never told me you liked dogs."

"Who doesn't like dogs?" said the portly cop. "Besides, I knew if we found your puppy, we'd be hot on the tail of the killer."

It made sense, but I couldn't help but conclude that the police sergeant had a soft spot for animals, particularly cute beagle mutts. Clarence must have sensed it, too. He ambled over to O'Halloran and licked his hand.

"Clarence wants to say thank you," said Doug. "He only gives kisses to people he really likes."

"And people who have recently used their hands to eat several pieces of cheese," I said, laughing.

"Now I have a question for you, Ms. Marshall," said Sergeant O'Halloran.

"I want to know how you figured out Janice Jackson was the killer, even before she tried to make you her next victim."

Dorian joined our group conversation. "I'd like to hear this explanation. All of a sudden, Kit hustled us over to the Jefferson Building and refused to tell me why."

"It was pretty simple once I thought of it," I said. "Two clues helped me put it together. First, when I saw the Librarian of Congress earlier in the day at Ford's Theatre, she said something that stuck in my head. She commented that Janice Jackson was always hustling back and forth between the Library's buildings and the congressional office buildings. As you know, an underground tunnel connects everything."

"Wasn't Janice seen on the surveillance video walking through the tunnel, headed over to a congressional office building after the preview event ended?" asked Lisa.

"Yes. And the fact she was on the video provided her with a supposed alibi, until I thought harder about it," I said. "I needed to know what she was wearing. I thought of it when I saw Joe Malden put on his coat to go outside for coffee on Friday when we visited him after his bat was stolen."

"What does a coffee break have to do with Gustav's murder?" asked Dorian. "I was there, and Joe didn't say anything incriminating about Janice."

"He didn't have to say anything. Just the fact that he was putting on his coat to go outside made me wonder whether Janice had worn a coat on that surveillance video," I said.

"But if she was only making an appearance in the tunnels to establish an alibi, it wouldn't matter," said Dorian.

"Exactly. I started to think about Janice's movements that night if she was the killer. Something had been nagging me for a while, but I couldn't figure out what it was," I said. "I had a suspicion she'd manufactured an alibi. I just needed to prove it."

"How did you figure out your hunch was right?" asked Lisa.

"I remembered that Congressman Chang asked for his coat when he left the preview reception. Why would he do that? He spent a lot of time at the Library of Congress. Surely, he knew he could use the underground tunnel to return to his congressional office. But then I realized he wore his coat because he knew the tunnel connecting the Library and the House of Representatives closes at eight o'clock in the evening on most days. He wasn't sure how late the event would run. If it lasted beyond eight, then he'd have to walk outside to return to his office, hence the coat."

"We keep the tunnel open later some nights, but since Chang was the only member of Congress attending the preview, we didn't bother to re-quest an extension," said Dorian.

"Surely someone who uses the tunnels every single day for her job would know the hours the tunnel is open. In fact, the Librarian reminded me of that fact when we chatted at Ford's Theatre," I said. "Janice wanted to establish an alibi, and she knew appearing before the surveillance cameras would be credible. If she was really intending to drop in on a staffer working late, as she claimed, she would have needed her coat. After all, she'd have to walk outside to get back to the Library after eight o'clock. But she didn't do that. Instead, she doubled back, probably using the stairwell to avoid additional security cameras. Then she slipped into the ceremonial to kill Gustav."

"I should have picked that up earlier," said O'Halloran. "At first, I was confused when you texted me, asking whether Janice was wearing a coat on the Library's security footage. I figured out it must have something to do with her alibi."

"Don't beat yourself up," I said, smiling. "Once you reviewed every-thing, it would have been staring you right in the face."

"I guess it goes to show that sometimes it's good to have more than one set of eyes on something," said O'Halloran. "Thank you, Ms. Marshall."

I felt my face blush. It was the first time our police pal had publicly acknowledged my role in solving a case. Had I become a legitimate sleuth in O'Halloran's eyes?

Dorian's eyes sparkled. "I can't wait to tell the Librarian that she gave you a critical clue to solve the murder. In fact, I might need to mention this to *Roll Call*. We're setting up an interview about the aftermath of every-thing that's happened." Dorian hustled off, probably to harangue as many Capitol Hill reporters as possible before the evening deadline.

"The other clue that pointed me in the right direction was the myste-rious disappearance of Joe Malden's bat," I said. When Joe heard his name mentioned, he edged over to join our group.

"How'd you know it was connected to the murder?" he asked, a glass of Prosecco in hand.

"I wasn't entirely sure," I said. "But you'd had the bat in your office for quite a while. It seemed like an odd coincidence that it would disappear only days after a murder and major theft."

"That's true," said Joe, who'd just stuffed a piece of broccoli into his mouth. "Why suspect Janice as the person who lifted it?"

"Process of elimination in my own mind," I said. "Quite frankly, I originally suspected Congressman Chang as responsible for the murder and Lincoln theft. If the same person who killed Gustav stole your bat, I knew it couldn't be Chang. He wouldn't have known you had a valuable Red Sox baseball bat inside your office. It also didn't fit his profile. His office was full of historical memorabilia, but there wasn't anything related to sports teams."

I continued. "Then, I thought about Lea Rutherford. Perhaps you gave her the bat and faked the theft to divert suspicion. But then we found out she was out of town. It didn't fit as an explanation."

"As I recall, you thought Gordon Endicott could have nicked it," said Dorian, who rejoined the group.

"Yes, he was a distinct possibility, especially if he'd stolen the Lincoln items to sell them for profit. Joe's Red Sox bat could fetch a tidy sum, I imagine. However, after Clarence was dognapped, I tentatively scratched Endicott off my list."

"Why?" asked Dorian.

"Whomever snatched Clarence had to have a car. That person tailed us from Capitol Hill to the house we visited in Falls Church. I knew from talking with Gordon previously that he was a subway rider. He'd even showed us his Metro card," I said. "Therefore, it was highly unlikely he'd followed us that day. You can't really steal a dog and then rely on an Uber or Lyft to make your getaway."

Dorian chuckled. "Good deduction. I hadn't thought of that clue."

"Then you saw me put on my coat to walk outside for coffee," said Joe.

"That's when I remembered what the Librarian said earlier about Janice dashing back and forth between the various Capitol Hill buildings, and I put it all together." I reached down to pet Clarence. "It was circumstantial but I hoped Dorian and I could confront Janice Jackson before the big congressional event and get her to confess."

"That's sort of what happened." The corners of Dorian's mouth twitching in a grin. "More or less."

"I'm just lucky I was nimble enough to avoid her using that slugger," I said. "She'd obviously stolen it because she thought Doug and I were onto her. She needed a weapon to finish us off. The bat was a convenient solution when she decided I was getting too close for comfort. She knew I would show up inside the Jefferson Building for the congressional event, and she wanted to be prepared. There's not many lethal objects floating around the Library of Congress."

"Thank goodness," said Doug.

Everyone laughed. Meg and Trevor heard the chuckles and wandered over. "What's so funny over here?" asked Meg. She tipped her glass of Prosecco in my direction.

"Kit and Sergeant O'Halloran just finished going over the details of how they solved the case," said Lisa.

"And how Lisa and Murphy found Clarence," added Doug.

"Glad you got everything sorted out," said Meg.

"Speaking of sorting things out, we took advantage of the quiet weekend and came to a decision." Trevor grabbed Meg's hand.

Meg's face was glowing. "Trevor and I have decided to date exclusively." She squeezed Trevor's hand. "I know it's been complicated, but I'm glad we took the time to figure it out."

"Congratulations." After I placed my glass of Prosecco on the serving table, I hugged Meg and Trevor. It was hard to say where that relationship was headed, but at least they had the courage to give it a shot and find out.

Dorian cleared his throat. "You know, Meg, I'd like to speak with you sometime about a position that just became available at the Library of Congress." He paused and looked at me. "With your supervisor's permission, of course."

My heart sank. Dorian wanted to hire Meg for the congressional relations job.

I recovered quickly. "Certainly." I forced a smile. "I'd hate to lose the best legislative director in the House of Representatives, but I'd never stand in anyone's way when it comes to career advancement."

"Do you mean Janice Jackson's job?" asked Meg, her eyes wide with surprise.

"Something tells me we're going to need a good person for that position as soon as possible. There's going to be a lot of questions to answer after this past week," said Dorian. "With your former boss as the chair of our oversight committee, I can't think of a better fit."

"Wow," said Meg softly. She turned in my direction. "I never thought about leaving Congress, Kit. But this might be a very good opportunity for me."

I nodded. "You should speak with Dorian about it and see if you're interested. I'm your boss *and* I'm your friend. Even if we don't work together anymore, we're forever besties, right?" I picked up my glass from the table and raised it.

Miriam Dunlap rushed over next to me. "Are you making a toast, Kit?" She shook her finger at me. "Really, that's my job."

"I wouldn't dream of it. Please, the floor is all yours." I stepped out of the way.

"Ladies and gentlemen, this has been a difficult time for everyone in this room," said the Librarian. She looked at myself and Meg. "In memory of our cherished colleague Gustav Gaffney, I'd like to propose a toast."

She raised her glass high in the air. "To the Library of Congress staff and those who support our mission. May we continue to serve the pursuit of knowledge." The Librarian's gracious toast was met with several calls of "hear, hear" along with a synchronized duo echo of "woof, woof."

THE END

COLLEEN J. SHOGAN has been reading mysteries since the age of six. A political scientist by training, Colleen has taught American politics at several universities and previously worked on Capitol Hill as a legislative staffer in the United States Senate, the Deputy Director of the Congressional Research Service, and as a senior executive at the Library of Congress. She is currently the Senior Vice President at the White House Historical Association and Director of the David Rubenstein Center for White House History. A member of Sisters in Crime, she lives in Arlington, Virginia with her husband Rob and rescued beagle mutt Conan.